BEAST
OF
DRACULA

JOHN PATRICK KENNEDY

2017

If you love somebody, let them go, for if they return, they were always yours. And if they don't, they never were.

— Khalil Gibran

CHAPTER
ONE

NEW YORK, 1927

C LUB MAZUMA beat like a pulse.
        Ruxandra Dracula—now Ruxandra Black, or Ruxie
        to her friends—stepped inside the smoky ballroom and
let her coat slide off her slender, pale shoulders. The red fox fur
collar tickled her arms as the garment fell into the waiting arms
of the maître d'. Ruxandra smiled. How she loved this city, this
time, and this club!

Jazz drums pounded a hard, fast beat, making the fifteen
crystal chandeliers shake. Men and women doing a frenzied
Charleston covered the sunken dance floor, their hearts pounding
in rhythm. Unlike the Cotton Club, which was strictly whites only,

Club Mazuma allowed anyone inside as long as they had money and behaved. People of all colors filled the dance floor and the two tiers of tables around it. Ruxandra felt each heartbeat, heard the blood rushing through each person's veins, and smelled the lust and love and exhilaration rising from the five hundred souls who filled the giant Harlem club.

Good thing I ate before I came in. Now, where is she . . . ?

She let her mind expand outward, sensing the emotions of everyone in the building. She felt their pain and pleasure, their joy or sorrow. Each person was unique in her mind, and each blazed with his or her own energy. She felt couples in love or angry with each other, people excited or nervous or scared or passionate. Some few, however, stood out. At a table in the back, two women burned with lust for each other, caressing each other's thighs and sending waves of pleasure through each. Near the dance floor, one man's backside burned and ached, making him squirm in his seat as he stared adoringly at a woman who beamed satisfaction and whose hand still hurt from beating him. Backstage, a man moaned as a woman took him in her mouth. And just beyond them . . .

Carolyn.

She was in the dressing room, humming with happy anticipation and laughing with the other dancers. Carolyn felt relaxed and happy and simmered with a lust of her own. Very soon she would come out on the dance floor. Ruxandra shivered with anticipation. She loved watching Carolyn dance, and afterward . . .

"Ruxie!" Jerome's voice pulled Ruxandra out of her reverie. She drew her mind back in, leaving Carolyn to her preparations, and smiled. He was a fine specimen, tall and wide, with skin the color of dark, fertile soil and a set of muscles that made Ruxandra itch to sink her teeth into them. He held out a hand to her. "Come dance with me, girl!"

They spun out onto the dance floor in a swinging Lindy hop. Ruxandra's red dress whirled high, the beading at her hips and breasts shaking and dancing with her. Her bobbed and marcelled red hair flickered like fire in the light as she spun. Jerome knew how to make a girl fly—legs up in the air and scandalous underwear occasionally on show for the table sitters. Jerome and Ruxandra spun and twisted through that song and the next. Then they did a fast-moving, hand-flapping foxtrot that made them both laugh and keep laughing as they wove their way through the crowd back to Jerome's table.

He ordered them two lime and tonics, slipping the waiter a little extra money to put in some gin. There were many wonderful things about America, but Prohibition was *not* one of them. Still, it added a certain bit of naughtiness to get one's booze under the table.

They chatted about inconsequentialities until the drinks came. Jerome took a long pull on his as soon as it arrived. Then he put his elbows on the table and leaned close to Ruxandra. "I understand I have some competition for your affections."

"Never, darling." Ruxandra took a sip of her drink. The booze tasted nowhere near as good as before Prohibition, but there were ice cubes in it, and the coolness felt divine. "You'll always be one of my favorite men."

"I know that, girl." Jerome squeezed her knee under the table. "But I know men aren't all you're interested in."

Ruxandra looked at him over the rim of her drink. "Is that a problem?"

"Not for me," Jerome said. "But there's others who won't like it. So you tell them Jerome Mobley is watching your back and that he packs heat and a razor."

"Jerome, that is so sweet!" Ruxandra leaned over and kissed his cheek. "I don't know what I'd do without you."

Jerome leaned close enough that his hot breath brushed Ruxandra's ear. "And if you break Carolyn's heart, I'll put you over my knee and see to it that you eat standing up for a month."

Ruxandra leaned up and nibbled his earlobe, feeling the blood pulsing in it. "For that offer, I may just have to . . ."

He threw back his head and laughed. "You're incorrigible, girl."

"I should hope so."

"Now, if you'll excuse me, there are some other ladies who *appreciate* my company." Jerome winked and sauntered toward a table where five dark-skinned young women wearing their sharpest dresses and fanciest hairdos waved and giggled.

The sharp, fast beat of a snare drum rolled through the room, drawing all eyes to the band. The dance floor cleared, and the MC, Big Mike Robinson, stepped up to the microphone in a white suit that set off his dark-brown skin and made him dapper and handsome despite his round body and bald head.

"Ladies and gentlemen!" Big Mike's voice rolled through the crowd like liquid velvet. "Please give a warm welcome to the Mazuma Dancers!"

The dancers took the floor like a dozen whirlwinds, with moves and speed that put even Jerome to shame. Like its patrons, Club Mazuma's dancers came in all colors: black and white and all shades in between. They danced with skill and abandon, making the audience clap and cheer and stomp their feet with delight.

In their midst, Carolyn shone like a star.

She was taller than Ruxandra, with dark hair, olive skin, and legs a mile long. She was strong, too, and could lift Ruxandra off her feet when they danced or made love. She wore a dazzling white flowing skirt that twirled up to show her long, strong legs every time she spun. The sight made Ruxandra burn with a lust hotter than the stage lights.

In the middle of a spin, Carolyn caught Ruxandra's eye and gave her a wink. Ruxandra smiled back. *Three months tonight. And three very nice months at that. It is going to be such a good night.*

Six hours later, the clocks struck two, and the club closed down. Ruxandra put on her coat and hurried around back to the alley and the stage door.

"Darling!" Carolyn ran forward and hugged Ruxandra and, with no one else around, planted a kiss on her with far more serious intent than the one Ruxandra had given Jerome hours before. The passion made Ruxandra gasp when their lips finally broke apart.

Ruxandra kept Carolyn in the circle of her arms, reveling in the warmth of her flesh and the quick pulsing of her blood. "My place?"

"Oh yes, please."

They giggled and gossiped all the way back to the Ansonia Hotel. The cab pulled up in front, and the valet opened the doors, saying, "Good evening, Miss Black. Good evening, Miss Mendez."

"Good evening, Patrick!" Ruxandra and Carolyn chorused. They managed to look almost respectable as they walked across the ornate marble foyer with its big desk and into the red-and-brass elevator that took them up to the seventh floor. When Carolyn winked, Ruxandra's knees grew weak. For the sake of propriety, she turned her eyes forward and pretended not to see, though her lips twitched in a smile.

"Now be quiet in the hall," Ruxandra whispered as the elevator vanished from sight. Antagonized neighbors were nosy neighbors, and she did not need nosy neighbors in her business.

"Don't you shush me, girl!" Carolyn pushed Ruxandra face-first against the wall, biting her ear and pressing breasts and hips hard against Ruxandra's back. She slid one hand up Ruxandra's side and gently squeezed her breast, while the other pulled up her dress and slipped beneath it. "Shall I make you beg?"

Moments later, Ruxandra bit her lip to keep from crying out as her body convulsed—a knee-trembler, they'd called it back in London, back in time, when she called Whitechapel her hunting ground. *Oh God, yes!*

Ruxandra grabbed Carolyn's hand and dragged her down the hallway. She fumbled with the door keys as Carolyn's lips and tongue ran over her neck and ears. At last she got the door open, and they stumbled inside. Ruxandra shoved the door shut behind them and kissed Carolyn hard, her own hands now wandering. Carolyn gasped with delight, and Ruxandra decided she couldn't wait for the bedroom.

She pulled Carolyn into the front room and pushed her down against the red velvet couch cushions. She kissed her long and slow and deep while slipping Carolyn's undergarments down and off. Then Ruxandra knelt between Carolyn's legs, tormenting and teasing again and again until the sweet, delicious girl cried out, convulsing in spasms of pleasure. As Ruxandra felt Carolyn's pulse race, smelled her hot sweat, and saw the flush of blood spread across her chest, it made other hungers far darker than passion stir inside her.

And that's the other reason I ate first.

She shook off her dark desires. Carolyn pulled her up and wrapped her in her arms. Ruxandra kissed her hard until Carolyn cried out again and fell back, exhausted.

"Oh my Lord, girl." Carolyn panted for air. Ruxandra leaned in for a kiss, and Carolyn stopped her with a hand on her chest. "If you want any more out of me tonight, you need to ply me with champagne. And salmon. And oranges."

Ruxandra grinned and stood up. "Your wish is my command, darling."

From the Frigidaire—possibly the greatest of all mankind's inventions—Ruxandra pulled out a plate of salmon, oranges, crackers, and cheese, and in the middle was a small box wrapped in silver paper. She tucked a cold bottle of champagne under her arm, grabbed two glasses, and brought it all out.

Carolyn spotted the bottle first. "That's the good stuff!"

"Only the best for you," Ruxandra said. "Open it up."

"One day, I must meet your sugar daddy." Carolyn's strong, sure hands made quick work of the cork and got the champagne into the glasses without spilling a drop.

"I don't have a sugar daddy." Ruxandra took a glass.

"Girl your age?" Carolyn shook her head. "Either you inherited it, or some man is paying your bills in exchange for your goods."

"I'm older than I look."

"Which makes you what, twenty?"

Ruxandra laughed and took a drink, letting the bubbles tickle her throat. She looked eighteen and could pass for early twenties, but she was far, far older than Carolyn knew.

"Ruxandra?" Carolyn sounded suddenly uncertain. She pointed at the box. "What's this?"

"*That*," Ruxandra said with satisfaction, "is for our three-month anniversary."

Carolyn's hand went over her mouth. Her eyes shone. "Oh, you shouldn't have! Oh God, I didn't get you anything!"

"I don't want you to get me anything," Ruxandra said. "I want you to open your gift."

Carolyn kissed her hard on the mouth and grabbed the gift. Her strong hands made quick work of the ribbon and quicker work of the wrapping paper. She opened the little box, and her eyes went wide. Inside, nestled in a bed of white velvet, lay a silver anklet with round turquoise stones.

"Oh my, Ruxandra. It's . . . it's beautiful." She kissed Ruxandra again, the touch of her lips and tongue sending heat through Ruxandra's body..

Ruxandra took the anklet and knelt, letting her fingers slip down the length of Carolyn's leg before sliding the silver chain around her ankle and doing up the clasp. "I knew it would look great on you."

"It's so wonderful!" Carolyn raised her leg to look. Then she leaned in and hugged Ruxandra tight. "God, I wish we could stay like this forever."

Nothing stays forever. Ruxandra looked away. The weight of time between them suddenly loomed large, pushing against her joy. She shook her head, shedding the past like a dog shedding water. She didn't want to think about it. Instead, she ran her hand up Carolyn's leg, feasting her eyes on the long length of it and the bare skin above the stocking. *Tonight, we have time . . .*

"Oh no you don't." Carolyn sat back and waggled a finger. "I've got plans for you, girl, and you're going to need all your energy. So eat something."

"I thought you'd never ask." Ruxandra knelt before her again. Carolyn clamped her legs together. Ruxandra kissed each knee and started working her way up. "You know what goes best with champagne . . ."

The doorbell rang.

"Relief!" Carolyn jumped to her feet. "I'll get it!"

Ruxandra stood, muttering, "Who in the *hell* . . ." Then she caught the woman's scent on the other side of the door. *Oh God. It can't be.* Ruxandra opened her senses. The woman waiting in the hallway blazed like a spotlight. *It is.*

"Maybe it's your next order of champagne," Carolyn said over her shoulder. Her heels clicked on the marble floor. "Or your sugar daddy come to call!"

Don't answer it. But Ruxandra couldn't get the words out. The woman on the other side knocked again. Carolyn reached for the knob.

Ruxandra moved faster than humanly possible. Her body slammed against the door, her hand tight around the handle. "No!"

Carolyn jumped back, eyes and mouth wide with shock.

"What are you waiting for, my love?" the woman on the other side whispered. Thankfully, Carolyn couldn't hear her.

"Ruxandra?" Carolyn looked at the door then back at Ruxandra. "What is it, Ruxie? What's the matter?"

"Ruxandra." The woman's voice grew louder. "Let me in."

Why now? Ruxandra closed her eyes. Her head slumped forward and hit the door. Then, because she really had no choice, Ruxandra's hand twisted the handle and pulled the door open.

The woman outside stood even taller than Carolyn and had long hair so dark it was almost black. She held a suitcase in her hand and wore a smile on her face. Ruxandra didn't smile back. "Hello, Elizabeth."

"Ruxandra, darling!" Elizabeth reached out her arms and engulfed her in a tight hug. Ruxandra caught only a glimpse of Elizabeth's long gray coat and the tight blue evening gown underneath before Elizabeth pressed against her so tightly Ruxandra could tell she wore no underwear. Elizabeth's thigh pressed up between Ruxandra's legs, and she leaned in for a kiss. Ruxandra turned her face away, and Elizabeth's lips hit her cheek. Elizabeth pretended to be unperturbed. "Darling, it is so good to see you!"

"Ruxandra?" Carolyn's voice came out at once uncertain and aggressive, like the low growl of a cat seeing something it isn't sure is a threat. "Who is this?"

"Just what I wanted to ask," Elizabeth said, her voice sweet and condescending as if speaking to a confused child. "Are you the help, girl?"

Carolyn's hands clenched into fists. She stepped toward Elizabeth. "The what?"

"Carolyn!" Ruxandra's voice came out louder than she meant it to and echoed through the apartment. Carolyn stopped moving forward, though her fists stayed clenched. Ruxandra pulled away from Elizabeth's embrace. "It's all right."

Carolyn sized Elizabeth up. "Ruxie, who *is* she?"

"Elizabeth Bathory." Ruxandra hoped the name meant nothing to Carolyn. Hoped even more that she wouldn't connect the tall woman in front of her with the legendary dark-haired countess who had murdered and bathed in the blood of more than three hundred girls *before* Ruxandra made her a vampire. "She's a friend."

"A lover, actually," Elizabeth said.

"*Ex*-lover." Ruxandra took Carolyn's hand, forcing her fingers between the other woman's until Carolyn's fist unclenched. "Why are you here, Elizabeth?"

Elizabeth batted her pale-blue, almost silver eyes—eyes the same color as Ruxandra's. "To see you, Ruxandra, dear. Why else?"

Carolyn's lips pressed into a tight white line. She pulled her hand free and shoved her chin in Elizabeth's direction. "And when were you going to tell me about this one coming to visit?"

"I didn't know about Elizabeth coming to visit."

"Charming as this little spat is," Elizabeth said, "I would much rather watch it sitting than standing. Or aren't you going to invite me in?"

"You're already in," Carolyn said, anger heating her words. "And no one invited you."

"Ruxandra?"

A long time ago, Ruxandra had learned to pitch her voice in a range no human could hear. She turned so Carolyn couldn't see her lips move. "Do *not* hurt her."

"I wouldn't dream of hurting anyone," Elizabeth said, without changing her voice. "Not even your little Spanish doll here."

Carolyn shoved Ruxandra aside. "What the *fuck* did you say?"

"Sit down, you foulmouthed little slut."

Elizabeth's words hit Carolyn like a slap. Her face reddened with anger. Her fists shook and pressed against her legs. Then, because Elizabeth had *commanded* her, Carolyn walked back down the hallway and sat on the couch.

It wouldn't last, of course. Commands never did. How long it would last depended on what you told them to do—hours, days, even a week, if it was a simple command. Commanding someone to kill herself was almost impossible.

Ruxandra stepped close enough to Elizabeth to smell the blood on her breath. "Don't you *ever* do that again."

"Oh, please." Elizabeth waved Ruxandra away. "She's just a human."

"I like her. Now, what are you doing here?"

"Visiting," Elizabeth said in a pleased, sing-songy voice. She stepped past her and walked down the hall, heels clicking and skirt swishing. "It's a very small place, isn't it?"

Ruxandra followed. "It's big enough for me."

"You two left your underwear on the floor. How cute. No wonder it smells like sex." Elizabeth wrinkled her nose as she looked back over her shoulder. She was very beautiful—would always be beautiful. Once, long ago, Ruxandra had fallen for that beauty.

"And food. Why do you have food, Ruxandra?"

"To eat," Carolyn said, her tone making it clear what she thought of the question.

Elizabeth sat in Ruxandra's favorite chair. "Fattening you up, is she?"

"Rude, are you?"

"Behave, Elizabeth." Ruxandra sat down beside Carolyn. "I mean it."

"Fine, fine. I was only joking," Elizabeth said. "Well. Let's all get better acquainted, shall we? Ruxandra, do you have anything to drink?"

Ruxandra held back a growl, knowing Elizabeth was baiting her. "Champagne, brandy, coffee."

"Yes, darling." Elizabeth looked at Carolyn the way a snake regards a mouse. "But do you have anything to *drink?*"

Ruxandra glared. Elizabeth shrugged. "Later, then. So tell me, how did you and this charming young . . . *lady* meet?"

She paused long enough before "lady" to make the word an insult. Ruxandra took a firm grip on Carolyn's hand. "At a club. Carolyn is a dancer. A marvelous dancer. The best."

"I see," Elizabeth said, drawing out the phrase. "Did Ruxandra fuck you that night, or did she wait an entire day?"

Carolyn's voice sounded cool and hard, like sharpened steel. "It must kill you to see me with her for you to act like such a bitch."

Elizabeth laughed. "Silly girl. I had Ruxandra long before you."

"Yeah? You start when she was twelve?"

Elizabeth's eyebrows went up. "Oh my, you are innocent, aren't you?"

She can't. Not here, not now. "Elizabeth . . ."

"Oh, dear," Elizabeth said with a cold laugh. "Haven't you told her?"

"Told me what?" Carolyn stood up. "I don't know what your game is, and I don't care how long you've known Ruxie—"

"Ruxandra," Elizabeth said.

"*Ruxie.* She's with me now. If you don't like it, you can fuck off."

"It isn't that easy, is it, *Ruxandra?*"

"I can make it easy," Carolyn said. "I can—"

In the time it took to blink, Elizabeth appeared in front of her, an inch away from Carolyn's nose. "No. You can't."

"Enough!" Ruxandra pushed Elizabeth away and turned her back on her. "Please, Carolyn. Don't argue with her."

Carolyn's eyes bored into Ruxandra's. "You taking her side?"

"No, I—"

"Maybe I should just go."

"Excellent idea," Elizabeth said.

"Shut up!" The words came out in an animal snarl, and deep within Ruxandra, the Beast, dark and vicious and always ready for violence, stirred.

The Beast was a legacy of the hundred years Ruxandra spent in the forest, refusing to drink human blood. Her mind had faded, her body had changed shape, and a new, separate personality had emerged. It was a primitive mind, dedicated wholly to survival. It did not comprehend the human world. People—even Ruxandra—were "Woman" or "Man." Everything else that moved was "Prey" or "Enemy" or "Thing."

Even now, three hundred years after she had regained control of her mind, the Beast still lived inside her head. Mostly it slept, but hunger or fury always made it stir. Then it would try once more to take over her mind and her body.

Don't get so angry. That's what it wants. She shoved the darkness and the Beast down inside her and took Carolyn's hands. "Please, Carolyn. This isn't about you."

Carolyn pulled away. "Feels like it."

"You're not that important, dear," Elizabeth said. "This is about Ruxandra, who's coming with me back to Los Angeles."

"What?" The word flew out of Ruxandra as a bark of laughter. "You can't be serious!"

"But I am."

"You're not going to Los Angeles with her!" Carolyn grabbed Ruxandra's arm. "Tell her!"

"Don't be silly," Elizabeth said. "Of course she'll come with me. Won't you, Ruxandra?"

"She will not! Ruxandra?"

"Enough!" *So much for not waking the neighbors.* But if they kept arguing, it would not end well. Ruxandra put her hand over Carolyn's and pulled her to the bedroom. "Elizabeth, I will talk to you in a minute."

Ruxandra closed the bedroom door behind them as if that would give them privacy. It was an illusion, of course. Elizabeth could hear everything in the apartment—everything in the building if she wanted. But the shut door would make Carolyn feel better, and that was all Ruxandra wanted because Carolyn was *furious.*

"Where the *fuck* does she get off?" Carolyn stomped back and forth across the floor. "Who is she, Ruxandra? What, did she fuck you when you were a kid and now wants to take you back? The bitch looks thirty at least. She had no business messing with you, *ever.*"

"Carolyn, calm down."

"I *won't* calm down. That fucking *puta* wants to take you away from me!"

"Carolyn!" Ruxandra caught Carolyn's face between her hands. "I'm not hers. I'm yours. And I'm not going anywhere."

"You're damn right you're not." Carolyn grabbed Ruxandra and pushed her back against the door, kissing her hard on the mouth. "You're mine, you hear? *Mine.*"

Carolyn kissed her again and ran her hand hard down the front of Ruxandra's body. She shoved Ruxandra's skirt up, shoved her fingers inside. Ruxandra gasped and grabbed Carolyn's shoulders. Carolyn's other hand tangled into her hair. Her tongue pushed past Ruxandra's lips as her fingers thrust hard inside her. Ruxandra moaned. Carolyn pulled her mouth off Ruxandra's and slammed her fingers into her harder and harder. Ruxandra's knees buckled and she cried out as the climax took her.

"There." Carolyn's fingers slipped out, leaving Ruxandra open and empty and wanting more. "That will show that bitch out there who you belong to."

It really won't. Ruxandra kissed her lightly on the lips. "My love."

"You'll tell her to go now, won't you?" Carolyn's eyes were wide and serious. "You're not going to let her stay here."

"I must." Ruxandra put a finger over Carolyn's lips before she could protest. "But I'll get rid of her as soon as I can. I promise."

"Why not now?"

"It's complicated. She's an old friend—"

"She's a bitch."

"Yes," Ruxandra said. "But she's also someone I must deal with. And then I promise to get rid of her."

"Do that," Carolyn said. "Now walk me out."

Ruxandra opened the bedroom door. Carolyn stalked out, grabbed her coat and purse, and picked her underwear up off the floor.

Elizabeth leaned back in her chair and smiled. "So *nice* to meet you. I'm sure I'll see you again. Soon."

Carolyn stomped past without answering. Ruxandra followed. "I'll see you tomorrow night at the club, all right?"

Carolyn kissed her long and hard on the mouth. "You'd better."

Ruxandra watched until the elevator came and Carolyn stepped inside. Then she closed the door, locked it, and returned to the living room.

"Quite the little alley cat," Elizabeth said. "When are you going to drink her?"

"What do you want, Elizabeth?" Ruxandra's voice came out flat.

"I told you. I want you to come back to Los Angeles with me."

"Why?"

"Do I need a reason?"

"Yes." Ruxandra picked up the champagne glasses and drank them both.

Elizabeth shuddered. "How can you drink that?"

"It tastes good." Ruxandra picked up the bottle and the plate and took them to the kitchen.

Elizabeth followed her. "Why are you cleaning, darling? Just leave it and let's go."

"I am cleaning because this is my home. And I'm not going *anywhere* with you."

"Because of that girl? She's a dago tart. You can find a hundred like her in Los Angeles."

"I like Carolyn. And I'm *not* going to Los Angeles."

"Well, if she's so important to you, I'll get her," Elizabeth said. "I can tell her all about you."

Ruxandra dropped the plate and bottle on the counter. "Don't. You. Dare."

"Maybe about our time in Castle Csejte? Or the Beast? I'm sure she'd love to hear how you spent a hundred years as an animal."

"You stay *away* from her!"

21

"Why? It's not like you're going to turn her."

"I . . ." Ruxandra turned away and tossed the food into the garbage. "I might."

"No, you won't," Elizabeth scoffed. "You haven't turned anyone since me."

It was true, and Ruxandra knew it. The problem was she hadn't found anyone she wanted to turn. Anyone who craved being a vampire wasn't anyone she could stand for a long period of time. And anyone who didn't, she wouldn't curse with it. As for Elizabeth . . .

Elizabeth screaming and contorting as her human flesh became immortal, tearing out the throats of a dozen women as the initial hunger ripped through her. The deep, dark smell of blood and slaughter and death spilling out through the whorehouse.

"Given how you turned out," Ruxandra said bitterly, "are you surprised?"

"Tut-tut." Elizabeth waggled a finger, her vulnerability vanishing. "Mean, Ruxandra. So then, are you going to kill her when you're done with her? Because that's the only other choice."

Ruxandra put the plate in the sink. "Unlike you, I know how to deal with humans."

"You killed the one in Paris. Kade told me."

"One out of five in Paris."

"And the one in—"

"Enough!" Ruxandra's fist came down hard enough on the marble counter that a crack ran the length of it. *I am not like you.* "Why are you here?"

"I told you."

"No, you told me what you wanted. *Why* are you here?"

Elizabeth went to the living room. She opened her suitcase, pulled out a newspaper, and held it out to Ruxandra.

Ruxandra turned her back and poured the champagne down the sink, just to make Elizabeth wait. Then she walked back to Elizabeth and took the newspaper. The headline sent a chill through her:

"Vampire Killer Stalks the Streets"

"Oh, Elizabeth," Ruxandra said, her voice barely a whisper. "What have you done?"

"That's the problem," Elizabeth said. "It isn't me. There's someone new out there."

NEW? BUT *that's not possible. Not unless . . .*

"You mean you *made* someone and let them get out of control?" Ruxandra scanned the article. "Six kills? In public? That's incredibly stupid. Especially these days."

"I noticed. And, again, it wasn't me. I didn't make this one!"

"Then who? Dorotyas?" Elizabeth's servant had been small-minded, petty, and vicious as a human. Elizabeth turned her into a slave vampire, taking her freedom in exchange for immortality. It had done nothing to improve her. "I can see her being that stupid."

"Dorotyas is devoted to me. She can't turn anybody without my permission."

Unless she's gotten sick of you. "Then it has to be one of Kade's."

Kade was the only male in their little group. He was also a sorcerer. The ability to manipulate the world around them with thought and ritual was rare, both among humans and vampires. All his human magic vanished when he became a vampire, and he spent years learning to use vampire sorcery. Ruxandra, Elizabeth, and Dorotyas all tried it themselves, but none had been able to work it.

Elizabeth shook her head. "Kade has been in Germany since the war."

"One of his couldn't take a ship?"

"Not without his permission. You know what he's like."

True. Kade had begun experimenting with creating other vampires in the late eighteenth century. Several of his "children" ran wild, and the humans tracked them down, reducing the vampires' lair to rubble with cannons and fire. Kade only escaped by digging deep into the cellar and staying there while the castle burned down above. He had been fanatical about control ever since. *If it isn't one of his . . .*

But that's not possible. There're only the four of us.

Ruxandra had made Elizabeth into a vampire. Elizabeth made Dorotyas. Kade drank Elizabeth's blood after Ruxandra beat the woman almost to death. And Ruxandra . . .

"I send you out instead, my child, "the fallen angel said, "to sow chaos and fear, to make humans kneel in terror and to ravage the world where I cannot."

The fallen angel pushed open Ruxandra's mouth and slipped the finger inside. "Soon you will be freer than you have ever dreamed."

A drop of blood dripped from her finger onto Ruxandra's tongue. Burning pain blossomed in her mouth. It enveloped her head then her entire body. Every fiber of her being burned. Ruxandra opened her mouth and screamed . . . .

Her father, Vlad Dracula, thought to gain the power to defeat his enemies by sacrificing his daughter. Instead, she'd ripped his head off and drunk his blood before killing everyone else in the cave.

In her first months as a vampire, killing horrified Ruxandra. She ran away from human society, hiding in the woods and living off animal blood. For a time she thought that would give her enough control to survive. Then she met Neculai, a woodsman, and in a few short weeks fell in love with him and murdered him for his blood. After that, she retreated deep into the forest, determined to die rather than drink human blood again.. The more animal blood she drank, the more her humanity faded until only the Beast remained.

One hundred years later, Elizabeth found her. Beautiful, charming, vicious Elizabeth, who fed her human blood. Who brought Ruxandra back, even as she used the Beast's madness and hunger for her own ends. Elizabeth who loved her and cared for her and manipulated her and told her that if they could be together forever, everything would be better.

I made Elizabeth.

Elizabeth made Dorotyas.

Kade drank Elizabeth's blood when she was injured to become a vampire.

And that's all of us.

Ruxandra had traveled the world. She'd heard legends and rumors from almost every culture she had visited. She'd found evidence other vampires existed before but had found none alive anywhere on earth. While Elizabeth and Dorotyas had made others in the past, none still lived as far as she knew.

None except us.

Ruxandra's eyes narrowed. Her voice hardened. "This isn't something you put together just to get me to come with you, is it? Because *that*—"

"No, it isn't," Elizabeth cut her off, her own voice cold and angry. "Even though you should be with me."

"No. I shouldn't."

Elizabeth closed the distance between them. "We were wonderful together."

Elizabeth's mouth landing on hers, her tongue ramming between Ruxandra's teeth. Her hands grabbing Ruxandra's breasts and pushing her up against the wall. One hand slipping down, pulling up her skirt . . .

"I don't want to," Ruxandra whispered. "Please."

Ruxandra shook her head. "It was wonderful for *you*."

"It was wonderful for *us*." Elizabeth's voice turned as gentle and as soft as when she seduced Ruxandra three hundred years before. Even now, Ruxandra shivered at the sound of it. "I missed your touch, you know." Elizabeth's hand landed on her shoulder, gentle as the brush of flower petals. "I'm sure you missed mine."

Ruxandra brushed her hand off and turned away. "You just chased my girlfriend out of my apartment, Elizabeth. Don't try to start something."

Elizabeth's body pressed tightly against hers, her breasts and hips pushing hard against Ruxandra's back. Her long fingers wrapped around Ruxandra's shoulders. Her mouth pressed against Ruxandra's ear. "She isn't your girlfriend. She's your plaything, and you know it."

Ruxandra didn't move. Elizabeth's smell—a new dusky perfume mixing with her own scent—threatened to overwhelm

Ruxandra. The touch of her, the *presence* of her sent shivers down Ruxandra's spine in a way no human could.

Elizabeth's lips caressed her ear, then her neck. Her hands slipped down to Ruxandra's breasts. "We are Blood Royal, Ruxandra. She is only human."

Ruxandra caught Elizabeth's hands, pulled them off her, and stepped away. "I *like* humans. Humans are fun."

"Humans are food."

"Humans don't try to run my life."

Elizabeth crossed her arms. "Now that's not fair."

"Fair? You wreck my evening, drive off my girlfriend, and show me *this*." Ruxandra thrust the newspaper toward her. "And you want me to be fair?"

"Fine." Elizabeth snatched the paper from her hand. "Forget her, then. I need your help, Ruxandra. I need you to find this stupid creature and stop it."

"You have Dorotyas. You have *you*. You don't need me."

"Dorotyas and I didn't spend a hundred years hunting our food through a forest with our noses."

"No." Ruxandra grabbed Elizabeth's bag and headed for the guest room. "It's almost sunrise."

Elizabeth tossed the paper on the coffee table and followed right on her heels. "We need a tracker, and that's you."

"No." Ruxandra put the suitcase down in the guest room. "You sleep here."

"We need to talk more about this."

"Not now, we don't." Ruxandra left Elizabeth in the guest room and went to her own bedroom. She shut the door and leaned her head against the cool wood. Her body trembled— with anger, with fear, with the knowledge that everything could go bad so very easily. She closed her eyes and sighed. The room smelled of Carolyn. *Oh God, why now, Elizabeth? Things were going so well here.*

An hour later, while Elizabeth slept, Ruxandra put on a full-length skirt with thick stockings underneath, a wool jacket over her blouse, gloves on her hands, sunglasses on her eyes, and a wide-brimmed hat. She slipped out of the apartment and down to the predawn streets. Even at this hour people were about, walking to or from jobs or sweeping the streets.

Ruxandra had no time to move at human speed.

Ruxandra discovered 350 years ago that she could move about unnoticed. It wasn't invisibility, though close to it. She simply wished not to be noticed, and people ignored her. She could stand between two people talking, and they would never acknowledge her presence. Now, Ruxandra became unnoticeable and ran faster than the cars on the street. She wove in and out of the people on the sidewalks, racing the sun before it became high enough to shine down on her and burn her through her layers of clothes.

In less than a minute, she'd crossed the half mile to the Western Union office and stepped inside. She turned notice-able, and the man behind the counter smiled at her as if she had always been there. He gave her a pencil and paper and told her to take her time. Ruxandra thanked him and stood at the counter thinking.

The problem with the telegram is that it completely lacks privacy. At least two people would read it, possibly more. It needed to be clear but give away nothing. It took her two minutes to compose the message, two more to write it legibly. She handed the piece of paper to the man behind the counter and then stood and watched as he typed it into the machine:

MEMBER OF CLUB MAKING PROBLEMS LOS ANGELES
STOP ANY OF YOURS ON THIS SIDE OF POND STOP ELIZ-
ABETH WANTS COMPANY STOP REPLY SOONEST STOP

Ruxandra stepped outside and looked up. It would be a race home to avoid the sun, but she didn't want to go back yet. She vanished from notice again and ran south to Fourteenth Street. Between Seventh and Eighth Avenues sat Little Spain, where Carolyn lived with her family. Carolyn never allowed Ruxandra to go there for fear her mother would realize the nature of their relationship. Ruxandra followed her home once anyway, just to be close to her.

Carolyn's father owned a small cigar shop in a brownstone, and the family lived above it. Ruxandra easily jumped onto Carolyn's windowsill and peeked inside. Four girls lay in the bed—Carolyn and her younger three sisters. The smaller ones looked like miniatures of their sister, long legs showing beneath their nightdresses, long hair tied up for the night. They cuddled around Carolyn like puppies. Ruxandra felt a stab of envy.

Carolyn wasn't asleep. She stared out the window—directly at Ruxandra, though she didn't notice her. Tears streamed down her face, and her breath hitched with slow sobs. Ruxandra heard her praying in whispers.

"Please, God, I know I'm a miserable sinner. I know what I do is against your laws, but please, please don't let that woman take her from me. Please." The last word came out louder than

Carolyn meant, and one of her sisters stirred. Carolyn jammed her fist into her mouth to keep quiet.

Ruxandra bit her lip to keep from calling out to her lover. She kissed her fingertips and pressed them against the glass before jumping down. Then she ran, racing the sun back to Ansonia.

I don't want it to end. Not yet. Not like this.

By the time Ruxandra woke up, the sky was fading from dark blue to black. Ruxandra sent her senses and mind out. Elizabeth wasn't in the apartment, or even the building. *Which means she's out causing trouble somewhere.*

Ruxandra cast her mind wide. It took some effort, but she sensed every living thing aboveground for five miles around, from pigeons on the roof to rats in the gutters to the people in the streets. She even sensed the vermin in the sewers, though not anything deeper. Earth and rock reduced her ability to sense life from miles to mere yards. The pigeons and rats glowed like sparks in her mind. The humans burned like torches. And in the middle of Central Park, Elizabeth's presence blazed like a bonfire.

Dammit. She can't hunt there. It's too close.

It only took five minutes for Ruxandra to go from naked to cleaned up, made up, and dressed up. With no time to marcel her hair, she combed it into a plain bob and pomaded it into place. Pale was fashionable, which made things easier. Dark eyeliner, gray eye shadow, dark-red lips. She didn't bother with eyelashes because hers looked fine, and curling them always felt silly. Then she slipped into a dark-green dress with matching hat and shoes, and she put on her dark-gray coat.

Not as elegant as Elizabeth, though.

Ruxandra could manage cute without trying and beautiful with very little work. But though she put on a good imitation of elegance, Elizabeth had it down in a way that Ruxandra, even after three hundred years of practice, despaired of ever matching. *Fortunately, I don't need to tonight. I just need to keep her overly elegant self from causing me too much grief.*

She took the stairs down to the lobby. Patrick smiled. "Good evening, Miss Black."

"Good evening, Patrick," Ruxandra said. "Did you see my friend leave? Tall, dark-haired woman who came in last night?"

"I did," Patrick said, his white teeth flashing out from between his ruddy lips. "She came through about an hour ago. Had a nice conversation with her before she went out."

Conversation? "What about?"

"Your friend Carolyn. Wanted to know what club she danced in. Said she wanted to visit there this evening."

Oh God. "Thank you for telling me."

"My pleasure. You have a good evening."

"And you, Patrick."

An hour. How much trouble could she get into in an hour? God, I don't want to know.

Ruxandra turned unnoticeable the moment she stepped outside. She reached the park in less time than it took humans to cover a single block. Elizabeth stood beside a tree near the menagerie, her hand on the bark and her eyes on a young couple. Ruxandra slowed down and stopped beside Elizabeth. The woman smelled of fresh blood. *She's already hunted.*

"See those two?" Elizabeth pointed with her chin. "Just came out of the woods."

Ruxandra looked. The woman wore a happy smile, and her hips swayed when she walked. The man looked smug. Both smelled of sex and sweat. "I see them. So what?"

"So, *he's* wearing a wedding ring and *she* isn't." Elizabeth licked her lips. "I think someone needs to teach her that girls who do that with married men get punished."

"I think you need to stop avenging your husband's infidelities," Ruxandra said. "He died three hundred years ago."

"He wouldn't have strayed if the sluts hadn't thrown themselves at him." Elizabeth's lips stretched into a grin. Her pupils became slits like a serpent's, and fangs slid out from between her lips. "Though I did like hearing them scream."

Ruxandra stepped in front of her. "Where is it?"

Elizabeth's head tilted to the side. "Why, Ruxandra, whatever do you mean?"

"There's blood on your breath. *Where is the kill?*" The last four words came out in a low growl.

Elizabeth laughed. "Why should you care, *Ruxandra*? It was just a human."

"It's trouble if someone traces it back to me. Where?"

Elizabeth stepped around her. "I'll tell you when I'm done with this one."

"No." Ruxandra's hand latched onto Elizabeth's arm, the grip tight and sure. Elizabeth growled, anger blazing in her eyes. Ruxandra didn't let go.

A moment later the blaze died out. Her eyebrow rose. "You never used to be so stubborn."

"Times change. What was she and what did you do with her?"

"*It*," Elizabeth corrected, "was a sixteen-year-old whore whose cunt hurt from the ten men she'd fucked today. All she wanted was to stop, so I granted her wish and then put her in the water." Elizabeth cast a longing look at the couple. "We could share them."

"I ate yesterday. I'm not hungry." *And you aren't, either. You just fed.* She didn't say it out loud. She'd never won an argument with Elizabeth, not in three hundred years. She tried another tactic. "Come with me."

"Where?" Elizabeth asked. "To see your girlfriend dance?"

"I thought we'd see a movie." *I have no intention of letting you get near Carolyn again.*

"A movie?" The distaste in Elizabeth's voice made it sound as if Ruxandra had invited her to muck out a stable. "Why would I go to one of those?"

"Because they're amazing." *And maybe it will keep you too occupied to wreck my life.* "I'll take you through Times Square on the way."

She put her arm through Elizabeth's and led her back to Broadway and the trolley. She kept it there for the short ride south to Times Square. Elizabeth used it as an opportunity to get closer, sitting hip to hip as they rode. Ruxandra didn't care.

As long as I can keep an eye on her.

The trolley pulled to a stop, and Elizabeth's eyes went wide with surprise.

Times Square shone as bright as day despite the late hour. The garish, glaring, giant signs selling Lucky Strikes and Maxwell House Coffee and Squibb's Dental Cream lit up the crowd in the square. People came and went from the theaters and clubs, chatting and laughing. Ruxandra led Elizabeth off the trolley and took a deep breath. The smells of humanity, of lust and fear, of sweat and soap and perfume, filled her nose.

"This is Times Square?" Elizabeth looked around her, lips pursed with distaste. "It's so garish."

"Isn't it?" agreed Ruxandra. "I love it. It's loud and silly and always filled with people. Now come, the movie theater is just a little way back up on Broadway."

"If it's up there," Elizabeth asked, "why bring me here?"

"Because Times Square is something everyone should see."

"No," Elizabeth said, her voice filled with distaste. "It isn't."

Three hundred years and you still haven't changed. Ruxandra, once she'd regained her senses, wanted to see the world, to experience everything in it. Elizabeth had been content in the castle, spinning webs of power and pain.

They flowed through the crowds until they reached the Capitol Theatre and a late-night showing of *My Best Girl.* Ruxandra loved the scent and sense of so many human lives almost as much as she loved the movies. She opened up her mind to feel the people's emotions as the lights went down. She laughed with the crowd at the silent gags, feeling their joy as well as her own. She sensed the men lusting after Mary Pickford and the women after Buddy Rogers. She smelled the lust and heard the movements of the couples kissing and groping in the back. It felt like living a hundred lives at once—ordinary, uncomplicated lives untainted by blood and hunger and the dark, violent past. But most of all, Ruxandra loved the movies for themselves. She marveled at the black-and-white moving pictures and the way the orchestra timed their accompaniment.

Elizabeth, on the other hand, radiated boredom.

Good. Maybe she'll go back to Los Angeles faster.

"That was wonderful," Ruxandra declared as they left the theater. "Let's see another one."

"That was terrible, and no." Elizabeth shook her head in disgust. "Is this how you spend your time?"

"It's fun," Ruxandra said.

"It's worse than opera."

Ruxandra shook her head. They first heard opera in Vienna when it was new, back when the Beast still raged within her. The voices rising so high and so powerful stirred her, even as they calmed the Beast's baser instincts. She basked in the pleasure of human emotion refined and patterned into art. Elizabeth, on the other hand, had been bored senseless. "You never appreciated culture."

"Culture is for little minds. Power is better." Elizabeth grabbed a big man by the arm, stopping him dead.

"Hey," he protested. "What's the big—"

"*Tell me where Club Mazuma is*," Elizabeth commanded. "*Now.*"

"Harlem." The big man pointed south. "That way on 144th Street."

"Thank you." Elizabeth released the man's arm and smiled at Ruxandra. "See?"

"Elizabeth . . ."

"Oh, don't worry. I'm not going to hurt your little friends." Elizabeth climbed into a cab beside the theater. "Club Mazuma. Coming, darling?"

Ruxandra fumed but got in.

Twenty-five minutes later they were in Club Mazuma. The gin was just as cold, the beat throbbed as hard as ever, but for once, Ruxandra felt not at all happy there. Especially when the drums rumbled and the horns blared and the Club Mazuma dancers came out like twelve whirlwinds.

Carolyn spotted Elizabeth and Ruxandra sitting together as soon as she came out. For a split second, she looked ready to kill.

Then her jaw set. She whirled faster, kicked higher, and smiled wider than the rest of the dancers. And every time she turned their way, her eyes locked on Ruxandra.

Just as the dance reached its climax, Elizabeth stood up.

"Well, this is boring," she said loud enough for everyone—including Carolyn—to hear. Her voice changed frequencies and only Ruxandra heard the next words. "I'm hungry. Take me where you hunt, or I'm eating the coat check girl."

That miserable . . . A dark, helpless rage made Ruxandra's skin crawl and her stomach tighten. Elizabeth walked away. On the dance floor, Carolyn's lips flattened into a tight line, and her eyes locked on Ruxandra, though she didn't miss a single step.

But Elizabeth didn't make idle threats.

I'm so sorry, Ruxandra mouthed at Carolyn. *I have to go.*

Ruxandra caught up to Elizabeth in the foyer, wrapped an arm through hers, and dragged her out onto 144th Street. The bright neon light from the Club Mazuma sign turned Elizabeth's lips from red to black. Ruxandra yanked her arm, putting them face-to-face. "What the *hell* do you think you're doing? You might as well piss on me like a cat marking its territory!"

"I'm hungry," Elizabeth said, ignoring her question. She sized up the passersby. Her eyes glinted in anticipation, shining silvery-blue and serpentine. "Take me hunting."

You just ate. You won't be hungry for days. Ruxandra went unnoticeable and pitched her voice below human hearing range. "Why not put it on the radio and tell everyone!"

"Maybe I should." But Elizabeth changed her voice and turned unnoticed just the same. She watched a trio of young dark-skinned women walking by dressed in bright yellow, scarlet, and blue, and giggling as the men tipped their hats. "You know we've never hunted together? Even after all this time? Take me out. Show me where you hunt."

Ruxandra's teeth ground together. *Fine, if it keeps her from being stupid.* "All right. But we hunt where I want, on my terms."

Elizabeth shuddered. "You're not going to make me take that hideous trolley again?"

"No." Ruxandra slipped off her shoes and picked them up. "We're running."

It took them five minutes to cover the eight miles to the Bowery. Ruxandra slipped her shoes back on her feet and took Elizabeth's arm again. "We're a pair of girls out for a bit of fun and a bit of money, got it? I'll find the prey."

Elizabeth put on her own shoes and looked in disgust at the worn-down houses and the worn-down men who inhabited them. "Here? In this godforsaken place? Why?"

"Because," Ruxandra said, "when people from godforsaken places go missing, no one goes looking. Now let's walk and show the men what they want."

They made themselves visible and walked, arm in arm, heads high, down the darkened street. People still prowled the streets despite the late hour. The women either clung to men's arms or stood near alleyways offering their bodies. Visiting sailors roamed from bar to bar, while poor men huddled in alleys. Ruxandra opened her mind and her senses wide, reading a thousand emotions.

Near the mouth of an alley, she found what she wanted.

He stood tall with broad shoulders and a predator's eyes and strong arms covered in sailors' tattoos. Ruxandra slowed her walk and smiled. Elizabeth rolled her eyes, and Ruxandra yanked on her elbow.

"Hello, sailor," Ruxandra said. "New in town?"

"Not completely." The man's accent was low-class British. "I've been here before."

"And what brings you here tonight?" Ruxandra stepped closer, letting the man breathe in her musky scent. "Looking for anything in particular?"

The man looked them both up and down. His eyes lingered on Elizabeth's large breasts. "I am."

"Hey." Ruxandra caught his arm. "Before you go looking at her, there's something you need to know."

The sailor's eyebrows rose. His voice went cool. "What is that?"

"Everything we do, we do together." She looked into his eyes. "Everything. Understand?"

A grin split the man's face.

"Good," Ruxandra said. "Now, do you have a room, or shall we start in that alley there?"

"I got a room." The sailor grabbed each of them by the arm, his grip tight and painful. Elizabeth looked bored. He hauled her in close. "You think you're better than me, whore?"

Elizabeth's eyes narrowed.

"Oh, she does." Ruxandra rubbed her body against his other side and breathed into his ear. "Right up until a man gives her a good, strong correction. Then she likes to apologize. On her knees."

The sailor's smile grew wider. He pulled Elizabeth closer. "We're going to start in the alley. I'm going to beat your ass hard enough you won't sit for a week. And that's just for a start."

Elizabeth glared at Ruxandra and let the man pull her into the alley. Ruxandra followed, clinging on the man's other arm.

He fought, at first. Then he begged. Then he started scream-ing. But this was the Bowery, and no one came looking until long after his screams stopped.

"For someone who said they were hungry, you sure wasted a lot." Ruxandra said as they walked through the near-empty streets to her apartment. She looked at the blood spatters that covered her. *I liked this dress. And this coat.*

Elizabeth shrugged. She wiped a large drop of blood from her face with her finger and licked it clean, her tongue as quick as a cat's. "You said we didn't have a lot of time, so I made the most of it. If we'd taken him back to his room, we could have used him for days."

Ruxandra rolled her eyes. "This is New York, Elizabeth. Even in the Bowery people tend to notice someone screaming for days."

"What if they do?" Elizabeth said. "It's not as if they could stop us."

"They stopped *you*," Ruxandra said. "Or have you forgotten?"

"You stopped me," snapped Elizabeth. "And no, I have not forgotten."

Or forgiven, apparently. "We can't go into the lobby like this."

"Afraid of Patrick? He won't even notice—"

"We'll drip on the floor. Come with me."

Ruxandra led Elizabeth around the building until they stood below her apartment. She jumped to the first window ledge, two stories above. Three more jumps brought her to her balcony.

Elizabeth, still on the ground, laughed. "You've grown weak." She bent her knees and leaped.

Ruxandra watched Elizabeth sail up past the balcony, then slam down hard as she landed on it, breaking one of her high heels.

"That's why I didn't jump it all at once." Ruxandra almost managed to keep the satisfaction off her face. She started opening the balcony door and froze. "Oh, shit."

"What?" Elizabeth glanced at the apartment and her eyes went wide. "Oh. Your little toy is here."

"Stay unnoticed," Ruxandra said. "We slip in and get changed, then slip out again."

"Oh, I don't think so." Elizabeth pushed open the balcony door. "Carolyn, darling! We're out here!"

Goddamn it! "I don't need a fight in my apartment."

Elizabeth ignored her. "We hardly expected you so soon. I'd have thought you had lots more *entertaining* to do."

Carolyn couldn't miss the emphasis on the word. She opened her mouth to reply when Elizabeth swept into the living room. Carolyn's eyes went wide. "What the hell happened to you?"

"Carolyn!" Ruxandra stepped in front of Elizabeth before the other could speak. "*Nothing happened. Don't notice the blood on us.*"

Ruxandra hated to command Carolyn but there was no other choice. Carolyn's eyes slid away from their blood-spattered dresses and met Ruxandra's. "Where the fuck have you been?"

"Commanding her?" Elizabeth's eyebrows rose. "Tut-tut. So much for trust in your relationship."

"Shut up."

"Yeah, shut up, *puta.*" Carolyn slurred the words. Her rumpled dress looked as if she'd fallen a few times in it.

"Been drinking, dearie?" Elizabeth asked.

"Fuck you." Carolyn lashed out her hand at Ruxandra's face. Ruxandra saw it coming long before it hit. She stayed still anyway. The hard flat of Carolyn's palm smacked against Ruxandra's cheek, making her wince. Carolyn glared. "You walked out of my show!"

"I had to."

"Because of the bitch here?" Carolyn shoved a thumb toward Elizabeth. "Why? She decide she needed to revisit old times?"

"No." Ruxandra reached for Carolyn's shoulders. "It wasn't like that at all. Please, Carolyn."

Carolyn shoved her hands away. "Then I come looking for you and what, you're too busy messing around on the balcony to answer the door?"

"I didn't hear the door—"

"Patrick let me in." Carolyn pushed Ruxandra back. "I told him you were letting me stay here."

"So you're broke as well?" Elizabeth said. "You do know how to pick them, Ruxandra."

Carolyn spun, spitting out fast, furious words in Spanish at Elizabeth. "*Tú eres más fea que el culo de un mono.*"

Elizabeth smiled. "*Me cago en tus muertos.*"

Carolyn swung a fist. Elizabeth was across the room, sitting in Ruxandra's favorite chair, before it landed.

"You stupid little girl." A dark, dangerous smile spread across Elizabeth's face. "You have no clue what you've stumbled into."

Carolyn stared at the air where Elizabeth had stood. "What the *hell*?"

"I'm telling her, Ruxandra."

"No!" Panic welled up inside Ruxandra. "Please, don't do this, Elizabeth."

"Oh, but I must." Elizabeth's smile grew wider. "You want your girlfriend to know the truth, don't you?"

Carolyn advanced on her. "What the fuck are you talking about, *puta*?"

"Ruxandra is a cold-blooded killer." Elizabeth's eyes bored into Carolyn's. "Or did you think she got her money from investments?"

"Fuck you, bitch."

Ruxandra reached for her. "Carolyn, it's not what you think—"

"Ask Ruxandra where she took me after we left the club," Elizabeth said. "Ask her what happened in Paris."

"Shut up!" Carolyn spun around, her eyes locking onto Ruxandra's. Her lips trembled. She no longer sounded drunk, and her words came out fast and staccato and scared. "She's full of shit, right? You didn't kill anyone. Right?"

"Carolyn . . ."

"It's not true. Say it isn't true." Carolyn's voice rose, and her eyes went wide. "Say it isn't true!"

"Oh, it's true." Elizabeth purred out the command. "*Look at the blood on the floor.*"

Carolyn looked.

"Ruxie?" Carolyn's voice broke. All her bravado vanished. The change in her voice struck Ruxandra like a punch. Carolyn stared at the spatters of blood that dripped from Ruxandra and Elizabeth's clothes. Slowly she raised her eyes. "Ruxie, who . . . who did you kill?"

"Who?" Elizabeth asked. "Oh, little girl, better to ask how many."

Goddamn it, Elizabeth. Ruxandra felt her heart breaking, felt everything she had built crumble around her.

"You." Carolyn's face turned red again. She moved toward Elizabeth. "You made her kill them, didn't you?"

"Me?" Elizabeth laughed. "Don't be stupider than you must."

"No wonder you're trying to get rid of me." Carolyn stumbled toward her, one finger jabbing out as if she could skewer Elizabeth with it. "If she's a murderer, *you* made her into one."

"Actually"—Elizabeth's eyes changed to serpent slits and her mouth stretched wide, revealing her fangs—"she made me."

Carolyn's scream rang through the apartment. Elizabeth clamped onto her throat with a clawed hand, cutting off her air, and slammed her against the wall. She raised her other hand, its nails now silver talons, and slashed four deep, bloody furrows across Carolyn's breast. "No one *ever* takes what is mine!"

In the moment it took for Ruxandra to move, Elizabeth plunged her teeth into Carolyn's throat and ripped the flesh away, sending blood spurting across the room.

CHAPTER
THREE

RUXANDRA'S FIST SMASHED against the side of Elizabeth's head with enough force to stave in her skull. Elizabeth yelped in pain and dropped Carolyn. Ruxandra kicked Elizabeth across the room and caught her lover with the same motion. She heard the crack of plaster where Elizabeth hit the wall but didn't care.

Carolyn convulsed and gasped. A hole gaped in her throat. Blood spurted from torn arteries and poured down over her dress. She tried to scream but no sound came out.

"Hush, sweetheart." Ruxandra cradled her in her arms. *Die Quickly. Die Quickly.*

Carolyn's hand came up, pawing at Ruxandra's chest, unable to grasp. Ruxandra caught it and held it tight. "Hush, love. I've got you."

It's not fair. Ruxandra's heart collapsed as her lover gasped for air that would not come. "I'm so sorry, love."

Carolyn's eyes went wide. Her mouth opened and closed, shaping words that could not come out. Then her eyes dulled, and she was gone. For a long moment, Ruxandra clutched the corpse in her arms. Carolyn's eyes stared sightlessly at the ceiling, her face frozen in horror and disbelief, the desperate cry of *not yet* forever locked away in broken, unmoving flesh.

Gently, slowly, Ruxandra laid Carolyn on the marble floor and straightened her dress. *My glorious dancer. My sweet girl. My love.*

"And now you're free to come with me," Elizabeth said. "Wasn't that easy?"

Rage shot through Ruxandra like an electric shock. A deep animal snarl, born in the Transylvanian forests and unused for centuries, rose from her chest. The Beast inside her clawed to get free. Ruxandra ignored it. *She* wanted this fight.

Ruxandra caught Elizabeth by the hair as she dodged and slammed her head against the wall, cracking both. Elizabeth raised her arms to protect her face, but Ruxandra batted them aside. She drove her fist against Elizabeth's face, again and again, shattering nose and cheekbones and sending silver ichor spattering against the floor and walls.

It wasn't enough.

Ruxandra shifted her grip and rammed her knee into Elizabeth's ribs until they broke under the barrage. She grabbed her arm, flipped her, and threw her hard. Elizabeth slammed against the floor, her neck and spine cracking. Ruxandra sat astride her chest, smashing her fists down until Elizabeth's head turned into a pulped, unrecognizable mess.

Ruxandra's vision narrowed. Another snarl, deeper and much more primitive, burst past her clenched teeth. The Beast wanted to turn fingers into claws and to rip and rend, to sink its teeth into flesh and tear chunks out while Elizabeth screamed and writhed. It wanted to shred Elizabeth's body and stomp on the pieces until nothing remained but the stains of her silver blood spattering the room.

No! Ruxandra hurled herself off Elizabeth and scuttled across the room on her hands and knees. *I won't let you take over. I won't!*

The Beast inside tried to claw her way out, to take over Ruxandra's mind and body and be free. Ruxandra shoved it back. *It's not supposed to be so strong. Not after all this time.*

She stared at Carolyn's bloody corpse remembering the love-making and the dancing and the joy of their nights out together. Ruxandra crawled across the room and took her dead lover's hand. As Ruxandra brought the cooling fingers to her lips, grief and loneliness welled up inside her and took the place of blind rage.

She used the emotions to force the Beast back down. It howled and struggled. It wanted to be free to destroy, dismember, and kill. But Ruxandra kept pushing it down until the Beast's angry snarls grew faint.

Then Ruxandra had control once more.

On the other side of the room, Elizabeth moaned in pain. Her head made wet crunching sounds as it shifted back to its original shape.

"Tha ee eee uuuu," Elizabeth moaned. Another crunch came, then the sound of jagged bone pulling from meat.

"Rullee . . . Ruxanra . . ." Elizabeth slurred the words from between her broken jaws, but Ruxandra still heard the reproach in them. "Yyy ouud you do that? You know you can't kill . . . ee like that."

Elizabeth stopped talking and cried out in pain. A dozen more wet pops sounded in rapid succession like a string of muffled fireworks as Elizabeth's face shifted back into shape. "So I really don't know why you bothered."

"It made me feel better." Ruxandra didn't take her eyes off Carolyn's torn throat and sightless eyes.

"She was only a human."

Tears welled up in Ruxandra's eyes, spilled over, and ran down her face. "She was my friend."

"No, she wasn't. *Ahh!*" Elizabeth stopped talking as her spine reformed, and her ribs snapped into place. At last she sat up, hissing with effort and pain. "*I* am your friend. I've known you for three hundred years. *She* was a toy for you to use to pretend you're one of them for a while. Nothing else."

"She wasn't!"

Elizabeth's words rode right over Ruxandra's angry cry. "And when *I* need help, when I need *you* to come to *me* for the first time in three hundred years, you'd rather sit here and play with your toy than help!"

"That isn't fair!"

"*Now* you care about what's fair?" Elizabeth's voice went up an octave. "When I found you, you were nothing but a mindless, naked animal feeding off the blood of squirrels. I fed you and gave you clothes and brought you back to civilization. I was your lover before that girl's great-grandparents were born, for God's sake! I did *everything* for you, and all you've ever done is leave."

Ruxandra didn't look at her, couldn't look at her. She felt like taffy in the hands of a candy maker, everything being twisted and pulled in different directions. She stared at the pool of blood around Carolyn's body. "You shouldn't have killed her."

"You shouldn't get so attached to your toys," Elizabeth said with deliberate, unyielding cruelty. She stretched her arms up, and the last of her bones clicked into place. "We're Blood Royal,

Ruxandra. Humans are playthings. Now we need to get cleaned up and go if we're to catch the morning train."

"We're not catching it."

"Ruxandra—"

"I'm not going anywhere until I take care of her!"

Elizabeth let out an exasperated sigh. "Don't be ridiculous. No one will miss her."

I will. She didn't say it. Elizabeth wouldn't care. "Her mother. Her father. Her sisters. Her friends. The people at the club. All of them will miss her."

They'll always wonder what happened. They won't understand. They won't know. Ever. The pain of it—hers and theirs together—brought fresh tears to her face. "They'll come looking for her. Here."

"Oh, very well," Elizabeth said. "But be quick. I want to be shut of this city."

Ruxandra let go of Carolyn's hand and wiped the tears from her face. *I'll cry later,* Ruxandra promised. *Right now, there are things to be done.*

There are always things to be done, after.

Ruxandra straightened Carolyn's legs and crossed her arms over her chest before pushing her eyes closed. Ruxandra kissed the dead girl on the forehead, then grabbed the rug's edge and pulled it out from under the furniture. "If she just vanishes, everyone will wonder what happened. They'll all watch me, asking if I know. This way, they'll know she's dead."

"So, you're going to drop her in an alley and let everyone believe someone tore her throat out with their teeth?" Elizabeth's voice dripped with sarcasm. "That's clever."

Ruxandra ignored her. She laid Carolyn on the rug and rolled her up, then she stripped off her own blood-and-ichor-stained clothes.

"Naked?" Elizabeth sounded amused. "Or do you want sex now? Because I—"

"Shut up." Ruxandra went to the kitchen and grabbed a long thin-bladed knife.

"And where are you going to carry that? In your purse?"

Ruxandra raised the knife and jammed it into her own forearm, sliding it between the bones until the handle pressed against her skin. It burned, the pain sharp and exquisite, and Ruxandra refused to show any of it.

Elizabeth's smug expression slipped for a moment. Then she put it back on and smiled again. "Am I supposed to be impressed?"

Ruxandra lifted Carolyn's carpet-wrapped body and stepped out onto the balcony. The sky had begun fading from black to dark blue, but there was still plenty of time before the sun rose again.

"This is silly, Ruxandra," Elizabeth called from inside. "Leave the girl alone. We need to go!"

Ruxandra shifted Carolyn's body to her shoulders and went unnoticeable. The carpet would be unseen, too, as long as she carried it. *Not that anyone watches the rooftops anyway.*

She jumped from her balcony to the roof across the street, landing off-balance. She adjusted the carpet as she ran across the roof and then jumped again. It was a tricky way to cross the city but, as Ruxandra had learned in the French Revolution, one of the best ways to do so without being spotted.

Halfway between Club Mazuma and Carolyn's parents' house in Little Spain, Ruxandra found an alley that turned out of sight of the street. Filthy, tall, soot-blackened warehouse walls rose on either side. Rats scuttled in the shadows.

Ruxandra jumped down and unrolled the carpet. She arranged Carolyn's body on the ground with the limbs askew and knelt astride it. Then she grabbed the handle of her knife and pulled. The skin and muscle had already closed around it, and Ruxandra had to cut them open again to make it come out. She pulled it from her forearm slowly, letting the flesh heal as the knife came out so none of her own silver blood fell into the alley. The pain was a sort of penance.

Not nearly enough, though. It's never enough.

Some of her lovers lasted only a day or a week. Some lasted months, like Carolyn. A few lasted years. Most times, Ruxandra left them behind without grief, changing taverns or clubs or cities or even countries. Sometimes, though . . .

Julio, the Spanish bullfighter who tried to strangle her to hide his affair from his wife.

Lauren, a Prussian spy in Venice, poisoned by the doge.

Johanne, in Finland, who saw her feeding and ran her through with a spear.

Audra who'd tried to turn her over to the Inquisition.

Ellissa, the London actress who'd been knifed in front of her outside the Haymarket Theatre.

Delfino, in France during the revolution, who'd tried to kill her with a stake and a cross and screamed for the mob with his dying breath.

She finished pulling the knife out of her arm and leaned over to kiss Carolyn's cold lips. "I'm so sorry, my love. But at least this way your family will know you're not coming home."

Sorrow overwhelmed her. Tears slid over Ruxandra's cheeks. Sobs racked and twisted through her, shaking her to her core and leaving her almost broken, though she made not a single sound.

Then she raised the knife and rammed it into Carolyn's body again and again. Ruxandra hacked and slashed, tearing open the girl's chest and stomach and her beautiful face until Ruxandra barely recognized her.

Ruxandra stood and stumbled back, letting the rest of her tears loose as she turned away from the ruin of her friend. She rubbed and snuffled away her tears, then she rolled the carpet back up and ran south to the bay. She threw the knife in first, sending it spinning out over the water. A flash of light from the rising sun glanced off it as it arced out high and far. She found a dozen rocks and rolled them up in the carpet. Two quick rips gave her cloth to tie the ends shut. Then she sent it flying out after the knife.

She didn't wait to see it hit.

Ruxandra sprinted. At top speed, she could outrun a cheetah, or a train for that matter. It wasn't a speed she could sustain for more than a minute, but that minute would be all she needed. Ruxandra wove through the predawn traffic and early-morning pedestrians, an unseen blur of movement and gust of wind that ruffled hair and rattled newspapers as she dashed past. She felt the sun rising higher. It hadn't hit the street yet, but even the refection of it off the windows would burn her terribly.

Patrick stood outside giving the sidewalk one more sweep before he headed home. Ruxandra skidded to a stop. *He let Carolyn in last night. Dammit.*

Commanding someone didn't last. Ruxandra usually used it for getting past drunks, or getting money out of rich men more interested in their bank accounts than her. But her other choices were to make a thrall of the man—drinking just enough of his blood to make him her slave or kill him, and Ruxandra didn't want to do either. Instead she slipped up beside him, still unnoticed, and whispered her command: *"Don't look around, don't stop what you're doing."*

Patrick started but kept working, his broom moving smoothly over the pavement.

Ruxandra leaned closer.

"If anyone asks you, tell them you did not speak to Carolyn last night. She did not ask you to let her in. You were here all night, and she did not come by at all. Do you understand?"

"I do, Miss Black."

"And this conversation never happened, either."

"Of course, Miss Black." A worried note crept into his voice, though he didn't—couldn't—turn around. "Is something wrong, Miss Black?"

Ruxandra bit her lip to keep more tears from flowing. "No, Patrick. It's all right. Everything is fine."

"That's good, Miss Black."

Ruxandra left him and raced around the building to jump up to her balcony. The command had been simple enough and would last a few days—long enough for him to answer anyone that came snooping around. Pale orange tinged the gray sky above. Ruxandra closed the doors and reached up to draw the curtains, then stopped. Blood covered her arms from her fingertips to her elbows. She swore and turned away, then she saw the true extent of the problem.

The apartment looked like a slaughterhouse. Blood and silver ichor spattered the walls and the furniture and sat in sticky congealing puddles on the floor. In the midst of it all, Elizabeth sat in Ruxandra's chair. She had bathed. Her skin shone. She wore a thick red bathrobe open wide at the neck and hip to show off the round curve of her breasts and the pale length of her legs. "I had begun to worry."

"Shut up." The cupboard where the maid kept the cleaning supplies yielded a bucket and a mop and rags. Still moving vampire-fast, Ruxandra managed to wipe the balcony doors clean and close the curtains just before sunlight peeked inside the apartment. Then she started on the rest.

The cleaning became another sort of penance. Three hundred years' experience taught her a great deal about cleaning up blood. Meticulously, with many trips to the bathtub to dump the bloody water and rinse the rags, she scrubbed the floor clean and blotted the wallpaper to pull the blood from it. The furniture took more water and salt and a great deal of scrubbing.

Elizabeth stayed in the chair and kept her mouth shut the entire time.

It took until noon to clean up the rest of the blood. Ruxandra closed her eyes and sniffed. The entire apartment smelled like lemon and bleach, except for her. Without a word to Elizabeth, she went into the bathroom and stood under the hot blasting shower, cleaning her body and hair with the same meticulousness as she had her apartment.

Sometime in the middle of it, she began crying again and kept crying as she dried off and crawled into bed. She curled up around a pillow, remembering the nights of passion and the smell of Carolyn's sweat and her sounds while they'd made love.

Eventually, sleep took Ruxandra, blotting out the pain the way she'd blotted the blood off the walls just a short time ago.

Elizabeth was asleep in the guest room when Ruxandra woke up. *Too much to hope she'd go back home.*

Ruxandra slipped out of bed and pulled on a kimono, then she went to the kitchen to fill a kettle and put on the gas. She took a French press, a grinder, and a bag of coffee beans down off the shelf. She ground them fast, making as much noise as possible, then put them in the press. When the water boiled, she poured it over the coffee, filling the apartment with its deep, rich smell.

Elizabeth hated the smell of coffee.

Since she'd become a vampire, Elizabeth refused to drink anything except blood. It was mostly an affectation, but the one thing that Elizabeth really didn't like was coffee.

Ruxandra poured a large mug and took it and the press into the living room so that Elizabeth could smell it better.

On impulse, Ruxandra went to the side table that held her phonograph and disks. She picked one, cranked the player, and put down the needle. Moments later, the newcomer Benny Goodman's clarinet led Ben Pollack and his Californians in a light, frothy jazz piece, with horns and drums beating in syncopation as Benny's clarinet flew up and down the register like a bird.

I hope she hates this, too.

Ruxandra sat in her favorite chair and waited. She drank half the coffee before Elizabeth came out of her bedroom still in her robe. She glared at the phonograph then at the mug in Ruxandra's hands. "Must you?"

"Yes."

Elizabeth sat down on the couch. "Yesterday. That wasn't the Beast that attacked me. Where did you learn to fight like that?"

"Fifty years in the Orient," Ruxandra said. "Before the Opium Wars."

"I see." Elizabeth looked at her hands. When she raised her head again, she wore the expression she used when doing something distasteful—face neutral, head high, chin up. "I'm sorry."

"No, you're not."

"I didn't think she meant *that* much to you."

"You knew *exactly* how much she meant to me, Elizabeth." Ruxandra's mug landed on the coffee table with a clunk. "And you killed her the first chance you got."

Elizabeth remained silent. Ruxandra waited.

"All right. I'm not sorry," Elizabeth said at last. "I meant everything I said last night. *All* of it. I need you, Ruxandra. I'm not a tracker. Dorotyas isn't a tracker. And that means neither of us have a chance in hell of finding the new vampire."

"*If* there's really a new vampire."

Elizabeth threw her hands up. "Good *God*, what must I do to convince you, Ruxandra? Do you think I came here just to ruin your life?"

"*Yes.*" The vehemence in Ruxandra's voice made Elizabeth sit back. Ruxandra let her anger pour into her words. "There are four of us, Elizabeth, plus whoever Kade turned. If it wasn't you or Dorotyas who made it, it must be Kade, so go bother him!"

Elizabeth's eyes narrowed and her brows went down. Her hands clenched into fists. Her voice came out cold and flat. "What if it's someone made the same way as you?"

"Humans barely believe in sorcery these days." Ruxandra picked up her coffee again, cradling her hands around the warm cup.

"Humans in the United States perhaps," Elizabeth said. "I spent eighty years in South America, and I assure you, they believe. Same with Russia and Africa and most of Europe. We *know* there were vampires before us. We've all read the legends. You talked to the fallen angel that first created vampires, for God's sake. So why won't you even entertain the possibility? Because I suggested it?"

Ruxandra didn't answer.

Elizabeth's eyes flashed red with anger. She stood up. "I'm going hunting."

Ruxandra's eyes came up. "You hunted last night."

"I spent most of my energy healing the mess *you* made of me." She stalked off to her bedroom. "I promise not to go near your club or any of your precious human *friends*. And while I am gone, I suggest you think about what is at stake here. Because if this one is willing to take on *me*, you can be damn sure it will have no qualms about taking on *you*. And how long will you be able to conceal yourself then?"

Elizabeth slammed the bedroom door. Ten minutes later, dressed to the nines, she stepped out, slammed it again, and walked out.

Ruxandra stared after her.

What if she's telling the truth?

Ruxandra remembered the desperate bloodlust that possessed her when she'd changed. It had happened to Elizabeth as well, and to Kade and Dorotyas, though Ruxandra hadn't seen it. It took over everything, took over all thoughts, all feelings. A new vampire drank until it was insensate.

If there is a new vampire, he's going to go through all that pain and turmoil, and worse. If he doesn't know there are more of us, or if he's scared of us, he could go insane. He might become another Beast. Or worse, end up under Elizabeth's control.

The thought horrified her for so many reasons.

Yes, she's the reason I'm not an animal and, yes, she was my lover, but she's a liar, and I can't trust her.

It took all of Ruxandra's strength to break away, and years longer to get over it. Even now, even with all that had happened, she still felt the bond, still felt a desire to make Elizabeth happy.

I should go to the club. To ask after Carolyn and allay their suspicions.

But Ruxandra had no desire to lead life like Elizabeth—the constant desire for power and the delight in the pain of others. The world was amazing. Addictive. More beautiful than Ruxandra could ever comprehend. Always so much more to see, so much more to do, so many bright and glorious people. To give it all up and go back? *Never.*

I should go to the club soon.

But she didn't. She stayed in her chair, still in her kimono, until Patrick knocked on the door at midnight.

Ruxandra slipped across the room and opened it. "Yes, Patrick?"

"Terribly sorry to disturb you, Miss Black." Patrick held up a small yellow envelope. "But the telegram boy said it was urgent."

"Of course." Ruxandra took the telegraph and ripped open the envelope.

"Do you want to send a reply, miss?"

"I don't . . ." Ruxandra read through the telegram twice before she finished the sentence. She folded it and put it back in its envelope. "No. No reply. Thank you, Patrick."

"You're welcome, Miss Black."

She closed the door and leaned against it, struggling to remain calm. The telegram had come from Kade:

ALL MY INITIATES ACCOUNTED FOR STOP NO ONE IN AMERICA STOP WHATS HAPPENING STOP

Ruxandra was back in her chair, the apartment light still off, when Elizabeth came in two hours later. She smelled of blood and sex and the sweat of a terrified human female. She smiled at Ruxandra. "Sulking in the dark?"

"No."

Elizabeth sat down on the couch. "Then what are you doing, Ruxandra? Because I need to get back to Los Angeles and—"

"We leave in the morning."

Elizabeth's face lit up. "Wonderful!"

"I'm only staying long enough to find your vampire," Ruxandra warned. "Then I'm coming back here."

"Of course." Elizabeth squeezed her tight. "I'll go pack my things. Then we'll go. I'm sure we'll catch the vampire in no time at all."

"I'm sure." Ruxandra stayed in her chair as Elizabeth practically danced into her room. *And as soon as I find him, I'm getting him the hell away from you.*

CHAPTER
FOUR

WHAT IS TAKING *so long?*

The morning sun shone down through the glass ceiling at Penn Station. Elizabeth had disappeared half an hour ago, ostensibly to buy tickets. Ruxandra, in her long summer coat, wide hat, gloves, and sunglasses, had found a shaded spot to stand on the platform to wait.

And wait.

It took Ruxandra six minutes to pack—the result of three hundred years' practice. In four minutes, her clothes—mostly practical for travel, with one formal outfit and three dresses for dancing—lay folded into her valise. In two minutes more, she'd opened her safe and packed her favorite jewelry and $10,000 in cash and gold coins into her purse.

Getting Elizabeth moving took considerably longer, including time for an argument over who would pack her bags, since Dorotyas usually did it. Then they took a cab to the station, and Elizabeth said she would get the tickets. Now Ruxandra couldn't find anywhere to stand without feeling like a steak being broiled. She glared up at the glass ceiling.

How long does it take to get tickets, for crying out loud?

Ruxandra growled and extended her senses through the station. Her mind wove through the crowds of people until she zeroed in on Elizabeth in a back hallway with a man. Both burned with lust, pleasure, and sexual energy.

Now? She's doing this now?

Ruxandra pulled her hat down farther and hurried through the morning light that drenched the station floor. She followed the blaze of Elizabeth's life force to a broom closet. As she got closer, she heard the man's thrusts, slamming Elizabeth against the shelves inside. Elizabeth's gasps and moans, the sounds feigned and real in equal parts.

So nice she's enjoying herself. Ruxandra pitched her voice below human hearing and snarled. "Going to be long?"

"Not . . . long . . . at all." The man pumping into Elizabeth gasped, his breathing erratic and his thrusts speeding up as he reached the edge of his orgasm. Elizabeth egged him on. "That's it. Fill me up. There's only one thing I like better than a man coming inside me. And that's a man dying inside me."

The man's groan turned to a cry of surprise. Ruxandra grabbed the door and yanked it open. Elizabeth's long legs were clamped tight around the dying man's waist, her fangs deep in his neck. Her lips clamped tight over the wound, draining the man's blood as he bucked and convulsed inside her.

"What the fuck are you doing?" Ruxandra hissed. She looked over her shoulder. The hallway was still empty, but chances are it wouldn't stay that way. "This is *not* the time for this!"

Elizabeth shuddered in pleasure. Her lips never left the man's neck, draining pints of blood from his body even as her own orgasm tore through her.

Ruxandra stepped in and pulled the closet door shut. Elizabeth's feet hit the floor a moment before the man's legs gave out. She let him drop, shuddered one more time, then pulled a dark-red handkerchief out of her pocket and blotted the blood from her lips.

"Are you insane?" Ruxandra demanded. "Doing this? Here? Now?"

"I needed money." Elizabeth held up the man's wallet.

"You killed him for his money?" Ruxandra could not believe it. "You should have just commanded him."

"But I wanted to be fucked, darling. I found listening to you and your little playmate the night before last most distracting." Elizabeth wiped between her legs and dropped the handkerchief over the man's face. "That is the best way to end a fuck with a mortal."

Ruxandra struggled to keep her voice even as anger flared inside her. "You realize if they find him they'll close the station to keep the murderer from escaping?"

"Then you'd better get our tickets, hadn't you?" Elizabeth tossed her the wallet.

"You said you would buy the tickets. Two sleeper compartments. Remember?" Ruxandra's eyes narrowed. "Or don't you know how?"

"Of course I know how. But I don't do that sort of thing. It's gauche. I make Dorotyas buy them."

For fuck's sake . . . Ruxandra threw the wallet back. "You haven't been a countess for three hundred years, Elizabeth. Buy the damn tickets."

"Fine." Elizabeth pulled the man's cash out and dropped the wallet. She stepped over his body, looking as satisfied as a cat in a creamery. "Come along."

Ruxandra fumed all the way to the ticket lineup. *Twenty hours on the Broadway Limited to Chicago. Sixty-three hours on the Los Angeles Limited. Then I am staying the hell away from her until I find the vampire.*

"One compartment for the two of us," Elizabeth said when they reached the counter. She looked at Ruxandra over her shoulder. "Far cozier that way, right?"

"Not with how you snore," Ruxandra pulled a billfold from her purse and peeled off two twenties. "Make that two, and non-adjacent, please."

Elizabeth raised an eyebrow but said nothing else until they left the counter. "Snore? Really?"

"Would you prefer 'you killed my girlfriend, and I'll be damned if I'll share a bed with you'?"

Elizabeth shook her head. "Stop being so sullen. You love to travel."

"On *my* terms," Ruxandra ground out between clenched teeth. "Not to fix your problems."

"*Our* problems, darling."

The train whistled, clanked, and started moving. Ruxandra lay down on the small bed in her compartment and closed her eyes.

She felt exhausted from the sun and the events of the last day. She was also getting hungry. *There will be no time to hunt before LA, either, unless I take someone on the train, which is risky. Maybe I could just find a snack.*

The kill gave nourishment. The passing of life force gave her strength and power, but she learned that a small drink slaked her thirst, at least temporarily, and it gave the mortal enough pleasure that he didn't remember the actual bite.

Which is what Elizabeth should have done in Penn Station. The image of the man convulsing as Elizabeth drank him floated through her brain. She shook her head and rolled over. *Stupid and careless even for her. She shouldn't have been hungry.*

She woke while the train rolled through the dark countryside. Ruxandra tossed on a pretty striped travel dress and finished her makeup and hair in five minutes. She found Elizabeth in the lounge car talking to a man.

Elizabeth wore a dark-green dress clung tight to her figure. Her hair was styled high, and her lips looked like wet rubies. The man in her company was tall, blond, and captivated.

Ruxandra took a seat nearby and pitched her voice so only Elizabeth could hear. "Don't kill him."

Elizabeth blotted her lips and behind the napkin said, "Why ever not?"

"Too conspicuous. No place to hide the body, and he'll be missed by his wife. Also, you ate this morning."

Elizabeth looked into the man's eyes as she stood up. "It is getting late. I should go to bed."

She headed for the door and whispered as she passed Ruxandra, "Don't be a spoilsport."

Ruxandra didn't move. "You already killed this morning. You don't need another."

"It's not about need, darling." Elizabeth tossed a glance over her shoulder that made it clear she expected the man to follow. "It's about desire."

No, it isn't. Ruxandra felt Elizabeth's hunger radiating from her as strong as her lust to cause pain. She watched the man leave money on the table and follow her. *So why is she so hungry?*

Ruxandra stayed in the lounge car until just before dawn, talking with the barmen and the other patrons, downing a few drinks—nonalcoholic thanks to Prohibition, but cool and fizzy. One man offered her a bit from his flask, which she gratefully took. She let the drink burn its way down her throat and wondered what Elizabeth was thinking. She couldn't find an answer in the bar car and knew Elizabeth wasn't going to tell her. Ruxandra sighed, thanked her table companion, and made her way back to her compartment in the predawn darkness.

"Wait a moment," called Elizabeth from behind her as she opened her door. "I want you to meet someone."

Ruxandra knew what Elizabeth wanted to show her and seriously considered not turning back. She did, though, and saw Elizabeth lead what was left of the man out of her compartment.

His arms had two extra bends in them, and the elbows pointed the wrong direction. Through his pant leg she saw bone poking out of one shin. Both his orbital bones were shattered, and his dislocated jaw pointed sideways from his face. Two deep holes in his neck showed where Elizabeth drained enough blood to make him a thrall.

Oh, fuck.

"Mr. James wants to stand between the cars," Elizabeth said. "Don't you?"

"Yuff." The man's agony radiated off him, but he could do nothing except what she asked. Elizabeth took the man's arm and tucked it into her own, making sure to bend the broken bone the wrong way. The man's body stiffened with agony, but no sound at all escaped his lips.

"Now come along, Mr. James," she said with a smile. "Show me how well you jump."

Stupid, sadistic . . .

Even when she had been human, Elizabeth treated others as objects, as toys to be played with and discarded. Back when Ruxandra was still in the Beast's grip and killing indiscriminately, she did not notice Elizabeth's cruelty. Humans hadn't mattered then.

Vienna, with its music and dancing and sculptures, had first reminded Ruxandra of what it meant to be human. After that, she wanted to explore and travel. Elizabeth's behavior became distasteful to her, then repugnant, as Ruxandra's eyes opened to the world.

Ruxandra had thought Elizabeth would change when she made her a vampire. But she never had and still hasn't. With no answers, and no hope of getting any, Ruxandra retreated to her compartment and went to sleep.

The train arrived in Chicago on a bright, sunny morning. Ruxandra double-checked that her clothes covered all of her skin and tried not to think about how fast the sun burned exposed skin. She led Elizabeth straight through the station to a cab. "The Continental Limited leaves at 7:00 p.m. from the Northwestern Terminal, just across the street from the Stevens Hotel."

"You know an astonishing amount about train schedules."

"I like traveling. We check in for the day, get baths, get sleep, and get going."

"I suppose you want separate rooms again." Elizabeth sighed and leaned back against the seat. "How dull."

"Assume that for the rest of the trip," Ruxandra said. She switched her voice out of human hearing range. "Don't kill anyone at the hotel."

"If you insist." Elizabeth shrugged and stared out the window. "Though I don't know how I'll entertain myself."

"Try reading a book," Ruxandra said. "Or you could go to the Stevens's bowling alley."

"Bowling?" Elizabeth sounded horrified. "What sort of a person goes to a bowling alley?"

"I bowl a perfect three hundred, thank you very much. And since we're going to be stuck here all day, I may just do that. Or go to the movies. They have those, too."

Elizabeth's mouth pursed as though she'd tasted something sour. "Your tastes are pedestrian, princess."

"You don't get to call me 'princess.'" Ruxandra remembered the last woman who had, two hundred years before in Moscow. "Not anymore."

Elizabeth behaved—as far as Ruxandra knew—and the day passed uneventfully. The Continental Limited pulled out of Chicago right on time. Ruxandra stayed in her compartment until sundown. Her hunger grew stronger—strong enough that she heard the Beast grumbling—and the smell of the people on the train became a taunt: their perspiration, their desire; the sounds of their breathing and their heartbeats; the sight of their throats, and the pulse of the blood flowing through them. All of it called to Ruxandra.

Only drinking all of a human's blood and feeding off his or her dying energy satiated her. But that was not an option. Fortunately, she didn't need to kill to take the edge off. Unfortunately, there were no seats left in the lounge when she arrived.

"Miss!" A well-dressed woman with curly brown hair and a bright smile stood up from a table. Late thirties, Ruxandra guessed, like the man who stood up with her. They had two teenage girls with them, one a year older than the other. "We're just leaving if you need a place to sit."

Ruxandra put on a smile. "I do indeed, and thank you."

The man stepped aside to let her in. "First trip to California?"

"It is," Ruxandra said. "Yours?"

"Indeed. Going out to visit my brother's farm. Maybe see some movie stars along the way, right, girls?" The two teenagers blushed and looked as embarrassed as every teenager does when their parents try to include them in a conversation. The man laughed. "Enjoy the ride, miss."

She sat down by the window and waited for them to leave before she turned her attention to the others in the car, several of whom looked her way. In short order, Ruxandra narrowed it down to three men whose eyes and scents signaled their lust. One woman looked interested, too, but seeing her made Ruxandra think of Carolyn. She sighed and glanced out the windows at the dark countryside rolling past.

A man will do. I can take enough to tide me over to Los Angeles, and he'll remember it as the best night of his life.

She picked a tall one with a broad chest and no wedding ring. She wasn't in the mood for conversation and so whispered a command to him and went back to her compartment. Ten minutes later he knocked on the door. Five minutes after that he knelt behind her, thrusting hard and groaning with pleasure.

Normally, she enjoyed feeling the hard, large length of a man—quite large, in this case. But as she inhaled his strong, musky scent and rocked her hips in time with his movements, all she could think of was Carolyn. The scent of her skin, the feeling of her mouth and hands, and the way she laughed in bed. Ruxandra felt tears coming and wiped them away.

"Turn me over," Ruxandra commanded. *"Kiss me."*

He did. She wrapped her legs tightly around his body. His lips came down on her, and his tongue roved in her mouth. She turned her head to kiss his jaw, kiss his ear. Her nails raked down his back, making him rear up with pleasure.

When he came down to kiss her again, she sank her teeth into his neck.

He gasped in pain and pleasure and grew even larger and harder inside her. The blood flowed into her, spreading through her body at once, a black dye that flowed through her veins, making them stand out through her paper-white skin.

He growled and convulsed and thrust wildly as his orgasm took him.

She released his neck and he collapsed on her, shaking in pleasure. He raised his head, opened his mouth to speak. She put a finger over his lips and shushed him. *"Get dressed, go back to your compartment for the night. Don't remember my name or that I bit you."*

Five minutes later he left. Ruxandra lay on the bed, her legs apart, feeling empty in a way that had nothing to do with her sex. Eventually, she wiped off, got dressed, and headed back to the lounge car. It wasn't like she could get drunk—even if they served alcoholic beverages, which they didn't—but at least she could find a distraction from her thoughts.

In the next train car, the smell of blood and fear hit her like a baseball bat. Ruxandra stiffened. She extended her mind outward, searching for Elizabeth. She found her in a compartment halfway down the car with a family of four, all terrified and in pain. Ruxandra ran to their stateroom door and knocked hard.

Elizabeth opened it and smiled. "Come to join the fun?"

The smell of blood and fear and despair surged in Ruxandra's nostrils and threatened to overwhelm her. The Beast, quiet for the last few days, snarled and slathered at the scent of blood. It wanted to join in and rend flesh and drink blood and feel the agony of the dying as she . . .

Stop it! Ruxandra shoved past Elizabeth and closed the door behind her.

It was the family from the lounge car. They'd taken two adjoining compartments, and now the mother stood in the doorway between them, her bleeding mouth jammed with three pairs of girl's underwear. Steel pens driven through her hands and feet nailed her to the floor and doorframe. The father sat in a chair, his hands and feet tied with torn sheets, his mouth also jammed with underwear.

And bent over the bed—naked, terrified, and bleeding—were the two teenaged girls. Elizabeth had tied their heads against the mattress, their mouths gagged with their stockings. Their hands were tied to their widespread legs, and their feet nailed to the floor like their mother. Each had deep cuts on their thighs and backsides from Elizabeth's talons.

She'd cut a hole in the floorboards to let their blood drain out. Ruxandra wanted to vomit.

You cannot do this.

But Elizabeth *had* done it, and short of throwing Elizabeth off the train, Ruxandra could not stop her. She brought her eyes up to meet Elizabeth's. "What the fuck is the matter with you?"

"Why, darling." Elizabeth ran a hand over the younger girl's breasts, leaving thin, bloody lines where nails cut through flesh, making the girl wail into the mattress. "Whatever do you mean?"

"You can't just indulge yourself—"

"I *can* indulge myself wherever, whenever, and however I want," snapped Elizabeth. "I am a Blood Royal! So are you, though you've forgotten what that means!"

The Beast growled at the challenge. *Be quiet.* "Avignon."

"That was different."

"Madrid. Rio. Ioannina. Istanbul. Every time you let things get out of hand, they track you down and burn you out." The smell of blood made Ruxandra dizzy and drove the Beast to a near frenzy. *I need to leave.* "Isn't this what that new vampire is doing? What you wanted me to stop him from doing?"

"*That one* has no idea how to cover its actions." Elizabeth slapped the older girl's backside, the force of it raising a deep-red bruise and bringing more muffled wails. "Mr. Gothrey's suicide note will show he was insane. Police will decide he spent the trip torturing his family before cutting their throats and draining their blood onto the tracks. Now, are you joining me?"

The Beast rumbled her approval. Ruxandra gritted her teeth. "No."

Elizabeth raked a clawed hand across the younger girl's welted buttock, opening up five bloody grooves in her flesh. The girl thrashed and screamed, the sound muffled by the gag and the mattress. "Then be a dear and close the door on your way out."

Ruxandra's hands started shaking on the way back to her compartment. Her hunger grew worse, but she wasn't going to give Elizabeth the satisfaction of seeing it or of knowing just how close she had been to joining in the bloodbath. *I'm better than that. Better than her. Better than the Beast.*

It was a fine line to walk, between killer and monster. Elizabeth had always been on the other side of it. And while Ruxandra had been there before, she couldn't anymore. She had *rules* now. Rules that kept her sane, kept her from going back to being a vicious killer. But being near Elizabeth . . .

They were vampires. They fed on humans. *But what Elizabeth is doing isn't feeding. That's torture for the pleasure of it. She's always done it. If I try to stop her, she'll just do something worse.*

She locked the compartment door and stayed there for the rest of the trip.

Two days later at one thirty in the afternoon, the train pulled into Los Angeles and Ruxandra stepped out. The sunlight slammed down on her like a hammer onto an anvil, even though her travel outfit with its gloves and sunglasses and wide-brimmed hat protected every bit of skin. She wanted to run into the station and hide in a dark shadow but knew Elizabeth would be watching her. *I'll be damned if I show her any weakness.*

Ruxandra walked in the hot, dangerous light, taking in the station and looking as relaxed and calm as possible. *It's like Morocco. Only with less history and more art deco.*

God, I'm hungry.

Elizabeth swept past her, long legs moving at a brisk pace. She went right through the station. A Stutz limousine waited outside. Its immaculate bright-blue body, silver headlights and grille shone in the LA sun. A tall, thin black man with two scabbed-over holes in his neck stood by the door, waiting.

A thrall. Ruxandra wasn't surprised. Elizabeth needed humans, as well as Dorotyas, to serve her. And given how she treated them, making them thralls made sense. *I wonder how many more she has.*

The man opened the car door. "Welcome back, my lady."

"Thank you, Mason," Elizabeth said. "My friend, Ruxandra, is coming right behind me, and the porters are bringing our luggage. Please help them load it."

That is a nice car. Ruxandra's fascination with automobiles began when the first ones rolled into the streets. *Too bad about the owner.*

Elizabeth took the shady side, of course, forcing Ruxandra to sit where the sun set her skin itching even through her clothes. Mason loaded the luggage and stepped in. Elizabeth smiled. "To the apartment, Mason. And do close the curtains, Ruxandra."

The engine purred, and the car slid into the Los Angeles traffic. Ruxandra caught glimpses of sun-faded buildings through the gap in the curtains, but not enough to get a real sense of the place. They moved through bustling traffic, then through residential blocks to a wide-open spot in the middle of the city. Ruxandra caught a glimpse of a golf course—bright green despite the heat—and a sign that said "Wiltshire Country Club" just before the car pulled into the shade of a six-story white apartment building. Mason got out and opened the door for Elizabeth.

"The Country Club Manor, my lady."

Elizabeth led Ruxandra through the ornate foyer and up the elevator to the top floor. The apartment was much larger than Ruxandra's and much more luxurious. Red and gold furniture done in the Spanish rococo style filled the rooms. There wasn't a single piece in the room without ornate curved lines and a curlicue on it somewhere. The paintings all featured women, mostly nude, in pain and despair. On a table beside the door sat a neat line of morning papers—the *Los Angeles Times*, *Herald*, and *Examiner*.

Ruxandra glanced down and stopped walking.

"My lady." Dorotyas stepped out of one of the bedrooms. "Welcome back."

Elizabeth's servant was the opposite of her mistress in every way: short to Elizabeth's tall, dowdy to her elegant. While Elizabeth radiated beauty with clean-cut features a sculptor might carve into marble, Dorotyas's face looked like a dented hatchet, angled and craggy and sharp edged. Her eyes, the same pale gray blue as Ruxandra's and Elizabeth's, sat beneath a thick, hairy brow that overhung them like a cliff over two caves.

When she saw Ruxandra, Dorotyas put on a smile that didn't reach her eyes, and her tone sounded as clipped as if she were receiving a paint delivery. "Princess Dracula. It has been a long time."

Not long enough. Ruxandra disliked Dorotyas with a carnivore's visceral dislike of a scavenger. "It's Miss Ruxandra Black now."

"Nonsense," Elizabeth said. "Be who you like in New York. Here you're with family, princess."

"Don't call me that." She held up the *Los Angeles Times*.

"Vampire Killer Strikes Again"

"Two more corpses found with their throats ripped open.

"Police urging people to stay off the streets at night."

"See?" Elizabeth said. "I told you it wasn't me."

"Which doesn't mean it isn't Dorotyas." Ruxandra turned the paper toward her.

Dorotyas's lip curled up in a sneer. "Given how undisciplined and messy the attacks are, I thought you killed them."

Ruxandra closed the distance between them in an eye blink. "Is it yours?"

Dorotyas didn't step back. "I do nothing without my lady's permission."

Unless you're bored being her lickspittle. Three hundred years is a long time under someone's thumb.

"Dorotyas has not made anyone since Peru." Elizabeth's tone warned Ruxandra to stop. "He died in the fire there."

"He was weak," Dorotyas said, her eyes still locked with Ruxandra's. "Unable to stand the company of my lady."

"Unwilling to kowtow to your lady, you mean?"

"Enough," Elizabeth said. "Dorotyas, we are hungry."

"How can you be hungry? You killed four on the train."

"I let most of that drain away," Elizabeth said airily. "Now, I'm hungry. As are you."

"I have two in the large bedroom, my lady," Dorotyas said, "waiting for you."

"Then let's eat our lunch." Elizabeth smiled at Ruxandra. "This apartment is soundproof. I once tortured a girl for seven hours and no one heard a thing."

There's no way I'm eating here. The Beast inside Ruxandra rumbled her disagreement. She shoved it down, picked up her valise, and headed for the door. "I want to sleep. I'll get my own food later."

"Nonsense. You haven't eaten since New York." Elizabeth headed for the bedroom. "Come, have a girl, then you can get settled into your room."

You'd love that, wouldn't you? "I'm not staying here."

Elizabeth frowned. "Don't be ridiculous. Dorotyas prepared a room, and you'll stay in it."

"You play too much with your food." *And I have no intention of being under your control.* "Will the concierge downstairs call a taxi for me?"

Dorotyas stepped in front of her. "The lady wants you to stay."

"Move," Ruxandra growled. "*Now.*"

"Don't be ridiculous, Ruxandra," Elizabeth scolded. "Put down that bag and come eat."

Ruxandra didn't move. "You wanted me here, I'm here. You want me to find your vampire, I'll find your vampire. But I do it *my* way and stay where I like. Now get her out of my way before I break her into pieces."

Dorotyas's fangs came out, her pupils turning to serpentine slits. "I'd like to see you try."

"Dorotyas!" Elizabeth's voice cracked like a whip. "Move."

Dorotyas moved.

"Are you going to be where I can reach you?" Ruxandra asked.

"I must return to my ranch tonight," Elizabeth said. "But I'll be back in two days."

"Fine." Ruxandra escaped the apartment. The screams of a terrified girl, inaudible to humans through the thick walls, rang in her ears as she went down the elevator. She waited in the shade under the front awning until the cab arrived. Even with her sunglasses, the glare hurt her eyes. When the cab came, she sat in the middle of the back seat, as far from the windows as possible.

Her lips felt cracked, not only from the LA sun, but also from deep, constricting thirst.

"Where to, madam?"

"Where do the movie stars stay when they're in town?"

"Movie stars?" The cabbie looked over his shoulder. "Want to be close to the rich and famous, do you?"

Ruxandra manufactured a smile for him. "Exactly."

"The Ambassador is the best place. They all go to the Cocoanut Grove. You can see them there if you can get a seat."

"Then take me there," Ruxandra said. She watched the Country Club Manor slip away behind her. *I need a hot bath and a change of clothes.*

And as I soon as I get them, I'm going hunting.

CHAPTER
FIVE

T
HEY DON'T DO *anything by halves, here, do they?*

Ruxandra leaned back in her chair at the Cocoanut
Grove wondering whom to eat. The place held a thousand
people, and it was full. Ruxandra managed to get a table only by
commanding the couple there to go home and spend the night
making love. Now, she sipped the cold fruit juice concoction the
waiter had brought her and sat back in her chair, brushing up
against one of the papier-mâché palm trees that decorated the
room. High above her, hanging from the tree trunk, a red-eyed
mechanical monkey stared down and grinned. Above that, twinkling electric stars covered the ceiling, and in the back, a water-
fall added its noise to the general clamor.

She felt ravenously hungry.

She let the waves of music and talking and the scents of a
thousand people wash over her as she thought about prey. On
the stage, the band played up a storm, and gyrating couples filled
the polished floor in front of it. Men and women laughed and
talked and danced and drank. Ruxandra felt the pulse of every

single person in the room thrumming and vibrating through their bodies. She wanted to feed—*needed* to feed before the Beast inside her started rumbling again. But one could not hunt inconspicuously at the Cocoanut Grove.

These were the rich and famous. If anyone went missing from this group, it would make the papers. Ruxandra went through the crowd with her eyes, picking out movie stars. *Clara Bow, holding hands with Gary Cooper. John Barrymore. Laurel and Hardy talking with Mae Busch. Douglas Fairbanks and Mary Pickford are sitting in the back, smoking.* Ruxandra shook her head. *I should have brought an autograph book. Now that would appall Elizabeth.* Ruxandra smiled, imagining Elizabeth's horrified expression. *She'd probably drink Clara Bow just to spite me.*

"Well, that's much better," said a man with an Austrian accent. "I so hate to see a pretty girl with a frown on her face."

He was tall and fit, with brown hair and eyes, and Ruxandra recognized him at once. "Joseph Schildkraut. *Young April, Shipwrecked, Meet the Prince* and *The Road to Yesterday.*"

His eyes twinkled when he smiled, and Ruxandra saw what made him an idol. "That is I, yes."

"Well, Mr. Schildkraut," Ruxandra said, switching to German, "do you always talk to pretty girls uninvited?"

"Whenever possible," said the actor, also in German. His smile grew wider. "So good to hear someone who speaks German. I don't recognize your accent, though."

"You wouldn't," Ruxandra said. "I travel a great deal."

He sat without waiting for an invitation. "May I buy a pretty lady a drink?"

"Not in this country."

Joseph laughed. "How very true. Do you dance, lovely young lady?"

"Not tonight," Ruxandra said. *Because you look divine, and if I stand that close to you, I'll drink you on the spot.* "I just arrived today and am quite tired."

"A pity."

She turned on her most flirtatious smile. "But I will be here tomorrow night, I'm sure."

"As will I." Joseph pulled a pack of cigarettes out of his coat and extended it to her. She took a cigarette and then the light he offered her. He lit his cigarette and sat back. "I am between films, so I have time to enjoy the nightlife."

And there's an opening if ever I heard one. "Do people still enjoy the nightlife, then? After all I've read in the paper, I should think people would be afraid to go out after dark."

Joseph's smile vanished. "Ah, the *vampir.*"

Ruxandra let her eyes go wide and her head tilt—the very picture of skeptical disbelief. "Surely not."

He shook his head. "Of course not. Stories to scare children. But still, it is a bad man who does these terrible things. I am not yet convinced it is not an animal. Someone's pet leopard or tiger escaped and running free."

Ruxandra called up a girlish shiver of fear. "A leopard? Now I really don't want to go out."

"The animal—or man, if it is one—avoids crowded, noisy places. It only attacks people alone in badly lit rough areas." Joseph put his hand on Ruxandra's, the touch as much a pass as a reassuring gesture. It sent a different kind of shiver up her spine. She felt quite ready, she realized, to take him into a back room and do to him what Elizabeth had done in Penn Station. He must have seen part of her thoughts on her face, because he smiled again. "If you go out with me tomorrow night, I will take you to crowded clubs and light-filled streets in areas that are not at all rough."

Ruxandra smiled back and hoped she didn't look like a cat sizing up a canary. "Then I hope I see you tomorrow night, Mr. Schildkraut."

"Joseph, please."

"Joseph." She finished her club soda and rose. He stood with her and bowed as she passed by.

Quite the gentleman, she thought as she stepped outside and vanished from notice. *Pity I don't have more time for him.*

She breathed deeply, spread her senses wide, and looked for the places where hunger, desperation, and anger were the most prevalent. She'd dressed for the hunt this evening—a red dress and shoes, hair upswept, and makeup done to make her look frail and pale, easy to overpower.

The better to attract a predator.

She knew Dorotyas was there a moment before the woman said, "What do you think you're doing?"

The woman's tone raised the hackles on Ruxandra's neck, and she barely managed to keep her fangs covered. Dorotyas emerged from the shadows looking entirely too proper in her calf-length skirt and pleated white shirt under a gray sweater. *After three hundred years, you'd think she'd learn to dress up a bit.*

"I'm going hunting, Dorotyas. Then I'm going to search for the vampire."

"Why didn't you just eat at Elizabeth's apartment? You could be looking for the vampire already." Dorotyas's voice sounded tight and angry. She held her chin high and was doing her best to look down her nose at Ruxandra despite being the same height. "You should do as Elizabeth says, not go off on your own."

"Doing as Elizabeth says never works out well." Ruxandra turned her back on Dorotyas and let her mind go wide again. "You know that better than anyone."

"I knew Elizabeth long before you came along. I served her as chamberlain and steward of Castle Csejte. I trust her."

"Then go back to her and leave me alone."

"Elizabeth wants you to come to the ranch."

"No."

"Why must you be so contrary?"

"Maybe because she dragged me across the country to deal with a problem that you two should be able to manage on your own?"

"She misses you." The tone—a mixture of annoyance, anger, and envy—made Ruxandra turn around. Dorotyas looked at her like an ungrateful child who ran away from home. "Before Elizabeth left, she talked about how much she needed you. How without you, things felt empty and meaningless. And the first thing you do when you arrive is abandon her."

Ruxandra squared off against the other woman, letting her hunger feed her anger. "Did she tell you what she did in New York? Or on the train? On *both* trains? If she didn't, you'll sure as hell read about it in the paper tomorrow."

"Elizabeth needs her entertainments—"

"Elizabeth," Ruxandra said stepping closer, "is insane. She's dangerous and she's out of control, which is why I left in the first place, why I'm not staying in her apartment, and why I'm getting out of this city as soon as I find this vampire."

Dorotyas stiffened. "She wants you with her."

"I. Don't. Care. Go away, Dorotyas."

Ruxandra turned on her heel. Dorotyas caught Ruxandra's arm in a tight grip and held her. "You need to learn your place."

Ruxandra looked at the hand on her arm. "My *place?*"

"Elizabeth is the reason you're here and not crawling through the woods like an animal. She's the reason you think and act like a vampire instead of just being the Beast."

It was true, of course, and that made it a great deal more irritating. "Let go of my arm, Dorotyas."

"You *owe* her, and you should repay her by showing her some respect for her wishes."

Ruxandra reached over, caught Dorotyas's thumb, and bent it at an unnatural angle. Dorotyas let go abruptly and tried to pull back. Ruxandra shifted her hands and locked her wrist, forcing the other woman to stay close. "You should learn to be something other than a servant. Anything I owed Elizabeth, I long since paid back. And since I am here looking for your vampire *just like she asked me*, get out of my way."

She let go of Dorotyas's wrist and watched the other woman stumble back. "Go back to Elizabeth and keep her from making this a bigger mess."

"I should have tamed you back when we first found you," Dorotyas hissed, "like all the other little girls who came to the castle showing airs."

"Pity you didn't try," Ruxandra said. "I'd have drunk you dry and wouldn't need to deal with you now."

Dorotyas cradled her wrist and glared but didn't come any closer. "Try Sunset Boulevard, northeast of here, if you're hungry. You'll fit in perfectly."

So nice to know her opinion of me hasn't changed.

Sunset Boulevard stood smack in the middle of the red-light district, and the prostitutes were out in force. They stood on the street corners or in front of doors leading up to small, grim apartments in the buildings that sat between the fancy clubs and bars that dotted the area. Ruxandra heard the sounds of paid sex from the apartments above and several of the alleys. Men groaned and thrust and emptied themselves into women's bodies and mouths. She smelled alcohol in the backrooms of the bars and opium in the basements of several apartment buildings. Exactly the sort of place she wanted.

After she'd left Castle Csejte, Ruxandra swore not to hunt innocents again. She swore never to hunt the girls that Elizabeth liked to torture, never to cut off a life that still had potential. Sometimes, she fed off the dying, taking away their pain in their last moments. But mostly, Ruxandra hunted predators.

She opened her mind and searched through the crowd's emotions. Many of the predators on Sunset Boulevard looked like respectable gentlemen but ached to inflict injury as they took their chosen whores up the stairs to their rooms. Some were the women themselves, planning how to pay the men back for injuries inflicted by others long ago. Some stood in the shadows, watching the whores they controlled or sizing up the people on the streets for robbery or worse.

One of them sized her up.

She felt his hatred, his desire to hurt. She spotted him inside an alley and caught a glimpse of the knife under his jacket. She was too far away for him, though.

Ruxandra crossed the street, pretended her shoes were troubling her, and stepped into the alley to fix them. The man caught her around the waist and slapped his hand hard on her mouth, whispering, "You stay quiet or I'll gut you right here."

Ruxandra stayed quiet and let him drag her deep into the alley. He shoved her face-first against the wall and pressed the knife against her neck. His other hand went to her hair, pulling her head back. "You little slut, walking around like you own the place. Someone needs to teach you a lesson."

"Oh, please," Ruxandra said, her voice bland and bored. "Don't hurt me, I beg you."

He grabbed her hair, spun her, and slammed her back against the wall, holding her in place with his knee. The knife danced in front of her eyes. "You think I'm playing a game, bitch? You think I'm just out to fill your stinking hole? I'm going to—"

He didn't see Ruxandra take the knife. He didn't see how she managed to spin him and pin him up against the wall. He *did* see the glowing red of her eyes with their snake-slit pupils and the large fangs that protruded from under her lips. He felt her hand between his legs, cupping his testicles through a tear in his trousers and underwear that hadn't been there a moment before. He felt the tips of her talons poking into his flesh.

"*Don't move; don't make a sound,*" Ruxandra commanded. She opened her mind wide again as she sank her fangs into his neck. *Because the last thing I need is to be caught.*

She gasped in pleasure as the blood flowed into her. It spread through her body at once, like the finest brandy on the coldest night. The man trembled in silent pleasure and pain.

Halfway through draining him she felt a burst of agony at the edge of her range. She pulled her lips off her victim and stepped away to concentrate. Someone was being killed in a horrible, painful way, his body being drained of blood. *It's the vampire. Has to be. But why can't I sense him? If it's a vampire, I should be able to sense him.*

She vanished from notice and began running, leaving her victim standing in the alley unable to move and bleeding to death. *Too bad I can't finish him off myself.*

The wind shifted, and the smell of human blood, faint before, grew strong. A large amount of blood had been spilled, more than was sensible to waste. *But what if he's not sensible? Maybe he's insane and needs help. Or worse . . .*

The sense of agony cut off as the man's life faded away. Ruxandra put on a burst of speed, closing in on the scent of blood like a hound after a fox. She raced through the city, crossing Santa Monica and Melrose and Beverly in a flash of motion. She passed the Ambassador Hotel and continued straight down Mariposa Avenue to Rosedale Cemetery. Someone far too strong to be human had bent the front gates open.

Well, that's not a cliché at all, is it?

She stopped to listen and smell and spread her mind wide. There was no sense of a vampire anywhere, no feeling of its presence, only the overwhelming smell of blood. Ruxandra slipped through the gates and followed her nose.

The man lay sprawled on the ground, his eyes wide with horror. His throat was torn open, and his shirt shredded. The skin and muscle beneath it had been raked with claws until bone showed through. Ruxandra circled him, her eyes on the ground, her nose twitching as she searched for the scent of the killer.

The dead man smelled like blood and piss and shit, like all the corpses she'd seen. Blood and offal from the man's ripped-open intestines spattered the ground around him for five feet in every direction. Ruxandra sniffed the air, then the ground. She circled wider, away from the corpse and the mess.

There.

Beneath the scent of blood came something deeper, and it wasn't a human smell. She smelled no sweat, no pheromones, no scent of a person. Just a faint smell of rot and filth, like a dead mouse hidden somewhere in the walls of a house.

Maybe he lives in a different graveyard, hiding like some silly creature from a story.

She followed the scent across the graveyard, over the wall, and through the streets. The vampire was long gone from the range of her nose or her mind. There was only the trail. She followed it at a jog faster than a human's best sprint. The trail led her north and east through the city. She put on bursts of speed, hoping to catch the thing. He stayed ahead of her, stayed out of range of her senses. Even with a nose as sensitive as hers and hundreds of years' tracking experience, she couldn't go too fast without losing the trail.

She wove through the streets and parks and came out at the Los Angeles River, which looked like a creek this time of year. Its shallow water rippled between the stones and grass covering its bed. The trail led right to the water's edge and vanished.

Does he know I'm following him? Or is this just the quickest way back to his lair? If it's the second, the trail would pick up again across the water. Ruxandra took off her shoes and carried them across.

And there's no trail here at all.

Dammit.

She crouched on her haunches, bringing her face close to the earth. She smelled dirt and insects and rats and the faint scents of humans who passed days before but not blood or death or rot.

She went south first, nostrils flaring and face staying just above the ground, moving like an animal. She went slowly and cursed the need. Picking up a scent trail from the water's edge was tricky, and she couldn't afford to lose this one. She spent two hours going down the riverbank until the river became a concrete-encased canal trickling past the railway tracks. The smell of steel and tar and oil filled her nose, making it harder to catch the other scents. Even so, she kept going south until it became a river again.

She found no scent of the vampire at all.

She crossed the river and went back up the same way, in case he turned back on his trail to confuse her. It wasn't likely—if the vampire had passed her, she should have smelled or sensed it.

She stopped when she found a faint scent of her own perfume where her legs had brushed the grass on the riverside. She crossed again and went north, sniffing and scanning the ground for footprints. Three hours later, near the aviation field in Griffith Park, she caught the scent and found a footprint sunk into the damp ground by the river. *Male, from the size of the feet.* She stared down at the footprint: round-toed with no heel. *Wearing simple shoes or sandals. Heavy.*

The trail led east through the suburbs, past houses large and small, and then out into the hills with their low cover of grasses and cacti. There were no trees here, nothing to hide behind or under. Ruxandra felt an itch between her shoulders as if the sun had already started blistering her skin. Above her, the sky grew lighter. Dawn would not come for hours, but Ruxandra had no desire to be in the middle of nowhere when it did. *But neither does the vampire, so that means he has a place close enough to hide in before the sun rises.*

She started jogging again, following the trail over the grass and the stones, spotting the occasional footprint in the dirt. The smell grew stronger the farther into the desert she went, allowing her to move faster, racing against the coming dawn. *If I turn back and run now, I can still make it into town . . .*

The wind shifted and the scent came stronger than ever.

But why can't I sense him? Maybe there's some vampire magic that hides us from one another. I'll have to ask Kade. But if he knows that, he can't be new at this. And if he's not new at this, what is he doing? Why is he so careless?

The scent went around a hill, then another, strong enough that the vampire couldn't be more than half a mile away. Ruxandra sprinted, leaving the trail, following the scent of blood and death and rot in the air, charging over the hill and down into the valley beyond.

A white shirt and a pair of white pants, both spattered with blood and offal, lay in a heap.

Shit. He led me right where he wanted—

The attack came from behind in a whirlwind of snapping fangs and slashing claws. Claws ripped open the flesh of her back, making her arch in pain and hiss even as she avoided the teeth trying to sink into her neck.

Found the bastard. She spun and flipped in the air, landing in an animal crouch with her fangs out and talons extending from her fingers. *Now, I just need to get him to . . .*

The thought died in her mind as the *thing* charged toward her again.

It wasn't human. It wasn't a vampire. It was a twisted, broken combination of both. Blood and bits of meat dripped from its jagged, curved nails. Its long, red-stained teeth dripped with blood and drool. Its naked skin was the gray of death. Its eyes glowed red with no intelligence in them, nothing except the desire to feed and kill.

Something in Ruxandra broke open, and she stumbled back in shock and surprise.

Oh God. A ghoul.

CHAPTER
SIX

T HE GHOUL HOWLED with a sound no mortal throat could make, a noise made of pain and rage and unending hunger. It crouched low, baring its yellow, misshapen fangs in challenge as it tensed to attack.

From within Ruxandra, the Beast howled its response and tried to claw free.

No, no, no, no, no! Ruxandra leaped backward, landing on the top of the hill. The ghoul sprang after, bounding up the hill in long leaps. Ruxandra stared at it in horror. *Why make a ghoul? How could it know how?*

A ghoul was a human who a vampire drained almost dry. At the moment of death, when the soul moved to leave the body, the vampire caught it and held it, trapping it as the mind shut down. The creature that resulted became a weak shadow of a vampire: brainless, savage, and constantly thirsting for blood. The vampire who made it could bend the creature to his will. He could even see out of the creature's eyes and sense what it sensed. A ghoul had no thoughts of its own, no desires except to feed and kill, and no emotions except hatred for its maker and rage at everything still alive on the earth. It destroyed everything in its path.

Four hundred years ago, before Elizabeth, before the Beast, when Ruxandra did not understand what she could do, she made a ghoul. It had been a year after she became a vampire. She was hiding in the woods, digging into the earth or hiding in the hollows of trees during the day, coming out at night to drink the blood of whatever small creatures she caught. She was filthy and scared and sick in her heart. She still craved the sun, though the touch of it burned. She'd get up before dark and watch the last light fade from the sky.

He was such a handsome boy.

She'd left her clothes on the edge of the pond and gone in to scrub the dirt and blood from her flesh. She'd ducked under the water, and when she came up he was there, watching. She'd shrieked and gone back under. He'd turned away and stammered out an apology. But he'd come back the next night. And the night after. And the one after that.

Ruxandra knew what might happen if she got too close. But he'd been such a handsome young man, and she felt so lonely. So, although she'd held her distance at first, after three days she'd spoken to him. Then she'd let him kiss her—her first kiss from a boy. Soon after that, she'd lain on her back and felt the warmth of his arms around her, his weight on her body . . .

And then she drank him.

He screamed so loud, fought so hard. I tried to let go, but I couldn't. Not after months of drinking only animals. His blood tasted so sweet and so divine, and I desperately needed it even if I didn't know it at the time.

When he'd collapsed on her, body convulsing in death, she'd felt his soul struggling to break free and gathered it to her own, not wanting to lose him.

The next night he'd turned into a ghoul and gone after her, because more than anything else, a ghoul hated the one who created it. When she'd figured out how to make him stop attacking her, he'd gone after his human family. She'd barely stopped him from killing them all, and then only by offering him her own silver blood instead.

Ruxandra shuddered, remembering what happened next. *I was so stupid.*

The ghoul in front of her howled and sprang, reaching out ragged claws to rip into Ruxandra's flesh. Ruxandra leaped again, landing thirty yards away. It hissed and spat, then turned and fled. Ruxandra stared after it, frozen in place as the Beast and the past both threatened to overwhelm her.

I never told Elizabeth how to make ghouls. I told Kade, though.

In 1872, Kade experimented with ghouls in Northern Ireland. He made three and practiced controlling them. He thought they would protect him from attackers.

Ruxandra found all that out later. She'd been going to visit him when she ran into the ghouls in a village near Kade's manor. The Beast, quiet for fifty years at that point, broke free and ripped all three to shreds in moments. It took a week before it calmed enough for Ruxandra to regain full control.

And now there's another one. And it's getting away.

Ruxandra snarled from deep in her chest; the Beast echoed her frustration. It wanted to be free, wanted to shred the abomination with claws and teeth. Ruxandra forced the Beast back. *I will not let you take control. That thing might lead us to its master.*

She sprinted, eating up the distance between them.

The ghoul ran on, loping through the dry hills. Ahead, the horizon grew brighter and brighter. Ruxandra felt the sun's heat even though it hadn't crested the horizon yet.

Come on, you stupid thing. Where do you go to ground? What's your hiding place?

The ghoul turned and ran straight at her. Ruxandra snarled, caught it as it leaped and smashed it against the rocks. The creature screamed and twisted and charged. She slammed it down again. *Lead me to your master, dammit.*

The ghoul raced up the hill. Ruxandra followed on its heels, hoping to keep it in a panic. It topped the hill and sprinted forward out of sight. Ruxandra came up a moment later.

Right into the light of the rising sun.

She screamed and threw herself backward, twisting and tumbling down the hill. Her hair burst into flame. She slapped at it, burning her hands as she doused the flames. Her forehead boiled with blisters.

From up the hill she heard flames crackling and the creature howling, coming closer. Ruxandra looked up and saw the ghoul, its entire body on fire and its flesh melting from its bones, leaping straight at her.

The Beast howled fear and pain, but Ruxandra refused to let it out.

She slammed into the ghoul, her talons ripping through the burning flesh like paper, scattering the flaming bits even as they scorched her. The thing stumbled and fell, and Ruxandra slashed with both hands, sending the ghoul's head flying from the shredded remains of its burning neck.

Sunlight touched the hilltop behind her, the scalding heat hitting Ruxandra like a lash. She searched the gully floor for a place to hide and found nothing.

Fuck, fuck, fuck, fuck.

The Beast screamed in animal panic. Instinct and fear made Ruxandra drive her hands into the earth, talons on her fingertips breaking through the hard-packed soil. Dirt flew in all directions. Deeper and deeper she dug, until the earth turned cool and loose instead of sunbaked hard. Ruxandra changed direction, digging sideways to make a narrow slot. She squeezed into it. The dirt brushed her face, pressed in on her breasts and hips. Above, rays of sunshine marched mercilessly across the land.

The last time she'd done this she'd been trying to kill herself. She'd dug her talons into a tree and let the sun hit her naked flesh. She'd woken up buried in the earth. She hadn't remembered digging the hole or pulling the dirt down on her burning body, only the desperate panic of being buried alive.

At least this time I know what is happening.

Ruxandra reached up and brought the trench down on top of her, burying herself in darkness and dirt. Inside her head, the Beast screamed in fear.

Ruxandra lay underground until the last vestiges of daylight faded. She didn't sleep but seethed the entire length of the day, furious at herself for getting into this predicament and even more furious at Elizabeth—*for getting me into this predicament*. But as the earth cooled into night, Ruxandra had bigger problems—

PAIN, PAIN, PAIN, HUNGER!

Ruxandra hadn't heard the Beast's voice in years. It terrified her. It was the sound of loss of self. The animal inside her wanted to break out and tear her from the nightclubs and cities, from human company and love and the touch of another's hand. She stayed calm, though it was an effort ignoring her still-burning-hot flesh and her hunger and the screaming creature inside her.

When the sun's heat vanished, she clawed her way out of the earth, spitting and horking dirt from her mouth and nose. Her entire body itched, as if a dozen beetles had crawled into her dress and laid their eggs on her flesh. She wanted to shake the dirt from her body, to put on her shoes, but her forehead still boiled with pain, her hair stank of burning, and inside, the Beast howled, *PAIN, HUNGER, BLOOD, PAIN, PAIN, PAIN, HUNGER!*

She knew she should search for the ghoul's clothes or its remains, should see if she could find a scent or a sign to help her pursue the vampire, but hunger, fear, and pain brought out the Beast, and right now it was more awake than it had been in centuries.

Too long without feeding. Stupid of me.

HUNGER, BLOOD, PAIN, HUNGER, BLOOD!

She raced across the desert back toward Los Angeles, her senses and mind wide open, searching for someone, *anyone*, she could take as prey.

God, I hope it isn't a child.

The man stood beside his car, filling the steaming radiator with water. He was forty or so with auburn hair and the smell of one who worked indoors. Ruxandra snarled and leaped, landing on top of him before he saw her coming. They tumbled to the earth, her legs locked tight around him the way she used to do with the deer in the Transylvanian forest. Her teeth sank deep into his neck and she drank hard, pulling every drop of blood out of him.

When she stood up, she could still hear the Beast howling. It still wanted out, wanted to take control and run. Ruxandra shivered with fear.

To have it come out so easily . . .

She looked at the dead man. He hadn't been a predator, hadn't been anything except some poor bastard who was in the wrong place at the wrong time.

I won't let it take over. Not again. She picked up the man's body and slammed his head against the engine block, opening his skull. She wedged his neck against the radiator, letting it burn away any evidence of the bites. Everyone would assume he fell. The Beast rumbled in delight and howled for more.

I need people around me. I need music and people and laughter. She ran back to the city. She felt her forehead healing and her hair growing back as she went. *Any longer in the sun and I wouldn't be healing nearly so quickly.*

Ruxandra turned unnoticed as she reached the city limits and stayed that way until she reached her room. She stood under the shower and scrubbed until all the dirt and bugs and itches washed away. Then she put on her second-best dress—the ghoul had destroyed her best—and went down to the Cocoanut Grove.

Joseph was there as promised, talking to a girl. He saw Ruxandra and smiled. "I feared you would not return."

"And I can see you were bereft," Ruxandra said. "Please dance with me? Now?"

"He is in a conversation right now," the girl said.

The Beast's snarl didn't pass Ruxandra's lips, but the girl saw it in her eyes. She went pale and leaned far back in her chair, her eyes wide. Ruxandra forced a smile onto her face. "I really, really need to dance, if you don't mind?"

The girl managed to nod. Ruxandra grabbed Joseph's hand and dragged him to the dance floor. The band struck up a new tune and away they went.

Joseph danced almost as well as Jerome, and they twirled through a foxtrot and a Lindy hop before she allowed him to take her back to the table. She asked for the coldest drink they had, and the waiter brought her a silver bowl piled high with extra ice cubes. She reveled in the feel of the ice on her lips and tongue and against her teeth. Joseph introduced her to the girl, then to other members of the Hollywood elite. Ruxandra turned on her own considerable charm and soon had everyone smiling. She also learned that Joseph was *not* the jealous type. In fact, he rather enjoyed the idea of sharing.

The rest of the night passed in a whirlwind of dancing and drinks, wide-ranging conversations and alcohol-infused passes. Ruxandra accepted them all. By closing time, she'd danced with a dozen of Hollywood's rich and famous, kissed Joseph (quite passable) and Greta Garbo (much *more* passable), had her ass patted by Stan Laurel, and had been finger-fucked hard in a bathroom stall by Lilyan Tashman.

And with each dance, with each kiss and touch and conversation, the Beast's growls grew a little quieter until they faded away.

Ruxandra slipped away when the Cocoanut Grove closed for the night. The air felt cool, with a breeze blowing off the ocean leaving the tang of salt spray on Ruxandra's lips. She breathed in the scents, enjoying the silence and calm as much as she had the excitement of the Cocoanut Grove. Then she went back to her room to do some serious thinking about what had transpired the night before.

Why the desert? She stripped out of her clothes and slipped between the clean, cool sheets. *There was no shelter, no place to hide, so why go there? And why did the ghoul come after me in the end? Because the vampire doesn't want anyone to find it? Because it wanted to kill me? Why?*

Ruxandra put her hands behind her head and stared at the ceiling.

I can't let it keep making ghouls. It's too dangerous. For the humans, for the rest of us . . . The Beast's reactions to the ghouls blazed up in her mind. She shuddered. *And especially for me.*

The papers held no mention of an attack the next evening, just the story of a poor unfortunate who slipped while repairing his automobile. Ruxandra sighed with relief and went down to the Cocoanut Grove. *Thank heaven for small mercies.*

She wanted to go back out and see if she could find some evidence on the ghoul's clothes. First, though, she wanted human company again, carefree, good-looking human company whose sophisticated but unserious banter helped rebuild the prison of civilized behavior that kept the Beast sealed away.

And so she sat with Joseph and Lilyan, allowing each to put a hand on her thighs. She pretended to listen to their conversation and the music while her mind opened wide and ranged through the city. She felt neither vampire nor ghoul within five miles.

"You certainly look different tonight," said Joseph.

"I like it," purred Lilyan.

"I'm a cat burglar," said Ruxandra, winking. She wore black britches and a black turtleneck sweater with a pair of black knee-high lace-up boots on her feet. The outfit wasn't fashionable, but it was acceptable and gave her much more freedom of movement than her other clothes. She considered going out naked, but she might need to talk to people when she searched, not to mention how hard being naked made getting a drink. These clothes would get her strange looks, but not enough to be considered scandalous.

She started to make her excuses and head out but then she sensed Elizabeth and Dorotyas five miles away and closing. *Guess I'll stay here a little longer, then.*

Fifteen minutes later, Elizabeth swept into the club in a pale-yellow dress and shoes. Her bold makeup highlighted her pale-blue eyes and ripe lips. She looked as elegant as a queen and every man's eyes went to her.

Of course she's all dressed up. Is she ever not?

Dorotyas followed right behind wearing a plain gray suit and looking every bit the private secretary. Elizabeth surveyed the room with a hungry look, her eyes lingering on the younger women. Ruxandra sighed. *Now everything is going to get a lot less fun.*

"Ruxandra, darling." Elizabeth homed in on her like a hawk stopping on its prey. "How *wonderful* this place is."

Lilyan raised her eyebrows at Ruxandra. "Friend of yours, I take it?"

"Long story," Ruxandra said. "Don't ask."

"Who *is* she?" Joseph's voice filled with admiration and thinly disguised lust.

"A man-eater, I bet," said Lilyan with a hint of jealousy. "Or does she eat girls?"

"You have no idea." Ruxandra stood up. "Lizzie! Darling! How wonderful that you're here! Do sit down."

"Thank you, my dear Ruxandra." Elizabeth gave her a hug. Her voice switched to vampire tones. "Do *not* call me Lizzie."

"Then call me Ruxie," Ruxandra said on the same frequency. She kissed both Elizabeth's cheeks. "And behave."

Elizabeth sat down and looked around the room like a cat looking over a pen filled with mice. "This is quite the place."

"You've never been before?" Ruxandra feigned surprise. *Of course she hasn't. It's too crass, too modern, and she can't kill anyone here.*

"I certainly would have noticed you," Joseph said.

Elizabeth turned her smile on him. "And I, you."

"You must forgive Elizabeth," said Ruxandra. "She never goes to the movies or the theater and has no idea who you two are." Ruxandra waved at the table of stars behind her. "She doesn't even know which one is Charlie Chaplin!"

"Sadly true," said Elizabeth, casting her best fake smile at Lilyan and Joseph. "*Go to another table and don't bother us again this evening.*"

Joseph and Lilyan rose at the command. Joseph bowed over Ruxandra's hand and kissed it. "If you will excuse us."

Ruxandra put on a pout as they walked away. "Well, there goes my tour of the studio."

"Humans are play*things* not play*mates*," said Elizabeth. "This place is gauche beyond belief."

"I know. Have you seen the monkeys?" She pointed up.

"Enough." The word came down like a butcher knife. "What do you think you're doing?"

Ruxandra leaned forward, elbows on the table. "Recovering."

"From what?" Dorotyas asked. "Overeating?"

Ruxandra's growl made Dorotyas sit back, though she kept the haughty expression on her face.

"Enough, children," Elizabeth scolded. "Recovering from what?"

"From almost getting fried by the sun and having to fight back the damn Beast."

"The Beast?" Elizabeth's left eyebrow arched up. "I thought you had it under control."

"I did." Ruxandra changed her voice so the humans couldn't hear it. "Then I saw the ghoul."

"The *what?*" Elizabeth's voice cracked like a whip, drawing stares from other tables. She changed her voice to vampire frequency. "What did you say?"

"A ghoul." Ruxandra forced her voice calm. She watched for any sign of guilt, but saw only shock and anger on Elizabeth's face. Dorotyas just looked outraged. Ruxandra sat back and waited.

Dorotyas spoke first. "Are you sure?"

"Of course I'm fucking sure!" The words came out loud and furious. "It had no brains. It had no sense. It had nothing but hate and hunger, and it lured me out into the fucking desert. I almost died!"

"A ghoul isn't strong enough to kill one of us, surely," Elizabeth said. "You told me it was . . . a shadow thing, something that a vampire made that was like us but not."

"It can also be controlled by the vampire who made it. The damn thing led me into the sun."

"Rather stupid of you," Dorotyas said.

Ruxandra ignored her. "Do you know how dangerous those things are?"

"Only what you've told me." Elizabeth leaned forward. "How do you make one?"

"I didn't tell you before, and I'm sure as hell not going to tell you now."

"Fine." Elizabeth stood up. "We won't get anything done here. Let's go."

Ruxandra rose with her. "I've been reaching out for the last hour. There's nothing within five miles."

Elizabeth led them outside, blowing exaggerated kisses at Joseph and Lilyan as she passed by. "What do ghouls feel like?"

"Like a human, but with pain and hunger and anger intense enough to make a human insane." She followed Elizabeth into the Los Angeles night. "We need to find the vampire, Elizabeth, before it makes more ghouls. Or before one gets past its guard and feeds from him."

"Why?" Dorotyas asked. "Wouldn't that solve our problem?"

Ruxandra gave her a look that would wither a cactus. "When a ghoul drinks our blood, it becomes just like us, except it's still a ghoul. It grows as strong as we are, as dangerous as we are, and just as hard to kill."

"Back to my apartment, then." Elizabeth looked over Ruxandra's outfit. "I'll feed and get changed into something more suitable. Though I doubt I own anything as interesting as that."

The warm, rich scent of fresh blood filled Elizabeth's apartment. A large metal trough sat in the living room, quiet sobbing coming from inside it. Elizabeth reached down with one hand and pulled a girl up by the hair. She was dark skinned, dark haired, and young. Her eyes darted back and forth, though no sound escaped her lips. Welts and cuts crisscrossed her skin. She was tied to another girl.

The corpse of another girl, Ruxandra realized. That one's throat was ripped open, and her eyes stared lifelessly as her head lolled back and forth, her long hair matted with blood. *Christ, Elizabeth. Why do you do this?*

Because Elizabeth was damaged, was the answer. Far more damaged than Ruxandra had realized back when she'd first turned her. And when she found out, it had been far, far too late. *She shouldn't make them suffer like this.*

Elizabeth bit the live girl and sucked at her until her screams faded to nothing and she collapsed. "Dorotyas, please clear the apartment. I'll get changed."

"Of course." Dorotyas hoisted the girls' bodies on her shoulder. "I'll have Mason take them away."

Elizabeth stepped into the bedroom. "You said the ghoul led you out into the desert?"

"Yes." Ruxandra found a comfortable high-backed wing chair and sat. Her fingers drummed the arm of it. She felt nervous, and she hated it. She wanted to find the vampire. She *didn't* want to face more ghouls.

"Did you find any sign of the vampire last night?"

"No." Ruxandra thought for a moment. "If you wanted to avoid being seen in Los Angeles but still stay close enough to kill in the city, where would you live?"

She practically heard Elizabeth rolling her eyes in the next room. "Oh God, there're a thousand places."

"Narrow them down."

"Well, there're a dozen little towns close enough to reach in an hour's run, as well as ghost towns, farms, ranches, and orchards."

"Then the vampire could be living in one of them."

"Excellent thought." Elizabeth stepped out of her bedroom in dark-brown riding britches and a deep-red sweater. "We'll start searching them tomorrow."

"Elizabeth!" Dorotyas stood in the doorway. "There's blood on the wind."

Ruxandra beat Elizabeth to the balcony. She leaned forward on the railing and breathed deeply, catching the scent of fresh-spilled human blood. She opened her mind and pinpointed the source.

Oh crap, there're more than one!

Elizabeth stepped up beside her. She concentrated a moment, then smiled. "Two of them. You're right; they feel like humans. They've already killed, and they're running."

"Together." Ruxandra frowned. "Ghouls don't work together unless someone makes them. That means he's controlling them right now."

"He?"

"Or she. Does it matter? They're running north and east. What's north and east?"

"Of here? Most of Los Angeles." Elizabeth pointed. "Hollywood is the closest, then Griffith Park, then Glendale. Farther east is Pasadena."

"There're people everywhere."

"Yes," Elizabeth said. "Especially this time of night."

"We have to stop the ghouls before they're seen." *Before they kill again.*

Ruxandra launched over the rail and vanished from human notice in the same moment. She hit the ground running, zeroing in on the ghouls' rage-filled presence.

"Always so dramatic." Elizabeth caught up to Ruxandra, her longer legs making it easy. "What do we do when we find them?"

"Tear their heads off and put them someplace where they'll burn up. Then I'll backtrack their trails and find where they came from." Ruxandra took a sharp corner, then another. She raced Santa Monica Boulevard, dodging the cars. Elizabeth fell behind. *Probably never runs.*

The ghouls changed direction, heading east. *Back toward the Hollywood Cemetery. Maybe there's a connection.*

The ghouls ran past it and went south. *So much for that.*

She caught up to them in the mess of houses and low-rises on the east side of Hoover. They turned, fangs bared and talons out. One had been a woman, the other a man. The woman's tattered and filthy flower-printed dress could have come off the rack of any clothier in the city. The man wore torn and dirty workman's trousers and shirt. Neither ghoul wore shoes. Blood dripped from their bared fangs and down their chins.

Ruxandra came to a stop a dozen yards away. The ghouls dropped into crouches, misshapen beasts waiting to spring.

At least the street is dark and empty. With luck, we can kill them both and anyone listening will think it's a couple of wildcats fighting.

Both ghouls turned their heads in a whiplash of motion. Then they jumped away and ran at top speed across the lawn and into the backyard of the nearest house.

What the hell? Ruxandra raced after them. *They should come after me. Ghouls want vampire blood more than anything else. So what . . .*

She heard tires screeching and glass smashing. Ruxandra cleared the backyard fence with one long jump. She raced around the next house.

Oh, shit.

The ghouls were attacking a police car.

CHAPTER
SEVEN

*S*HIT SHIT SHIT *shit shit!*

The two policemen scrambled from the car clawing for their guns. The female ghoul leaped at the younger one. Ruxandra caught it in midair and slammed it against the ground hard enough to fracture ribs. The ghoul hissed and struggled, its face twisted with pain as its bones tried to knit. Ruxandra smashed a fist into its face, driving it back down and sending blood and bone spattering.

A revolver fired six times. The male ghoul screamed in pain and staggered back, three bullet holes in its chest. The older officer kept pulling the trigger, his empty revolver clicking. The younger officer stared in shock at Ruxandra.

Deal with him later. Ruxandra launched a spinning kick, snapping the male ghoul's neck when it connected. The ghoul collapsed like a marionette with its strings cut.

The female ghoul landed on Ruxandra's back, claws digging into her flesh, teeth slashing at her neck, seeking the veins.

Ruxandra grabbed the ghoul's face and hair, her talons piercing the bones of its skull. She hauled up the creature, ripping its claws from her body and swinging the ghoul high before smashing it to the pavement.

No, no, no, no, no! Ruxandra shoved the Beast back even as she snapped the ghoul's spine. She pummeled the back of the creature's neck, turning the bones and muscles within to powder and jelly. She leaped onto the male, giving it the same treatment.

"What the fuck are you doing?" the older cop yelled. "What the fuck is happening?"

"*Be still!*" Ruxandra commanded. She kept punching until the ghoul's head lolled back and forth on its neck like a rock in a leather sack. Its teeth still snapped, still tried to reach her, but it couldn't control its head at all. Ruxandra stood up and stepped away.

Elizabeth watched, her eyes cold and calculating, but didn't come closer.

"Thanks for the help," Ruxandra snarled.

"You took care of it," Elizabeth said. "After all, you're so much better at this sort of thing."

Useless, lazy . . . Ruxandra turned to the police officers and commanded, "*Get these into the back of your car. Keep your hands away from their mouths. Now.*"

"What are you doing?" Elizabeth asked as the policemen picked up the first one.

"Putting the ghouls in the desert." Ruxandra grabbed the female by one leg and hauled it around to the now-open rear door of the police car. "I'm going to pound on their necks until we can get there. Then I'm tearing their heads off and letting the sun destroy them."

"Excellent thinking." Elizabeth's eyes went to the young policeman. "What about these policemen? Shall we eat them after?"

"Because *that's* not going to draw attention." Ruxandra rolled her eyes. Be sensible, Elizabeth. These fine officers are going to assist us poor women who got mugged, then drive us home. *Won't you, gentlemen?*"

"Of course," said the older one.

"Very good," Elizabeth said. "I'll stay here."

"What?" Anger that had nothing to do with the Beast rose in Ruxandra. "I did all the work! You could at least help clean up the mess!"

"I am." Elizabeth pointed to the open doors around them and the people peering out. "I'm going to take care of the witnesses, and then Dorotyas and I will sweep the city for more ghouls and see if we can spot the vampire."

"Good idea," Ruxandra said grudgingly. She tossed the female ghoul into the car. A thought struck her. "And by 'take care of' you mean command them to forget, not kill them, right?"

"Of course." Elizabeth smiled, her fangs showing. "There're too many to kill quickly. But don't worry. They'll all hear me shout. Now run along."

"*Drive us to the desert, please,*" Ruxandra commanded the officers.

She crawled into the back seat and perched above the ghouls. She gave each of their deformed necks another stomp with her boot, more for the satisfaction of it than anything else. The cops got in, the older one behind the wheel. He started the car and drove east, heading for the desert. Behind them, Ruxandra heard

Elizabeth's raised voice, commanding everyone on the block to come out.

"Pity about the mugger," the younger cop said. "Most times they get away. Still, maybe we can get back and look for clues."

The older one snorted. "Clues. Listen to you. Two years on the force and he already wants to be a detective."

"I'm just saying."

"Clues?" Ruxandra leaned forward over the lumpy bodies. "What sort of clues?"

"Go on, Sherlock," said the older cop. "Tell her what you know."

The younger one blushed. "Well, normally they look for patterns. See where the muggings happen and when, and then go there to try and catch them."

Like tracking a bear. Her mind flashed back to Whitechapel. *Or the Ripper.* "Is that what the police are doing with these vampire killings?"

"Oh yeah." The young cop glowed with enthusiasm. "They've got an entire squad devoted to it."

Ruxandra considered this for the next half hour as they drove, leaving the paved roads for a bumpy, dusty trail. Finally she commanded, "This squad. *Introduce me. Tomorrow.*"

Before long, they reached empty desert. The darkness was complete, punctuated only by flickering stars overhead, and the occasional light of distant houses. They dumped the bodies, and Ruxandra took their heads. Then she told the young policeman how to find her the next evening, commanded both officers to forget what had happened, and sent them on their way. When their car disappeared around a bend, she ran out to where the previous night's ghoul had died. In half an hour, she covered the twenty miles to the charred bones and the pile of bloody clothes.

Peasant clothes. Cheap trousers, cheap shirt, sandals. She studied every inch of the fabric, looking for anything out of place, sniffing for any scent that wasn't part of the ghoul's own stink.

She found nothing.

Ruxandra sighed. She spread her mind wide while she dug a pit to bury the ghoul's clothes. She sensed rabbits and snakes, mice and rats, and in the distance, a pair of coyotes. There were farmhouses at the edge of her reach with humans asleep inside. She found no signs of any other ghouls or of the vampire who had made them.

Dammit. Ruxandra turned and ran back to the hotel. *Maybe the police know something. Or maybe I can see something they don't.*

The young policeman, Ian, showed up in the Ambassador's lobby the next evening. He wore a nice suit and had bathed with a clean-smelling soap that Ruxandra smelled as soon as she entered the lobby. She smiled. *He probably thinks he's on a date.*

Ruxandra wore the same clothes as the night before, cleaned in the sink and dried on her balcony. If Ian thought it odd, he said nothing about it. The sun had just dipped behind the horizon, and heat still blistered the air. Ian led her to his car and held open the passenger door for her. *A 1915 Ford Model-T Convertible.* Ruxandra flashed her best smile. "A gentleman's car! That's what my mother called them. Do you know why?"

"No." Ian gave the engine a pair of cranks to start it up, then hopped in the driver's side. He raised his voice over the noise of the engine. "Why?"

Ruxandra looked him in the eyes and smiled. "Because there's no back seat."

Ian turned an endearing shade of red and put the car in gear. Ruxandra kept her senses and mind wide open as Ian drove through the evening traffic on Santa Monica Boulevard. Dorotyas and Elizabeth were at the apartment. She saw no sign of any other vampire—*not surprising*—or of any ghouls.

Their route took them right past Grauman's Chinese Theatre. It was massive and red and made Ruxandra smile again. *Not quite Chinese, but close.* Then they zipped past it and turned north on Cahuenga Boulevard.

"There." Ian pointed to a three-story building with wide garage doors in the front of it. "Built it in 1913. Police and fire station all in one."

"Quite a building."

"The detectives are upstairs."

"Thank you." Ruxandra hugged his arm. "Can you show me?"

"Can't." Ian patted her arm and left his hand there. "They don't allow anyone up there unless they've got actual business."

"Well, then, *just park up the street*," she commanded. He pulled over on the next block. She patted his thigh. "*Wait here for me. I won't be long.*"

She stepped out, vanished from notice, and went back to the police station. Slipping upstairs, she found the door labeled Detective Squad. Inside were five men, older and rougher than Ian, wearing cheap suits with shirt collars undone. Two frowned as they studied a series of files under the yellow light of desk lamps. Two more talked with each other, smoking by a wall of black filing cabinets. The last sat alone, drinking coffee and staring out the window. The room smelled like cigarette smoke, burned coffee, and sweat.

On one wall hung a map of Los Angeles, with notecards attached to it by pushpins. Each notecard held the name, gender, age and date of death of one of the murder victims.

Ruxandra turned noticeable again. "Gentlemen, I need your help."

The detectives all jumped in surprise. One bore down on her, his face red and his brows drawn low over his eyes. "What the hell are you doing here?"

"Are you the detectives on the vampire murder case?"

"None of your damn business." The man took her arm and started pulling. "You get out of here, young lady."

Ruxandra didn't move. "*Tell me everything you know about the vampire murders. Now.*"

Two hours later, Ruxandra made her way down the stairs and out of the station. *Nineteen mutilations over the last three months. The kills getting closer together. No one saw anything.*

Assuming that's all of them. Ruxandra's mind flashed back to the corpse in the graveyard. *They might miss some, thinking they are animal attacks.*

Ian did not look happy when she reached him. "You said you'd be back soon."

"I am *terribly* sorry," Ruxandra said, and meant it. *It's not his fault I'm in this mess.* "Tell you what: why don't you take me to the Chinese theater? I'll pay for the movies, you buy the drinks."

"I don't know . . ."

"Please. I really want to see a movie tonight." Ruxandra slipped in beside him and put her hand high on his thigh. He jumped at her touch. "I like sitting in the back of the balcony. Don't you?"

Ian's face went red. "There's a cowboy movie playing tonight, I think. Do you like cowboy movies?"

"I do." *Which is true,* she thought as he started the car. *And more than that, I like sitting in the dark and thinking.*

It was a weeknight and the place was almost empty, which suited Ruxandra fine. They laughed through the two short films before the main feature—Keystone Cops and comedians racing across the screen and trying to catch one another. Ruxandra leaned against Ian's shoulder. She enjoyed the warmth and the fresh, clean scent and the pulse of life moving through his body. He put his arm around her and that felt good, too.

If only . . . She cut off the thought right there. If Elizabeth thought Ruxandra enjoyed someone's company, she'd no doubt kill him, just like she killed Carolyn. Ruxandra shuddered and shoved down the memory. She reached out with her mind and found Elizabeth and Dorotyas in their apartment feeding on a girl and a man, respectively. *Of course. God forbid they search for the vampire.*

Maybe all that torture gives Elizabeth such an appetite she has to eat every day. Or she's just grown gluttonous in her old age.

She looked at Ian. He smiled as he watched the horses racing across the plains, the good guys hot on the heels of the bad guy. *If I were Elizabeth, I'd kill him just to keep him silent.*

She put her hand high up on Ian's leg. He breathed in sharply. *Good thing for him I'm not Elizabeth.*

His eyes came down and met hers. She smiled up, leaned in, and kissed him on the mouth. He wasn't a bad kisser, which was nice. She let her hand wander higher, then put her mouth next to his ear and whispered, "Don't make a sound."

She slid off her seat and knelt at his feet, her hand reaching for the buttons on his trousers.

He came with a tight, quiet gasp just as Gary Cooper saved Betty Jewel from a runaway horse. Ruxandra swallowed, stood up, and whispered in his ear. "You're a nice boy, Ian, and I had a great time. *Don't try to follow me out. Don't try to see me again. Don't tell anyone else about tonight. Watch the rest of the movie.*"

She left Ian watching the screen, his face still flushed with pleasure.

—— ◆ ◆ ◆ ◆ ——

Outside the theater, she sensed a ghoul less than a mile away.

Ruxandra reached out with her mind and found Elizabeth and Dorotyas still in their apartment. *What the hell? They're supposed to be watching.*

She vanished from notice and ran. The ghoul was in Griffith Park, stalking a pair of humans parked near the municipal golf course. From the lust Ruxandra sensed coming off them, neither would notice the ghoul until it jumped on top of them.

Ruxandra ran the distance in one minute flat, not caring if the ghoul heard her coming. Griffith Park was green and lush and filled with trees, in stark contrast to the streets around it. The roads were smooth and well kept, and the golf course had several convenient parking places for couples wanting privacy.

Ruxandra spotted the lovers first, both in the passenger seat of a Stutz roadster. The woman sat astride the man, riding hard while he buried his face in her bare breasts. The ghoul crouched twenty feet away, preparing to pounce.

Ruxandra put on a burst of speed and caught the thing in midair, slamming it against the nearest tree with a thud as loud as a cannon shot. The woman in the car screamed, and the man shouted in surprise. The ghoul hit the ground with a howl of pain and scrambled to its feet. It used to be a black-haired, brown-skinned man, though its flesh was now pale and gray.

It saw Ruxandra and snarled like an angry trapped mountain lion. Its lips were ripped where its jagged fangs had torn through the skin. Blood speckled the remains of its white shirt and loose trousers and stained the tops of its boots. Its fingers ended in razor-sharp claws ready to tear Ruxandra's flesh if she let them. The ghoul screamed and charged.

Ruxandra kicked forward, her heel cracking the ghoul's sternum as if it were a dry stick. The ghoul squealed and fell, its momentum gone. Ruxandra jumped on it, fists swinging. She pounded its face, smashing teeth and cheekbones and bursting one of its eyes. The thing squirmed and thrashed and bucked, throwing her off before she got a good grip around it with her legs. She sprang up again, but the ghoul ran across the road and disappeared into the wooded parkland.

"Hey!"

Ruxandra turned. The man was running toward her, a tire iron in his hand.

"Hey! You all right?"

"Fine," said Ruxandra. *"Now get in the car and get out of here."*

Moments later, Ruxandra heard the car racing down the road behind her as she ran across the golf course. The ghoul had a head start, but Ruxandra caught up and stayed ten yards behind—close enough for the thing to see and smell her and stay panicked. It ran straight for the Los Angeles River.

Please, please, lead me back to your master.

The ghoul stopped at the riverbank, turned, and charged Ruxandra again. Its jaw had healed, and its regrown jagged teeth glinted in the moonlight. It stretched its claws out to tear into her flesh. Ruxandra used a move she'd learned in Japan seventy-five years before to throw the creature hard against the rocks thirty feet away. It bounced to its feet and charged. Ruxandra kicked it this time, driving it back.

"Come on, you stupid thing," she muttered as it stood again, "show me where you live."

Instead, it swiped its claws at her. She punched it hard, breaking its teeth again, and smashed a heel into its knee, driving it down. Her next kick hit the back of its head, sending its face onto the rocks on the riverbank. It started crawling away. Ruxandra gave it another kick. "Come *on*, show me where you live!"

It splashed through the shallow water and loped toward the other bank. Ruxandra followed, ignoring the water seeping into her boots. Halfway across, the ghoul turned and attacked her again. The mud and water slowed them both but did nothing to take away Ruxandra's superior strength. She threw the thing back in the water, punching and kicking until it splashed away from her and up the opposite bank into the streets of Glendale.

Same direction as the last one. So where's it going?

Ruxandra kept pace with it through the empty streets, past the city's outskirts, and into the desert beyond. They ran for hours. The night sky changed from black to dark blue. Still the creature kept running.

Goddamn it. It's trying to leave me stuck out in the desert when the sun comes up. Same as the last one. I don't have time for this.

Ruxandra scooped up a rock without losing her stride and threw it hard. It hit the back of the ghoul's head with a crunching splat and the ghoul fell. She jumped on its back and pinned it facedown with her boot. The ghoul struggled and tried to claw her. Ruxandra shifted position, squatted, and drove her talons through the sides of its skull. Then she straightened her knees and ripped its head from its body in a single motion. The creature convulsed once and went still.

Ruxandra sighed and pulled the body up a hill for the sun to burn it away. She dropped the head and knelt down, looking for some sign of where it came from or where it had been going. She leaned in closer, breathing deep, and caught a trace of perfume on its collar. It was so faint that at first Ruxandra wasn't certain it was there. She sniffed again. *A flower scent.*

She sat back on her haunches. *Maybe it's his wife's perfume. Or his mistress or his daughter. He could be a florist. He might like men and want to smell pretty for his boyfriend. Or . . .*

Or the vampire is female.

A hint of doubt crept into her mind as she looked at the headless body. *Elizabeth said it wasn't her or Dorotyas. She said they had nothing to do with it. And I never taught her how to make ghouls.*

Ruxandra looked at the brightening horizon. Time was getting short. *And Elizabeth never lies, right?*

Yeah, right.

Ruxandra ran but not back to the Ambassador. She went to the detectives' office. She left just before sunrise with a giant map of Los Angeles and the area around it and several boxes of brass and steel pushpins.

Back in her hotel room, she pinned the map to her wall. She began pushing in pins, each with a notecard that described the victim. In fifteen minutes, she recreated the entire map that had hung in the detective's office. Then she added pins and cards for the two ghouls who'd attacked the police car and where she'd killed the other two.

At least there's some benefit to a vampire's memory. She took her chair and sat in front of the map. *So what's the pattern?*

The ghouls struck in Beverly Hills one night, in Westgate two nights later, then in Maywood the next night. Then no attacks happened for a week before three in a row in Santa Monica, Vernon, and Pasadena. They weren't choosy about their victims, either. They took men and women, white, black, and Hispanic. Once they snatched a child.

Random. Ruxandra sighed and went to bed. *It can't be random. All of us have patterns. I just need to figure out this one's . . .*

I need to talk to Elizabeth about it all.

She woke as the sun set. A quick expansion of her mind showed Elizabeth and Dorotyas at their apartment along with two new girls. Ruxandra rolled her eyes and turned her mind elsewhere. *Never take a break, do they? Never go out looking, either.*

She thought about that while putting on her black clothes. *Are they that lazy? Or do they even want this creature caught?* But she couldn't think of how it benefited Elizabeth to have a mad vampire in her city or to bring in Ruxandra if she didn't want it gone.

She turned unnoticed and went out. She found no smell or sense of ghoul anywhere and, of course, no sense of the vampire. She sensed all the humans, though, and it reminded her that she had not fed in three days. She forced the hunger out of her mind and jogged to Elizabeth's apartment, taking enough time to arrive after Elizabeth finished her gory games.

Dorotyas answered the door, blood on her face and on the thick butcher's apron she wore over her clothes. "Finally decided to visit, did you?"

"Where the hell were you two last night?" Ruxandra demanded. She sniffed the air, ignoring the smells of blood and death and fear, searching for perfumes instead. "There was a ghoul."

"We noticed," said Elizabeth, emerging from the bedroom with a wide blood-covered strap over her shoulder. "We also realized you had it, so we let it alone and focused on looking for the vampire."

"Without leaving your apartment." Four perfumes floated in the air: two young, fresh ones from the dead girls in the bedroom, a deeper, muskier one from Elizabeth, and a surprisingly light, flowery one from Dorotyas. None matched the ghoul's scent. *Because that would be way too easy.* "How helpful of you."

Elizabeth passed the strap to Dorotyas. Then she pointed toward the dining table, covered with half a dozen open maps. "This is what we have been doing. If the vampire is making ghouls, he's not making them around here. Someone would notice."

"She."

Elizabeth stopped and stared at Ruxandra. "What?"

"It's a she," said Ruxandra, watching her. "I smelled perfume on the ghoul last night. Not a man's scent."

Elizabeth's eyebrow went up. "Now I suppose you want to smell my perfume collection?"

"I already checked."

"Really, Ruxandra." Elizabeth sounded exasperated. "Why don't you trust me?"

Experience. But Ruxandra didn't say anything, she just looked at Elizabeth and waited.

Elizabeth shook her head and walked over. She pointed at a small town on the edge of the map. "Tonight the three of us are going on a trip. Have you eaten?"

"Three nights ago."

"You should have come earlier. We could have shared."

I am not eating your kills. "I don't like watching you play with your food."

"Too bad." Elizabeth smiled. "They were delightfully squirmy."

"I'm sure."

"Well, it's too late to get anything now. Maybe we can stop for a snack on the way."

"On the way where?"

Elizabeth tapped the map. "North. We're going for a car trip. I want to find the bastard who's hunting in my town and put an end to her."

CHAPTER
EIGHT

"WHERE EXACTLY ARE we going?" Ruxandra asked as Mason drove them through Los Angeles, across the river, and up Chevy Chase Drive.

"We're following up on your idea," Elizabeth said. "You thought the vampire might be staying out of town. So we're going to search out of town."

Ruxandra nodded. "All right. So what's out this way?"

"The Angeles National Forest," Elizabeth said. "There are also a few small towns within running distance of Los Angeles for a ghoul. I thought we'd start with them."

Ruxandra frowned. "I'd think a farmhouse would be better. A vampire would be easy to spot in a small town."

"Not if it controls the town." Elizabeth smiled. "I remember a little place outside of Ouarzazate in Morocco. We ruled it for twenty-three years before anyone escaped."

"They had a large underground cistern." Dorotyas's eyes half closed as she reveled in the memory. "We controlled their water supply and kept them from leaving. They sacrificed girls and men to us. Especially travelers."

"It was a lovely time." Elizabeth smiled. "Now, once we get outside the city, we all stretch our senses. With luck, we can pick up the new vampire."

"Why aren't any of us staying in the city?" Ruxandra asked. "What if there's another attack?"

"Then we'll know she's closer to LA," said Elizabeth. "Or in another direction. We try east tomorrow and south the day after."

Needle in a haystack. Ruxandra looked out the window, watching as Los Angeles gave way to forest. It was larger than Ruxandra expected, and as they drove through it, she stretched her senses as far as she could. Plenty of animals, some humans. No ghouls, no vampire. She sighed and kept at it.

It took Mason three hours to drive them through the mountains. Ruxandra could run it in half that, but Elizabeth insisted they all stay in the car. "Running is far too much effort, darling, especially when we don't need to."

When they emerged into the farmland on the other side, Elizabeth sat up. She closed her eyes and cocked her head, listening.

"There," Elizabeth said. "Do you feel it?"

"Ghoul," Dorotyas said. "Near . . . about twenty people. It hasn't attacked anyone yet."

"Mason, turn left at the next road."

"I can run there faster," Ruxandra said.

"Dorotyas, go with her."

Ruxandra opened the car door and jumped, hitting the ground running. She heard Dorotyas land behind her, stumble, and then run hard to keep up. Ruxandra put on a burst of speed, eating up the distance between her and the ghoul.

Less than a mile.

She found the ghoul howling with frustration and rage, slamming its body against the door of a long, low barrack at the bottom of an orange orchard. She sensed eighteen people inside, all scared to death.. The door shook and rattled, the wood straining with each blow. Ruxandra heard the shouts of pain from the men inside leaning hard against it and felt the women and children's fear.

Children. Fuck.

The ghoul hit the door again and bounced off. It howled and circled the house. Then it took a run at one of the shuttered windows. Ruxandra slammed into it, sending it flying into the wall. The wood cracked as the ghoul bounced off it and dropped to a crouch.

Younger than the last one. Also male, also Mexican. Same peasant clothes, same sandals. Ruxandra sniffed. *Fresher than the last one, too.*

The ghoul launched at her. She slapped it down, beat it brutally enough to make it stop moving, and sat on it, one knee on its throat to keep it from biting. She grabbed its hair and pulled its face around.

"I know you're in there," she snarled at the vampire controlling the ghoul. "I know you see through this thing's eyes and hear through its ears. So you listen to me. What you're doing is dangerous to you and to all of us. I don't know if you're new at this or what, but we need to talk. So make this ghoul lead me to you. *Now.*"

"What on earth are you doing?" Dorotyas ran up beside her. "Kill the thing and be done with it."

"I will if it doesn't lead me to its maker. Now get back." Ruxandra tensed her legs and waited. As soon as Dorotyas moved out of the way, she jumped off the ghoul's throat and landed in a crouch forty feet away. "Come on. Lead me. *Now*."

The ghoul howled. Then it turned and ran.

"We'll take care of the witnesses," said Dorotyas. "You find that vampire and you bring it to us!"

Ruxandra didn't like the glee in Dorotyas's voice. She knew how Dorotyas and Elizabeth take care of witnesses. She didn't have time to argue, though. The creature loped back through the fields toward the Angeles forest. Ruxandra kept pace with it, staying close. The ghoul ran straight until it hit the forest. Then it began dodging in and out of the trees, trying to hide from Ruxandra's sight. She caught up to it, kicked it, and drove it to the earth.

"I've run in forests for four hundred years," she said as the ghoul struggled to its feet. It glared with so much hate that she braced for the next attack. "Don't even try it. Just bring me to you."

It ran.

Ruxandra chased the ghoul for three hours. It weaved and dodged, trying to throw her off. Ruxandra stayed close until the morning light started to fill the sky. The ghoul wasn't leading her anywhere.

The vampire wants to trap me in the sunlight. She closed in on the ghoul and let all her irritation and anger loose on it. *If that's her game, I'm not playing.*

When she finished she dragged the crushed, bloody, limp body of the still-growling creature to a clearing for the sun to burn. The creature tried to howl, but she'd driven its ribs through its lungs and the sound came out as a bubbling gasp.

"Believe it or not, I am *trying* to help." Ruxandra stood over the bleeding, snarling creature. "If Elizabeth or Dorotyas get hold of you, you will wish to God you were dead, so stop messing with me and come talk to me!"

She ripped the creature's head off and slammed it down so hard it broke open. She checked the sky. The sun sat just below at the horizon. Ruxandra swore and started running.

In Barstow, she found a fancy railway depot done up in a combination of Spanish and classical style with a bit of Moorish thrown in for good measure. It was at once an eyesore and glorious in its ridiculousness. It also, Ruxandra discovered, held a hotel called the Harvey House. In short order, after commanding the man at the desk not to notice the blood on her, she had a suite with a bath. Ruxandra spent half an hour washing the dust and blood off and sank into bed.

<hr>

She was starving by evening, and the Beast growled and snarled with discontent. She opened her mind, looking for a predator to kill, but there wasn't one. She considered taking the bellhop, who stared at her breasts whenever he thought she wasn't looking, but wasn't going to lower her standards. She turned unnoticed instead and ran out of town, heading back to the farmhouse and Elizabeth. *Perhaps I can take someone on the road.*

Ruxandra smelled blood and kerosene in the barracks from a mile out. The Beast inside her smelled it too and began howling. *Four days without feeding, and the Beast is already this close to the surface. What the hell is wrong with me? It's the ghouls. They're triggering it.*

One glance inside the barracks showed her enough to start her cursing in ten different languages. Blood spattered over the walls and floor, and the bent, broken bodies of women, men, and children lay around the room like toys thrown about in a toddler's temper tantrum. The Beast howled in frustration at being denied fresh blood. It wouldn't drink from the dead, and neither would Ruxandra. She opened her senses and found Elizabeth and Dorotyas in the big white house along with three men and two girls in terrible agony. Ruxandra walked through the grove, the sharp smell of citrus not doing enough to cover the stench of death and fear and spilled fuel coming from both the barracks and the house.

For God's sake, Elizabeth. Ruxandra stepped over the bloodless staring corpses of a well-dressed older white couple to get in the front door. *Probably the owners.*

The house's interior was a single space with a clear view from the front door to the kitchen and dining room on one side, and the large parlor on the other. Thick wooden beams ran the length of the ceiling. Three young strong men hung naked from the beams by barbed wire wrapped around their elbows and ankles. All wept and prayed in Spanish. Dorotyas stood before the first, a long talon extended out at the height of his groin.

The Beast wanted to leap up and land on the men's backs, to drink them one by one until it felt swollen and full. Ruxandra forced it back, ignoring the howls that filled her brain and the cravings that came up from her empty stomach. The effort left her shaking. *I do not kill prisoners. I am not a torturer or a slave owner. I will not eat like this.*

"About time you got back," Dorotyas said. "Find her?"

Ruxandra managed not to kick the woman through the wall. Through gritted teeth, she asked, "Where's Elizabeth?"

"In the kitchen." Dorotyas jabbed forward with her hand, spearing the man's left testicle. He screamed loud and high and thrashed. "She got bored waiting for you."

"I'm sure that was her excuse." Ruxandra walked to the kitchen. Two women sat at a long table, each with a fingerless hand pinned to the wooden table by a knife. The missing fingers lay on plates in front of them. They saw Ruxandra and pleaded for help. Elizabeth stood against the counter, smiling.

"Hello, Ruxandra. We're having a little contest. Whoever eats all their own fingers first gets to live." Elizabeth frowned. "So far, neither has managed it. I'm very surprised."

BLOOD, BLOOD, BLOOD, BLOOD, BLOOD!

The Beast's screams rattled around in Ruxandra's skull, making it hard to think. She fought to ignore them and planted herself in front of Elizabeth. "What the *fuck* are you *doing*?"

"Keeping entertained." Elizabeth looked at the women and commanded, "*Everyone quiet now!*"

The three men and two women fell silent at once, though tears continued to stream down their faces, and their mouths gasped for air.

"Much better," said Elizabeth, turning then to Ruxandra. "Want one?"

YES, YES, YES, YES, YES. DRINK, DRINK, DRINK, DRINK, DRINK!

Shut up! "No."

"Too bad. Dorotyas and I are both quite full."

"You're both insane, is what you are."

Elizabeth's eyes narrowed. "That's rather rude, Ruxandra."

"Fuck you!" Ruxandra's shout made the windows rattle. "Killing everyone in the barracks? Torturing everyone here? I thought you wanted to calm things down! To keep us from getting caught! How is this helping?"

"I don't care how many humans die." Elizabeth closed the distance between them, eyes simmering. "What I care about is making that bitch out there know that California is *my* territory, not *hers*. I need her to see that *I* decide who lives or dies and who is terrified. Not her."

KILL, KILL, KILL. DRINK, EAT, KILL!

Ruxandra stumbled away, grabbing her head and squeezing it until the Beast shut up. When there was finally silence inside her, she straightened up. Elizabeth watched, smiling, her ivory skin marred by a smear of blood on her chin. Ruxandra growled. "That's what this is? A power play? Elizabeth, there's an entire *city* full of terrified people out there. Now you want to drag in the whole *state*? How much more before they call in the army?"

"I've faced armies before."

"Not like this. Times have changed, Elizabeth."

"You think I don't know that?" Elizabeth's voice rose to a screech. "I have spent three hundred years living in the shadows! *Me*, who used to dine with the emperor!"

Ruxandra rolled her eyes.

Elizabeth tossed her head and walked to the woman facing Ruxandra. She ran a hand over the woman's hair, then down her neck and into her dress. She leaned close and licked the woman's face. "Things were better before, and I think we should make them better again."

Ruxandra's mouth fell open. "Are you serious?"

"I am Blood Royal!" Elizabeth spat out the words. "I'm tired of living like a common bourgeois, tired of pretending to be human and hiding."

She ripped her hand out of the woman's dress, taking flesh with it. The dress stained red at once, and the woman thrashed, her mouth wide in a silent scream. "You should be with me on this, but you *like* hiding. You like skulking like a common killer in the shadows. What has it gotten you? Nothing."

"Nothing?" Ruxandra felt the Beast responding to her anger, egging her on to violence. "I speak sixteen languages. I play eleven instruments. I saw the first opera in Vienna and watched the Eiffel Tower being built! I'm rich, and I go anywhere I like. How is that nothing?"

"No one respects you! No one fears you! No one even knows you exist!" Elizabeth waved at the room, making the blood hurry in snaky streaks down her wrist and forearm. "Remember the train? The family? This vampire bitch has seen that in the papers and she'll see this. She'll realize *exactly* what she is dealing with and she will be terrified. And as soon as you find her, we bring her to heel."

"I wonder," Ruxandra looked at the bloody mess around them and felt for the first time in many years deep shame that she had made Elizabeth immortal. *How much worse will the other one be if Elizabeth gets her claws into her?* "You two sound too much alike for comfort."

"I can control her once I find her," Elizabeth said. "With her and you together, we could take over the entire state. The entire country, in time!"

"The humans would kill us."

"They *can't* kill us!"

"The humans outnumber us a million to one, Elizabeth, and that's just California! They have machine guns now. They have artillery. They have airplanes and bombs and *flamethrowers*, for

God's sake. I was in the Great War. I saw what those weapons do. We can't survive a fight against them. And what do you think will happen when they see this place?"

"The humans will *never* see this place. Or is the Beast taking so much control of you that you can't smell the kerosene?" She stepped closer to Ruxandra, their bodies almost touching. "Real fear comes from not knowing. From realizing there is power out there they can't control. From realizing that they must kowtow to our wishes if they want to survive."

Elizabeth stepped closer; dropped her voice low. "Remember Castle Csejte? How much power we had?"

"How much power *you* had." Ruxandra looked at the bloody mess and the thrashing silent victims. The smell overwhelmed her, bringing horror and hunger in equal measure. Elizabeth's scent threaded through it all, musky, confident, and intoxicating. "I remember the constant stench of an abattoir. I remember having to fight the Beast every day just to stay sane. I was *glad* when they finally came for you!"

Ruxandra turned her back on Elizabeth, kicked open the back door, and stomped through it.

"Where are you going?" Elizabeth demanded.

"Back to the barracks." Ruxandra didn't stop walking. "If I can backtrack the creature's trail, I can find where it came from."

"Eat first." Elizabeth grabbed the woman's arm. The woman's flesh ripped away from the knife jammed in the table, tearing what was left of her hand in half. Her mouth opened wide in a soundless scream as she flew through the air. She landed with a crunch of bone at Ruxandra's feet. "I'd *hate* to see you lose control. Again."

The girl stared up at Ruxandra with hopeless eyes.

"Oh, I forgot," Elizabeth said. "*Everyone can talk again!*"

The screams and cries of pain and babbled prayers all started at once, filling the house with a cacophony of anguish that made the Beast howl for freedom and blood. Ruxandra's fangs and talons came out of their own accord, and her eyes turned red, the pupils becoming serpentine slits.

The girl lying on the ground in front of Ruxandra didn't scream. She just stared up, her eyes wide and filled with tears. She cradled her ruined hand.

"Please," she whispered. "Kill me."

KILL, DRINK, KILL, DRINK, KILL, KILL!

The Beast wanted to tear the woman's throat out, to feel her convulse and thrash as it drained the life out of her. Elizabeth stood in the doorway, watching Ruxandra struggle as the Beast demanded food.

Ruxandra reached out, wrapped her hand around the girl's neck, and snapped it with a single motion. Then she turned her back and walked away, ignoring the Beast's enraged screams.

"What a waste," Elizabeth said.

I am not a fucking animal. You hear me, Beast? I am not like her, and I am not like you. I choose my own kills. Not you, and not her!

With tears in her eyes from the strain of resisting the Beast and her own hunger, Ruxandra found the ghoul's trail, two days old now, and followed it. It led right back to the Angeles forest. It twisted and turned a hundred times, up cliffs and down hills, over trees and through swamps, and ended in the river. Ruxandra sank down into the cool mud by the riverside, her head in her hands. *Of course, it's a dead end.*

She shook with hunger and was more than ready to eat anyone who crossed her path. She wanted to scream with frustration, to smash her fist against a tree and watch it shatter. But any action like that just brought the Beast closer to the surface, and she couldn't afford that. *Not when it's so close to taking over.*

So instead she opened her mind and her senses wide and listened. She found a family in a farmhouse two miles east. A mile west, two couples camped together. South of her, four hoboes crouched around a fire, sharing a bottle. And a mile north of her, a self-satisfied woman drove a car with a terrified, angry man in the trunk.

Really? Ruxandra rose and followed the woman's energy. She reached the car just as it pulled over and stopped. *Perfect.*

A short brunette woman with pushed-up breasts under a tight blouse, and curved hips under an even tighter skirt stepped out of the car. She wore very sensible rubber boots. She held a gun in one hand and pointed it into the trunk as she opened it. "Here we are, Phillip. Time for you to dig."

"Please," the man in the trunk begged. "Please don't kill me. Think of my daughter . . ."

"Oh, but I am." The woman stepped back. "Especially that cute little ass of hers. I mean, now that you've left everything to me, and given how that little slut of yours treated me, I know how to make her earn her keep."

"Oh, I think not," Ruxandra whispered in the woman's ear. "I think not at all."

The woman didn't get a chance to scream before she died.

There's another ghoul. Ruxandra felt the creature as she reached the outskirts of LA. It loped through Laurel Canyon, three miles west of her as she emerged from the hills. She changed course, following it through the night. She felt angry and frustrated and more than ready to call everything off and go home. *Except if I do, Elizabeth will just come after me, and I'll never hear the end of it.*

She closed the distance between them but stayed far enough back that it couldn't smell her. The creature picked up its pace, heading west. Ruxandra stayed on its trail for another three miles and reached ahead of it with her mind. A few miles farther, a house blazed with the energy of at least thirty people, including a few Ruxandra recognized. *Joseph? And Lilyan? Oh, crap. If the ghoul eats them, the press coverage will reach the entire country, and there'll be hell to pay.*

Ruxandra sped up and caught the thing at the base of a hill with a sign saying "Pickfair," and a road leading up to a large house with lights on and laughter coming from within. She jumped on the ghoul from behind and snapped its neck. *Douglas Fairbanks and Mary Pickford's house. Of all the stupid places to go, why there? Those people are famous. It can't target them and expect to get away with it. Unless it doesn't care. Or it knows that I know them.*

She cast her mind wide as she dragged the ghoul into the open hills beyond the house. No sign of a vampire anywhere. She dropped the ghoul on the ground and pulled its head off. She knew she should talk to the vampire controlling it but was too angry. Instead, she went back to the party, turned unnoticed, and kept watch until the last partygoers left or slept in one of the rooms. Then Ruxandra made her way back to the Ambassador and spent a long, long time in the shower.

She knows I'm chasing her. She knows who I spend time with, and she probably knows I'm alone in the city. She dried off and climbed into bed, her mind spinning with ideas. *Tomorrow I'll go back and find the ghoul's trail. I might even find the stupid vampire and convince her I'm not a threat.*

Maybe I can even convince her to help me calm Elizabeth down . . .

She woke to someone knocking on her door. She sighed and rolled out of bed. *Probably Dorotyas come to . . .*

She froze when she smelled the man on the other side of the door.

How could . . .

The knocking came louder the second time. Ruxandra rose on shaky legs and put on her kimono.

He'd started knocking a third time when she pulled the door open.

He was tall, but then he'd always been tall. His dark-brown hair lay smoothed back against his head with pomade. He held his hat in his hand and his long, gray traveling coat over his arm. He wore a black wool suit with a deep-red tie and black shoes polished to a shine. His long, narrow face broke open in a wide smile, and he looked down on her. "Good to see you, Ruxandra."

"Oh my God." The words came out of Ruxandra in a whisper. "Kade?"

CHAPTER
NINE

"P RINCESS." KADE'S BARITONE voice sent vibrations through Ruxandra. "It's good to see you again."

Kade was Elizabeth's personal sorcerer when Ruxandra had been the Beast. He bound her to Elizabeth and refused to let her go until Ruxandra made him a vampire. Instead, Ruxandra almost killed Elizabeth. Kade took the moment to drink Elizabeth's blood and become a vampire. When he turned, his human magic disappeared, and Ruxandra broke free. She left Castle Csejte. Kade stayed with Elizabeth and Dorotyas for fifty more years and then left in search of vampire magic.

It took a hundred years for Ruxandra to forgive him.

In Moscow, they fought a fallen angel and became lovers. Since then they've stayed friends, keeping a longtime correspondence and seeing each other whenever they ended up in the same country. And now, he stood in her doorway, smiling.

Kade stepped forward, put his arms around Ruxandra, and kissed her on the forehead. "It has been far too long."

"The war." Ruxandra's arms went around his waist. She felt the long, lean strength of him under his suit, felt the effect of it between her legs. "You were on the German side, pretending to be an officer."

"You drove ambulances for the British," said Kade. "Remember the night we ran into each other, hunting in no-man's-land?"

"I remember." Ruxandra leaned her head against his chest. Tension she didn't realize was there began to melt from her neck and shoulders. "Thank God you're here."

He squeezed her again and walked her back, closing the door behind them. "I thought you swore never to spend time with Elizabeth ever again after Castle Csejte."

"She came to me." Ruxandra stepped away from him. "And messed up everything." She sank down onto the soft couch.

He sat beside her. "Tell me."

She did, from the moment Elizabeth came to her in New York to the death of Carolyn and everything that had happened since. Kade frowned as he listened and studied the map on the wall with all of its pins. "That sounds . . . strange. Even for her."

"Are you sure she's not one of yours?" Ruxandra asked. "Maybe someone who got away from you?"

"No one gets away from me." Kade's tone left no room for doubt. "I've been careful ever since the first time in Italy."

Ruxandra shook her head. "But if she's not yours and not Elizabeth's . . ."

Kade looked thoughtful. "Are we sure she's not Elizabeth's?"

Ruxandra's eyebrows went up. "Pardon?"

"I mean, if one of hers got away and decided she didn't want Elizabeth domineering over everything . . ."

"That explains why Elizabeth needs the help." Ruxandra rose and began pacing the sitting room. "If she knows the vampire, if she trained her, the vampire would know all about Elizabeth and how to keep away from her."

"If she wanted revenge on her for something, that's motivation enough to cause trouble." Kade studied the map some more. "Why is the Beast so close to the surface? I thought you had control of it."

"I do," Ruxandra said, then amended, "mostly. It's always there, but as long as I'm not hungry or furious, it keeps quiet. But the ghouls . . ." She stopped, then, trying to put her thoughts in order. Kade waited. At last, Ruxandra said, "You remember in Ireland, when I found your ghouls."

"I do." Kade smiled. "You were so angry."

Ruxandra nodded "The only ghoul I ever made was by accident when I was first a vampire. Before I knew anything. All I knew was that I liked him and he liked me, so I cleaned myself up, and one day we started to make love and . . . I drank him."

"You told me," Kade said gently.

"And you know what happened next."

"You turned him into one of us."

Ruxandra shook her head. "No. I hung onto his soul, even after it left his body. That made him a ghoul. I just didn't know it. Then I let him drink my blood. I turned a *ghoul* into a vampire, and it damn near killed me before I killed it, and then after . . ."

Her hands trembled as she spoke. She tried to stop them but couldn't. She stood up and started pacing just to get her nerves under control. "After, I went into the woods and only drank animal blood until I became the Beast. When Elizabeth found me, it took months of living in a cage and drinking human blood before I had enough control to stop turning into the Beast every time I got hungry."

"For years after, I've had to fight it. After I let it free in Moscow, it took months to control it again. Then I saw your ghouls and all that control slipped away. It took me five days to get the Beast back in its cage in my head. It was . . . frightening."

"I can imagine."

"No," Ruxandra said. "You can't. You're always in control, Kade, always taking charge of everything. And now . . ."

Kade waited. When no more came, he prompted her. "And now?"

"Now, every time I fight a ghoul, I feel the Beast trying to take control again." She shook her head. "Never mind. Did you ever make any more ghouls? Or tell Elizabeth how to make them?"

"No." Kade's voice was firm. "I promised you I wouldn't."

"Good."

"But it doesn't mean she couldn't have figured it out on her own." Kade looked thoughtful. "And if the vampire is Elizabeth's, she might have told her how to make a ghoul."

Ruxandra nodded. "Or she figured out how to make them on her own to use against Elizabeth."

"Yes."

"I should have thought of that. She swore it wasn't one of hers." Ruxandra stopped pacing. Her kimono had come loose, she realized, exposing her leg to the hip and most of one breast. He looked at her leg, and his expression stirred a primal feeling that had *nothing* to do with the Beast. She smiled. "Thank you so much for coming."

"How could I not, after what you telegrammed?" Kade stood up, leaving his coat and hat behind on the couch. "Concealment is our greatest asset. Especially in the modern age, when so few people believe in us. With the cities awake all night, no one raises an eyebrow at the man who prefers darkness. So much abundance at our feet, so many uprooted people who won't be missed. There has never been an age like this, so suited to our kind. For a vampire to be so blatant, to risk this—"

"Would be just like someone turned by Elizabeth."

Kade's smile grew wider. "Indeed. Should we go talk to Elizabeth, then?"

"Elizabeth is out of town, chasing the vampire." Ruxandra stepped closer, breathing in his scent. "It's just the two of us."

"Then perhaps the two of us—"

"Kade." Ruxandra stopped with her body inches from his. "How long since you've been with another vampire?"

Kade looked down at her body again. "Not as long as it's been for you, I suspect."

"You suspect right." Ruxandra knew he smelled her arousal. "This has been a *very* long, very trying couple of weeks. I have been on the edge most of the time. I can't trust Elizabeth or Dorotyas, and if I get too close to any humans, Elizabeth will drink them dry. So *please* just spend the next few hours fucking me."

His clothes didn't make it out of the sitting room. Her kimono fell off somewhere between the sitting room wall, and the doorframe, where she'd braced her arms as he'd bent her over and slammed into her until her knees gave out.

Ruxandra had almost forgotten how good it was with another vampire. It wasn't just that Kade had three hundred years of practice, though that helped. With him, she didn't need to restrain her strength, or sheathe her talons, or hide her true self. Kisses became bites of passion, fangs showing and eyes turning to slits as they allowed their vampire selves to come out. They sunk teeth into each other's flesh, tasting each other's silver blood as their bodies came together.

They took care not to destroy the hotel room.

They spent five hours engulfed in each other's bodies, riding and being ridden, on top and underneath, standing, sitting, facedown and face up, on every surface in the suite, until both collapsed.

Kade rose first, and Ruxandra watched him as he walked to the bathroom to wash off. He had been round, as a human. Becoming a vampire turned him lean and strong. His sculpted muscles shone bright white in the moonlight. When he stepped out of the bathroom, she smiled.

"Oh no," Kade said. "I know that look."

"But it's right here." Ruxandra rolled onto her hands and knees, bringing her head level with his crotch. "And I know it's good for another one."

"It is." Kade stepped beside the bed. "But I need to hunt while it is still night. Where do you go?"

"I haven't picked a hunting ground." Ruxandra crawled across the bed, the movements slow and sinuous, like a cat. "But there are both slums and docks nearby."

"Then we should go."

"We should go *soon*." Ruxandra rubbed her hair against his hip, then across his crotch.

Kade groaned but didn't move. "The sooner we go, the sooner we face Elizabeth."

"That's really *not* encouragement." Ruxandra kissed his length.

He groaned again. "I have not fed in two days."

Ruxandra replaced her mouth with her hand. "We are good for four or five, so I don't see the problem."

"*You* are good for four or five," said Kade. "I have thralls."

"Thralls?" Ruxandra frowned. "Why?"

"Because it makes it easier to maintain a proper household. But it means I need to feed more often."

"You can control them from here?"

"A little." He smiled and ran his hand through her hair. "Enough to keep the house clean. But if I don't feed, I lose the control."

"I've never kept one," said Ruxandra. "It was Elizabeth who figured out how to make them. I've never liked the idea of making someone else my slave like that."

"I would hate to lose them. Do you know how hard it is to find a good butler?"

"Very, I'm sure." She stopped stroking but left her hand on him. "Please, just a while longer?"

Kade's head tilted. "Why?"

"Because as soon as Elizabeth finds out you're here, everything will get much, much worse."

"It won't—"

"It will." Ruxandra put the full force of her feelings into the words, making sure he believed them. "And I really, really don't want to deal with that yet. All right?"

Kade let his hand drift over her cheek and then tapped the tip of her nose. "All right. But I need to feed before dawn."

"I promise," Ruxandra said. Then for the next two hours, neither of them talked much at all.

They reached the docks just before dawn and a mugger mistook them for easy. They shared him and dumped his body in the harbor. Then they curled up together in Ruxandra's hotel room and slept.

Ruxandra woke up in the evening feeling far better than she had in weeks. Kade lay still beside her. She sighed and stretched and ran a hand down his body. When she reached his groin, he grunted. She smiled and licked his belly. "Oh, good, you're awake."

"I am."

She rolled onto him and straddled him, her plump breasts poised just above his face. "Well, since you're up."

Kade put a hand between her breasts. "Wait."

Ruxandra stopped. Kade sat up, kissed her, and lifted her off him. Then he went to his coat and pulled out a large sheet of paper covered in circles that were inscribed with words in Latin and Greek.

Ruxandra craned her neck to get a better look at it. "What is that?"

"A spell for detecting vampires designed not to detect you, me, Elizabeth, or Dorotyas. When a vampire comes into its range—fifty miles more or less—I feel it."

Ruxandra rolled out of the bed and took a closer look. "That's amazing."

"I've spent two hundred years chasing down vampire magic. Most is for ensorcelling humans, though some tomes have spells against other, more dire creatures." He laid the paper underneath the bed. "I discovered that spells did not need to be written in chalk on the floor, which meant I could make them in advance."

"That helps."

"I'll make another one tomorrow for detecting the ghouls." He began chanting in a language that Ruxandra didn't recognize at all, though it sounded vaguely Arabic. She listened and watched as the lines and runes on the page glowed bright red, then faded. "There. Now we need to charge it."

Ruxandra caught the glint of mischief in his eye. "And how do we do that?"

"How do you think?"

"Oh, good," Ruxandra said as Kade climbed onto the bed. "I hoped you'd say that."

Another two hours passed in a pleasant haze. Somewhere in the middle of it all, they managed to shower. When they finally dressed, Ruxandra led Kade to the Cocoanut Grove. His eyebrows went high on his forehead. "Well, this is . . . impressive."

Ruxandra grinned. "Look up."

He did, and his mouth fell open at the sight of the red-eyed mechanical monkey. He laughed out loud.

"This way." Ruxandra took his hand and led him to the dance floor. "First, we dance, then we look for Joseph or Lilyan."

"And they are . . .?"

"Movie stars, silly." The band played a Viennese waltz, and they spun around the floor with grace and ease. Ruxandra grinned, remembering the salons in Vienna and the first time they'd waltzed together.

"As much fun as it is to meet movie stars," Kade began, but Ruxandra cut him off.

"They are also friends of Douglas Fairbanks and Mary Pickford, who own the Pickfair estate." She waited until he opened his mouth again before adding, "Where the last ghoul attack happened. So we go with them, I introduce you to Douglas and Mary, we get invited to tonight's party, and we have an excuse to be there while I track down where the ghoul came from."

"Good thinking." Kade let the hand on her back slide lower and gave her ass a quick squeeze. "How do you know there's a party there?"

"Because as near as I can tell, there's always a party there."

After the dance, she found Joseph and introduced him to Kade in German. Joseph was delighted, and the two chatted about Austria and Germany until Ruxandra made Joseph take them around. Lilyan looked at Kade as if afraid he would take away her playmate. Kade put on his very charming smile and soon won her over. In short order, he met Charlie Chaplin and Mary Pickford and Douglas Fairbanks and a half dozen others. At Ruxandra's quiet command, Douglas and Mary invited them all to Pickfair. They all packed into the movie stars' cars and drove out to the hills. Kade went with Joseph, who wanted to talk more about Austria. Ruxandra went with Greta Garbo and Lilyan, who both insisted on being kissed along the way.

As they passed the Pickfair sign, she breathed deeply, catching the ghoul's scent.

Up close, the house was magnificent: four stories high, with twenty-five rooms inside and its own outdoor in-ground swimming pool. The crowd inside was noisy, happy, and made up of Hollywood's elite. Ruxandra walked through the place admiring its ceiling frescoes and parquet floors, French antiques and Italian tapestries, some of which she remembered from the great houses of previous centuries. She treated Lilyan to a knee-trembler in one of the bedrooms before finding Kade deep in conversation with Douglas Fairbanks.

"I'm heading out," she said in a voice only he heard. "Have fun."

Kade nodded but didn't stop talking.

Ruxandra slipped back out into the yard and the darkness beyond. She turned unnoticeable and stripped off her clothes, hiding them in the crux of a tree. Then she spread her mind and senses wide as she ran to where she had first spotted the ghoul, hoping to pick up some sign of other ghouls or the vampire. It took her five minutes to cover the three miles. Then she began tracking, slowly and carefully, following the scent through the Santa Monica Mountains.

Two hours later, she had covered ten miles of winding, backtracking scent trails that ended in the Los Angeles River, just across from Universal City.

Of course.

She turned and sprinted back to Pickfair, stopping only long enough to dress. Kade met her by the swimming pool. "How was your journey?"

"Unhelpful," Ruxandra said. "It ended at the river."

"Like the others."

"Most went into the desert." Ruxandra thought about it. "But they all crossed the river at some point or other, probably to throw me off their scent."

"Annoying."

"Very. Anything interesting here?"

"Three women and two men approached me for carnal purposes," he said with a smile. "And one man who claims to be a producer and will make me a star."

Ruxandra smiled. "That was also for carnal purposes, I bet."

"I suspected as much. Shall we go?"

"I think so."

A slight breeze blew over them. Ruxandra inhaled deeply, finding a hundred other scents, from wildflowers to sagebrush to spilled gin to the sharp tang of a nearby coyote. And mixed with it all, the smell of rot and death.

Oh, shit. She opened her senses wide again. "Kade . . ."

He looked away, scanning the horizon. "Three of them."

"Coming this way. Shit."

"Close."

"Very. In the hills."

"We need to go."

"Already?" Joseph asked from behind them.

Ruxandra put on a smile and faced him. "I'm afraid so."

"Always gone before dawn." Joseph shook his head in mock sadness. He was tipsy, and the motion made him stagger. "If I didn't know better, I'd say you were *ein vampir.*"

Ruxandra laughed and hugged him and kissed him on the cheek. "Maybe I am." With her mouth close to his ear, she whispered her command: "*If anyone asks, we got a ride home. You don't remember with whom.*"

They left Pickfair behind and sprinted. Kade matched her pace. "Do you want to keep any of the ghouls alive?"

"Not this close to dawn," Ruxandra said. "Why are they here?"

"Because we are here, I'd say."

"How the hell did she know that?"

Then the ghouls charged them, and everything was reduced to a whirlwind of slashing claws and teeth and blood spraying on the rocks.

Kade fought without a single wasted motion, ripping the arm off the first ghoul as Ruxandra's foot smashed the skull of the second, sending it flying against the rocks twenty yards away. She spun, grabbed the shirt of the third one, and threw it toward Kade, who used the first ghoul's arm as a club to drive the creature to the ground.

The first one jumped up, wrapping its remaining arm around Kade's back and seeking to sink its teeth into his neck. Kade shrugged it off with ease and smashed it face-first against the ground. The third leaped to its feet and attacked again. Ruxandra's talons tore through the creature's neck, separating its head from its body. It collapsed, dead. She threw the head away and went after the one she'd attacked first. In several seconds, it lay broken on the ground. She turned back and found Kade dismembering the other one.

"Your style has changed," Kade said. "Less animal, more precise, more flowing."

"Fifty years in the Orient." Ruxandra felt pleased that he'd noticed. "You did well, too."

"Thank you. I like to keep in practice. And now?"

"We dump them on the hilltop to burn, and we get ourselves back to the hotel." *And add three more pins to the map. Maybe tomorrow night we might actually get somewhere.*

They didn't.

"Kade!" Elizabeth's voice echoed in in the hallway outside Kade's suite. He'd insisted they go there so he could change clothes the next evening. She'd agreed and everything had gone very well to that point.

"You open this door right now!" Elizabeth's voice wasn't in the vampire frequencies, and Ruxandra bet other guests would call down complaints soon.

Dammit. Ruxandra took her mouth off Kade, pulled her hips away from his tongue, and rolled to her feet. She grabbed Kade's shirt from the doorway and threw it on. "Told you everything would get worse."

"She's as subtle as ever," Kade grumbled, rolling up on the other side. "Seen my trousers?"

Ruxandra picked them up and tossed them to him. She buttoned the shirt as she walked through the sitting room. Elizabeth pounded her fist against the door hard enough to make it dance.

"Ruxandra!"

Ruxandra sighed and opened it. "Hello, Elizabeth."

Elizabeth's eyes turned red, her fangs and talons coming out. She looked ready to rip Ruxandra apart. "How *dare* you bring him here without telling me! When did you contact him?"

"In New York." Ruxandra stepped back. "To see if the vampire was his."

"I told you she wasn't!"

"And you've *never* lied to me before." She waved Elizabeth into the room. "Get out of the hallway before you cause a scene, Elizabeth."

Elizabeth stayed in the doorway. "When were you going to tell me he came to town?"

"She didn't know I came to town." The pale skin of Kade's bare chest shone. "I didn't tell her."

"You didn't tell me, either!" Elizabeth snapped the words out. "You should have telegrammed!"

"Given what happened, I thought it wiser to come in secret. I thought I might flush out the vampire easier if no one knew I was here."

Elizabeth glared. "Is that why you're here? Or were you planning to interfere with my life like you did in Rio de Janeiro?"

"My interference is the only reason you got out of Rio alive." Kade sounded calm and appeared unruffled by Elizabeth's screaming fit.

"Your interference is the reason we had to go our separate ways! We were all going to be together!"

"And we were." Kade's voice went cold. "Right up until you got careless."

"It was not my fault!"

"So someone else kidnapped a contessa?" Ruxandra put as much sarcasm into her voice as possible. "Because from Kade's letters, I'm pretty sure it was you."

"Don't you start with me!"

"Perhaps we could talk about this somewhere else?" suggested Kade, his voice moving into vampire frequencies. "Somewhere not surrounded by *people*, for example."

Elizabeth glared at him then back at Ruxandra. "Dorotyas is waiting in the car. We will all go to the apartment. Now."

Kade's eyes went to Ruxandra. "Perhaps we should talk alone, Elizabeth."

Ruxandra opened her mouth to protest, but Kade mouthed *please*. She frowned but didn't argue. *Maybe it's a good idea. Maybe he can get the truth out of her.* "Sounds good to me. I'll get changed and go on patrol."

"Can you do that while walking bowlegged?" Elizabeth asked, her voice sweet and catty.

"Ask Kade to help you find out." Ruxandra smiled. "Maybe it will improve your mood."

"Unlike you, I don't need someone between my thighs to be happy." Elizabeth turned and walked out. "Do hurry, Kade. The evening is wearing on."

"Thank you," Kade said as the door shut.

Ruxandra went back to the bedroom and found her clothes but didn't put them on.

"I suspect she's listening to everything we say." Ruxandra tucked her clothes under her arm. "I'm tempted to ride you once more, just to aggravate her, but I'm afraid of the damage the hotel would sustain."

"My presence was a shock to her." He stepped close and kissed Ruxandra on the mouth. "I will talk to her and learn all I can. Perhaps among the three of us we can solve this mystery."

"I hope so. Because I really want to leave this city." She leaned close to him and smiled, then raised her voice to make sure Elizabeth heard. "I meant what I said about fucking her. Anything that helps fix her attitude."

He smiled and caressed her cheek. "That's our Ruxandra."

She turned unnoticeable and slipped upstairs to her room. She grabbed a quick shower and put her blacks on. *Hopefully, there isn't anything that needs my attention, and I'll be able to stay within eavesdropping distance.*

She slipped down the stairs and through the lobby. She felt tempted to go to the Cocoanut Grove and get a drink before she went out. Unfortunately, Dorotyas was waiting for her when she stepped outside. "About time you got here."

Ruxandra didn't slow down. "Elizabeth decided to leave you behind?"

"She and Kade need to talk."

"Without you?" Ruxandra shook her head. "I guess she doesn't trust you."

"I already know all my lady's secrets." The acid in Dorotyas voice could eat through steel. "She needs me here because she doesn't trust *you* to find the vampire. Now, let us go. I'm assuming a ghoul came into town yesterday?"

"Three."

"Funny how they follow you around isn't it?"

RUXANDRA LED DOROTYAS into the hills around Pickfair
without going near the house. Dorotyas wore a skirt and
blouse, and her multi-chained leather-and-steel belt—not
the most sensible for hunting, but at least her shoes were flats,
and she could run enough in them.

"Bet you this trail ends at the river," Ruxandra said as she
started following it. "Ten dollars?"

"I don't carry money," Dorotyas said, her tone bored. "I don't
need it."

"Too bad, it makes going to the movies easier."

"I don't go to movies, either."

"How do you have fun?"

"I see how long I can make a man scream before he dies. My
record is ten weeks."

"Like mistress, like servant," Ruxandra muttered. "Open your
mind. Maybe we'll find something."

She started walking over the hills, her eyes on the ground.
She followed their footprints easily enough over the dirt, but

the thin grass and the rocks on the mountains made it harder. The scent stayed strong, though. She spread her mind wide as well, hoping to sense the vampire or the ghouls. *Not that there's a chance in hell of that.*

An hour later, Dorotyas broke the silence. "I can't believe you brought Kade here."

Ruxandra's rolled her eyes. "I didn't."

"Liar."

That made her stop and turn. "What?"

"You're lying." Dorotyas put her best superior look on her face, and her tone matched it. "There's no reason for him to be here. Not unless you asked him to come."

"I telegrammed him back in New York to see if any vampires he had made were in America," Ruxandra said. "He came over on his own, without me asking and without telling me."

"Which is why he spent two days fucking you as soon as he arrived."

"Not the whole two days." Ruxandra smiled. "Just most of it."

"You asked him to come," Dorotyas said. "Because you don't trust Elizabeth."

"Of course I don't trust Elizabeth," Ruxandra said. "She's a lying, manipulative, psychotic mess."

"Don't you talk about her like that!" Dorotyas's voice filled with venom. The hatchet-faced vampire's eyes turned red.

"It's true." Ruxandra turned her back on Dorotyas and started following the scent trail. "She's tried to run my life ever since she met me."

"She's doing what's best for all of us."

"She's doing what's best for her." The trail divided into three. Ruxandra swore and glared at the ground as if that would bring the vampire. "That's all she ever does. Why else did she make you a slave vampire instead of just turning you?"

"That's not true!"

"The ghouls went three different directions. Think you can track one?"

"You shouldn't talk about Elizabeth like that!" Dorotyas snarled. Her eyes went red, and her hand tightened around her belt. "Getting Elizabeth to do what you want. Bringing in Kade from across the globe. You think you're so special!"

"*What?*" Ruxandra shook her head in confusion.

"You think you're the center of the universe!" Dorotyas snapped out each word like fangs driving into Ruxandra's throat. "You think everyone wants to be around you. Everyone wants to be near you."

Ruxandra's mouth dropped open. She stared at Dorotyas in astonishment. "How did this become about me?"

"Elizabeth went across the country to get you." Dorotyas spat the words. "I bet it made you feel so important, didn't it?"

Ruxandra felt her blood rising. "I didn't *want* her to get me."

"But here you are!" Dorotyas slashed the air toward Los Angeles with her arm. "*You* came *here*. You could have driven her off in New York, but you didn't."

"I came here," Ruxandra said, enunciating each word, "because there's a vampire that Elizabeth *says* she didn't make and you didn't make."

"'Says'?" Dorotyas pounced on the word. "What do you mean, 'says'?"

Ruxandra's voice dropped to a growl. "I mean that Elizabeth *lies* and so do you. Who is the vampire?"

"I don't *know*." Dorotyas matched her tone exactly.

Ruxandra stepped closer. "I don't believe you."

Dorotyas met her halfway. "As if I care what you believe."

"Tell me." Ruxandra's voice went hard. "Tell me right now."

"Get away from me!" Dorotyas's hands slammed into Ruxandra's chest, sending her flying back across the hill. Ruxandra flipped in the air and landed on her feet, her claws and fangs out and an animal growl coming from inside her.

"Of course," Dorotyas sneered. Her hand wrapped around the thick multi-chained metal-and-leather belt at her waist. She pulled the buckle, and it opened into a five-tipped flail with razor-sharp metal woven through the leather lashes. Dorotyas swung it back and forth. "As soon as she's scared, she turns into the Beast."

"This isn't the Beast," Ruxandra said. "This is me wondering what is the *matter* with you."

"*You're* the matter." Dorotyas began stalking forward. "You and Kade. You come here like she belongs to you. Like you get to be the center of her world whenever it pleases you."

"I don't *want* to be the center of her world." Ruxandra started circling. "I hadn't seen either of you in three hundred years, and I liked it that way."

"Then leave! Pack up and get out. She doesn't need you here. *I* don't need you here."

"Because you're so successful at finding the vampire yourself?" Ruxandra put a huge rock between them. "So successful at stopping the killing?"

"No one *cares* about the killing!" Dorotyas yelled. "You're the only one who cares about the humans!"

"I care about us not getting discovered!"

"Liar! You just want Elizabeth for yourself. You and Kade! You've always wanted her. You've always tried to take her from me!" She leaped forward, the flail tearing through the air.

Ruxandra charged straight into it. The flail switched directions and the metal ripped through Ruxandra's shirt and the skin of her back even as she caught Dorotyas's arm and flipped her into the air. Ruxandra threw her hard at the ground, hoping the impact would knock some sense into her. Dorotyas spun in the air and landed on her feet, then she whipped the flail forward again. Ruxandra caught it with her bare hands, ignoring the metal biting into her skin, and ripped the flail in half. Dorotyas dropped it and tried to hit her in the head. Ruxandra blocked the punch, caught her arm, and threw her again. Dorotyas landed on her feet ten yards away.

"You all think I'm nothing," she hissed. "You all think I'm just Elizabeth's bootlicker. But *I* am the one who keeps her alive. *I'm* the one who keeps her supplied with girls. You're nothing but fair-weather friends who run away when they get what they want. Just like Kade the last time he was here!"

The last time?

"Neither of you care in the slightest what happens to her as long as you get your way! So why don't you just fuck off back to New York and leave us alone!"

Kade came here before? Why didn't he tell me about it? Ruxandra's eyes narrowed. "When was Kade here?"

Dorotyas straightened up, her face going blank for just a moment. Then she sneered and looked down her nose at Ruxandra. "As if you care about that. You don't care about anything but having your cunt filled."

Ruxandra smothered an animal urge to tear Dorotyas's head off. "I get it. You're jealous. You think Elizabeth cares more for us than she does for you. Wrong. Elizabeth doesn't care about anything but herself, torture, and power. That's all she's ever liked; it's all she's ever cared about."

"Liar."

"Three hundred years you've been with her." Ruxandra straightened from her fighting crouch. "Has she ever treated you as anything except a servant?"

"None of you have! At least she knows my value!"

"She revels in your *pain*, Dorotyas. She made you a slave vampire so you would never, *ever* be her equal. Stop acting as if she's the queen of the world."

"She *will* be queen of the world." Dorotyas spat the words like venom. "Just you wait!"

Dorotyas turned and ran. Ruxandra stared after her. *What in hell was that about?* She looked down at the three trails. *These aren't going to lead me anywhere. Where is Dorotyas going?*

She stretched out her mind, found Dorotyas, and followed her. Dorotyas kept moving. Ruxandra went unnoticeable. It wouldn't affect Dorotyas, of course, but it kept people out of her way. Dorotyas ran through the city, picking up speed as she went. Ruxandra stayed on the edge of her trail. She suspected that Dorotyas wasn't actively using her mind to search but didn't want to risk it.

Dorotyas went through Hollywood and crossed the Los Angeles River. She slowed then. Ruxandra risked moving close enough that she heard her, even if she couldn't see. She sorted through the babble of voices, the rumble of cars, and rattle of wagons until she heard Dorotyas's command: "*You three. Come with me. Now.*"

Three men, Ruxandra sensed, all healthy and strong, followed Dorotyas through the slum. Ruxandra heard a large door open and close and Dorotyas command, *"All three of you be silent."*

She's feeding. Ruxandra came closer, slipping up to the building—a warehouse—and inside a side door. Dorotyas stood in the middle of the building surrounded by crates. Ruxandra bet any sound made by either vampire or victim wouldn't make it out the door.

With a pair of commands, Dorotyas had one man on his knees in front of her, another behind. Both went under her skirt and licked her bare flesh as if they knew their lives depended on it. Dorotyas moaned in pleasure, then smiled at the third one. *"Come closer. Stand there. Don't move."*

Ruxandra peeked around a box. Dorotyas writhed under the ministration of the men's tongues. Her fangs and teeth came out, and one talon dug into the standing man's chest. He flinched and gasped in a breath. Dorotyas leaned forward, her eyes narrowing. "They think I'm foolish. I know that."

She pulled the talon slowly across his chest, ripping muscle and sending blood spurting. "They think I don't know what's going on or what's going to happen. But they're wrong. I know everything that's going to happen. Far better than that Transylvanian bitch. Oh. Oh!"

She convulsed and her talon dug deeper into his flesh. When she regained control, she looked down and patted the licking man's head through the front of her dress. *"You keep doing what you're doing. Your friend can stand up and put it in."*

The man behind Dorotyas stood up. Ruxandra shook her head and slipped away. Behind her, Dorotyas gasped with pain and pleasure, then commanded, *"You, my friend, can start screaming."*

So much for her. Ruxandra walked back across the shallow, burbling river. *And Kade is still with Elizabeth, I bet, which means they're probably killing or screwing or both . . .*

Or maybe they're still talking.

Why didn't Kade tell me he'd been here before? Anger bubbled up inside her, making the Beast stir and growl in hope. *Is that why he thinks the vampire is Elizabeth's? Because he's met her before?*

Maybe if I listen in. Ruxandra ran, covering the distance to Elizabeth's apartment in minutes. *If either is listening or watching, they'll know I'm here. But if not . . .*

She reached the country club across the street and leaned against the wall. She closed her eyes, listening. Elizabeth was right about the soundproofing. It took all her concentration to make out the voices both female, both begging for mercy.

Something leather cracked against skin and a girl screamed.

"They are a penny a dozen, I swear," Elizabeth said above the screaming. "They come north looking for work as farm labor or nannies or whatever they can find. Half the men end up in gangs, and half the women work as whores. It makes it easy to lure them. And best of all, no one misses them."

"Very efficient," Kade said, approval in his voice.

"I do enjoy blonds, though. So sometimes I need to indulge. You understand."

"I do." Kade's voice held enough sincerity that Ruxandra almost believed him. "You can always tell the lesser races by how homogeneous they are. It is in the superior ones that you find blonds."

Lesser races?

"So very true," purred Elizabeth.

I recognize that tone. Ruxandra sighed. *Now I know what they spent at least part of the last few hours doing. Hope he got something out of her for it.*

"But even so," Kade said, "what's happening is dangerous. It might expose us."

"Maybe we should be exposed." Leather bit skin again, and the second girl shrieked. "Maybe it's time we came out in the open instead of hiding."

"That is not possible," Kade said. "There are too many of them, too few of us. You know that."

"God, you sound like Ruxandra." Elizabeth's tone shifted, becoming seductive. "You want power as much as I do."

"True." Kade kept his voice neutral. "But I realized that subtlety and quiet manipulation work far better for gaining and maintaining power."

"Fear is the best way to gain power."

"Fear brings revulsion and revolution. As you know."

"That was the past."

"Humans have not changed since the past." Ruxandra heard the amusement in Kade's voice. "Except to become better armed."

"And yet . . ." Leather hit flesh twice more, and the girls wailed again. "Look how they cower."

"Girls," he said. "Young, alone—of course they're terrified. The more humans that band together, the braver they become. And some—many, very many in comparison to us—are smart and trained in the arts of war. Given the amount of trouble this . . . other vampire is causing"—his tone shifted just enough for Ruxandra to hear his doubt—"I suggest you refrain from burning down any more farmhouses. For the near future, at least."

"Always cautious." One of the wailing voices cut off, replaced by a gasp and a gurgle. A minute later, Elizabeth sighed. "Want one?"

"Thank you." The second girl's screams rose then were muffled as if someone placed a hand over her mouth. "Are you going to still maintain this course you're on?"

"Why, Kade." Elizabeth sounded flirtatious. "I have no idea what you are talking about."

"Yes, you do."

An edge crept into Elizabeth's voice. "I have a *competitor*, Kade. Yes, I will keep going after my competitor, if that is what you mean. If you mean anything else, well, why don't you take it up with Ruxandra, since she's listening outside?"

Of course, Elizabeth wouldn't be so careless. Ruxandra straightened up and called, "The trail led nowhere, and Dorotyas had to feed, so I thought I'd come see what you were doing."

"Nothing that concerns you," Elizabeth said. "Though it would be lovely if you found the damn vampire so I can get back to my life."

Fuck you, you lazy . . . Ruxandra thought but didn't say it out loud. "We'll try again tomorrow. Meanwhile, I'm going back to the hotel. Kade, you coming?"

"In a while," Elizabeth said. "I still need him, if you don't mind. Or at least part of him."

"Here I thought you'd already done that," Ruxandra said. "Still, if you need another—"

"His mind, girl," scolded Elizabeth. "Unlike *you*, he is trained to think and may find our solution, since your tracking skills have proven useless."

"I am still not forgiven, then?" Kade asked, though his voice held no contrition whatsoever.

"Not at all," Elizabeth said coldly. "Now hurry up and eat, and then we will discuss this matter further. Ruxandra, tell Dorotyas that we'll need a fresh supply tomorrow."

"Tell her yourself," muttered Ruxandra. She walked down the empty road, heading back toward the Ambassador Hotel. She listened as long as she could, but all she heard was Kade drinking the girl, then Elizabeth talking of her ranch and how the new vampire made it harder for her to stay there and enjoy herself. *Figures. Anything she really wants to say to him, she'll wait until she's out of range to say.*

But when Kade gets back, he's got some things to tell me.

Ruxandra spent the night stewing in her room. She grabbed a shower. Then a bath. Then she read a magazine. Finally, she dropped down onto her bed and glared at the ceiling. It wasn't that Elizabeth had sex with him. That rankled a bit, she had to admit, but a life span measured in centuries instead of years left little room for jealousy.

Ruxandra worried that Elizabeth was filling his mind with poison. If Kade started believing her . . .

He'll probably come back and try to tell me how to hunt.

Her eyes went to the map on her wall. She still did not see a pattern. The ghoul attacks looked random. *Which means whoever managed this knows something about hunting. Or about strategy. Which tells me nothing.*

She woke when Kade knocked on the door. A day ago she would have answered naked and proceeded to see how well she could make him squirm. Now, though, she put on her kimono and tied the sash tight. She also picked up his shirt off the chair and had it in her hand when she answered the door. "You made it out alive, I see."

"I did," Kade smiled and reached for her. "You're annoyed."

Ruxandra stepped back. "You didn't tell me you visited her here before."

"Ah." Kade nodded. "That."

"*That.*" Ruxandra tossed the shirt at him. "Put this away and meet me in the lobby."

"As you like," Kade said as Ruxandra closed the door.

She took her time dressing, choosing a plain gray skirt and white blouse with sensible shoes for walking. She also did her makeup nice and slowly, making sure it looked pretty and perfect. *There. I look like a fresh young thing on a night out.* She stared in the mirror and sighed. *I'm being petty. But he still should have told me.*

She took the elevator down and walked right past Kade. He sighed, stood up, and followed her out. Ruxandra vanished from notice and started running—back into the Hollywood Hills. Kade kept pace, silent, until she took them off the road and up the driveway to Pickfair. She slowed to a walk and Kade caught up and walked beside her.

The big house stood dark and silent, with no sign of life inside. Kade looked it over. "No party tonight?"

"They're at a film premiere. Joseph invited me the night before last." Ruxandra led him around the house to the hundred-foot-long swimming pool set amid formal gardens. She looked up at the stars. He stood beside her, waiting. At last, Ruxandra brought her eyes down to his. "Explain."

"Explain what?" Kade's eyes met hers.

"Explain why you didn't tell me you'd been here before."

"It wasn't relevant."

"Bullshit!" Ruxandra let her anger free. "Everything to do with her is relevant! Why did you visit?"

"Because I wanted to see how she was doing."

"Bullshit."

"And *what* she was doing," Kade said firmly. "She has very specific patterns, our Elizabeth. She likes torture, she likes terror, and she likes power. Wherever she is, she'll pursue all three."

"That mattered to you why?"

"Because I have my own pursuits." Kade closed the distance between them. "Every time that Elizabeth starts misbehaving, she messes them up. So I visited her, just after the war. She'd just left South America and settled in California. She wanted to live in the city, but I persuaded her that a ranch was a much better choice. Someplace away from other people, where she could pursue her desires without causing a disturbance. *And* without disturbing what I am trying to do in Europe."

Ruxandra glared, unsure if he was telling the truth. "What are you trying to do in Europe?"

Kade smiled, and his voice became self-mocking. "Following my pattern. Trying to create a place of safety where I can live in peace with others of my kind."

"Like Elizabeth?"

"No." Kade's voice left no room for doubt. "Not like Elizabeth. She is too uncontrolled."

"Just like I am?"

Kade heard the dangerous edge in her voice. "Nothing like you. You are wild. A free spirit. You enjoy everything life offers. Elizabeth . . ."

"Elizabeth," Ruxandra finished for him, "is insane."

"Yes." His voice became serious and earnest. "And if the humans noticed her insanity, in this day of telegraphs and radios and newspapers that reach across nations and oceans, and *scientists* that dissect anything different to learn its nature, well . . . it is dangerous. To us all. So I came. I convinced her to stay out of the city, and for ten years, it worked. Then you sent me a telegram."

Ruxandra glared a while longer, then sighed. She stepped to the pool's edge and began stripping off her clothes.

"What are you doing?" Kade sounded at once bewildered and amused.

"Swimming." She tossed her clothes on a chair while Kade watched. Then she dove, cutting through the water and reveling in the cool wetness. When she came up, she smiled. "Much better."

"Does this mean I'm forgiven?"

"No more than when you asked Elizabeth."

"Ouch."

"*Did* she create another vampire?"

"She says not. And I believe her."

"Someone new, then."

"It appears so."

Ruxandra went onto her back. The water felt blissfully cool, and the breeze that touched the tips of her breasts as they poked out of the water sent goose bumps over her skin. The scents of sagebrush, mint, and roses floated in the air, the smell as soothing as the cool water. She floated, trying to make sense of what Kade had said.

He could be lying. He could be hiding something, just like Eliz-abeth. But he really wants to take control and end this. Ruxandra smiled. *But then, that's part of his pattern.*

"Are you coming out?" Kade asked.

"Not soon." Ruxandra rolled over, letting the water cover her. A moment later she broke the surface again. "Will you come in?"

"No."

"Dorotyas hates us."

If the change of subject surprised Kade, he didn't say so. "I know."

"She's jealous of us. She thinks we want to take Elizabeth from her."

"Not really." Kade sat down on one of the chairs. "She's projecting."

Ruxandra frowned and drifted in the pool. "What?"

"A psychology term," Kade said, "from the writings of Freud. The idea that a person denies the existence of what they fear by shifting the responsibility to someone else. In this case, what Dorotyas fears isn't that we want to take Elizabeth from her, but that Elizabeth wants us more than she wants her."

"Interesting." Ruxandra put her elbows on the pool's edge. "That explains why she attacked me in the woods, and why she told me to leave her alone."

Kade frowned. "It might also create a desire for Elizabeth to need her . . ."

"By creating a crisis for Elizabeth to deal with." Ruxandra shoved off the pool wall and floated on her back again. *I wouldn't mind an estate like this.* "Maybe she's the one behind the mess?"

"I don't know," Kade said. "She is a slave vampire. She can do many things on her own, but I don't know if she can go against her mistress. She bears watching, though. If *she* created the vampire, that would explain some of what is happening."

Ruxandra thought about it. "The only question is how she could tear herself away from Elizabeth long enough to create a vampire. And nurture her through the first few weeks."

"Maybe she didn't." Kade leaned forward and put his elbows on his knees. "Maybe she just created her and left her, like the fallen angel did with you."

"Which explains the vampire's behavior." Ruxandra stopped floating and started treading water. "Think you could get it out of her?"

Kade shook his head. "She doesn't think much of me."

"Well, she didn't try to flay the skin off your back last night," Ruxandra said. "So I'd say you're ahead of me."

Kade nodded. "I am sorry, Ruxandra, I should have told you."

"Damned right." She splashed water at him, but he moved back far too fast for any of it to touch his suit. "Hold still."

"Not for the world," Kade said. "Now, how much longer will you be in the pool? Because I want to spend some time exploring the city. Maybe then I could figure out where the vampire hides."

"*If* she's in the city."

"True," said Kade. "But we will not find that out floating in a swimming pool."

"Spoilsport." Ruxandra let the water enfold her and sank down. For a moment, she imagined a house of her own with a pool like this and the ocean near. Then she pushed hard off the bottom, flying out of the water with an enormous splash. She flipped in the air and landed on her feet.

"Show-off," Kade said.

"Always." Ruxandra lay back in one of the chairs. "Now what?"

"Your place, first," said Kade. "I want one more look at the map."

"Why?" teased Ruxandra. "Your memory failing you?"

One side of Kade's mouth quirked up. The vampire memory was powerful enough that both could draw the map on the spot. "No, but I want to look at it again. Maybe it will give me a sense of a pattern, like where the trains or busses or streetcars go."

"Maybe." Ruxandra felt irritated she hadn't thought of the streetcars. They were one of her favorite places to find prey back in New York. "There're towels in the cabana. Get one for me, would you?"

Elizabeth and Dorotyas were both waiting in the Ambassador lobby when they got back. Elizabeth looked livid. "Where the *hell* were you two?"

"Swimming." Ruxandra started to walk past her. "And now we're going to my room."

Elizabeth's hand wrapped hard around Ruxandra's arm. "No, you are not. We have a problem."

Ruxandra looked down at Elizabeth's hand. "As big as the one you'll have if you don't get your hand off me?"

Elizabeth didn't budge. "Bigger. Listen."

Ruxandra's eyes narrowed, but she listened. From a radio behind the front desk, she heard a voice say, "The creatures, which is the word witnesses used to describe them, appeared outside of Grauman's Chinese Theatre during the premiere of *Lady Luck's Run Out*, a new comedy. At first, patrons thought they were some strange type of promotion, but the creatures—again, this is the word the witnesses used—attacked theatergoers and the crowd outside waiting to see celebrities. The police were there in force and managed to drive back the creatures. Even so, some dozen patrons received bite and claw wounds, as if from animals . . ."

They've gone public. The damn ghouls went public. Ruxandra didn't listen to any more. Her stomach sank, and her mind raced. Kade watched her with worried eyes. Elizabeth and Dorotyas both looked furious.

"There were reporters," Elizabeth said. "Dozens of them. And they took pictures."

R UXANDRA STRUGGLED TO get the panic rising inside her under control. "How many ghouls?"

"Two," Dorotyas said. "Only two."

"Why didn't you stop them?" Kade demanded. "You know as well as I that a public scene is one of the worst things that could happen."

"We weren't there." Elizabeth glared as if it were somehow his fault. "We first heard about it on the radio. And when we got there, they were gone."

"Then we need to track them down," Ruxandra said. "Now."

"How will that help?" Elizabeth demanded. "They were *seen*. By everyone."

Ruxandra's jaw clenched. Out of the corner of her eye, she saw Dorotyas sneering. She resisted the urge to slap both women through a window. "And what were you two doing while the ghouls stalked the streets? Eating again?"

"At least we were in the city," Dorotyas said. "Where the hell were you two?"

"Trying to track the ghouls from the night before last," Ruxandra lied. "You remember that trail, don't you? And how you abandoned it?"

Dorotyas opened her mouth to answer, but Kade's deep voice cut her off. "This is not the time to argue. We need to get this situation under control."

"No, we need to leave here," Elizabeth said. "Right now, before—"

"Before we get noticed?" Kade looked pointedly around the lobby. They were the only people there save the desk clerk and bellhop, both of whom watched them with great interest. "Dorotyas, please make them forget. Elizabeth, we will all go to Ruxandra's room and discuss this."

Dorotyas looked at Elizabeth, who nodded, before she went to the bellhop. Elizabeth turned back to Kade. Her eyes glinted red and the tips of her talons started to extend out of her fingers. Her posture and voice both filled with tension, like twin bowstrings about to snap. "There is nothing to discuss. They saw the ghouls. We need to get out of here."

"*No.*" Kade's voice was firm. "We need to contain this problem if *we* want to continue walking the streets with impunity. Now let us go upstairs and discuss this. *Please.*"

He held out his arm for Elizabeth to take. She growled but took it and went. Ruxandra followed right behind them, trying not to be annoyed that Kade offered his arm to Elizabeth instead of to her. *It's just to get Elizabeth to come along, after all. Unless he's on her side in this whole mess.*

The thought came out of nowhere and made Ruxandra roll her eyes. *This is not the time for more paranoia. I need to stop things before they get worse. If the papers print the pictures, everyone will start looking for the ghouls. And if they track some missing girls to Elizabeth . . .*

Shit.

Dorotyas joined them at the elevator, pushing her way past Ruxandra to stand beside Elizabeth. No one spoke on the ride up, and the tension and anger they radiated was strong enough that the operator cast worried glances at them the entire time. When they reached Ruxandra's floor, Kade led them to her room and strode over to the map.

"Where is Grauman's Chinese Theatre?"

Ruxandra tapped the spot on the map. Kade put a pin in it and looked at Elizabeth. "How long ago?"

"An hour." Elizabeth sat down on the small couch and crossed her arms. "Now it's all over the radio. Which is why we need to start packing and get out of here."

"The radio is only words floating through the air," Kade said. "If they have no proof, the story fades away into nothing."

"Did you not listen?" Dorotyas stepped between Kade and Elizabeth, blocking Kade from moving away. "There were dozens of photographers."

"Photographers need newspapers," Kade said. "Without them, they can do nothing. If the newspapers don't print photos, people convince themselves the entire event was the result of too much drink or a lunatic or someone who smoked something they shouldn't. How many newspapers are in Los Angeles?"

"No idea." Elizabeth leaned back in her chair and glared at Kade and Ruxandra. "And even if I knew them all, you can't reach them all, and you certainly can't stop them from printing the pictures."

"It is much easier to temporarily stop the presses than you think."

Ruxandra's eyebrows rose. Elizabeth and Dorotyas stared, looking no less skeptical than she. Kade smiled. "In Germany there are many papers, and we have, on occasion, needed to silence them. We just need to keep the editors from printing anything long enough for us to gather and destroy all the photographs. Because once the evidence vanishes, they cannot print anything more than wild speculation. It's not hard if we reach the editors in charge, but we need to find out their names."

"How do you suggest we do that?" Dorotyas sneered. "Buy the morning edition of each?"

"That will take too long. We need a list tonight."

"The police know all the newspapers," Ruxandra said. "And you can bet they're already interested. Especially the vampire task force."

Kade's eyes widened, and his brows went up, though he managed to keep his surprise out of his voice. "The what?"

"The task force of detectives assigned to catching the 'vampire killer.'"

Kade's eyes narrowed at Elizabeth. "You allowed things to get this far out of control?"

"No," Dorotyas said. "Ruxandra let things get this far out of control."

"*What?*"

"This is the sort of thing Elizabeth brought you in to stop! But you haven't prevented a single attack. In fact, ever since *you* came here, the attacks got worse! For all we know, you found the vampire the first night and have been working with her ever since!"

"I'm not the one who let it get this far in the first place." Ruxandra's words came out as a low snarl. "This isn't my city, and it wasn't my problem until Elizabeth showed up, remember?"

"So you say!"

Ruxandra stepped close to Dorotyas. "We've already had this conversation. So unless you want to repeat *your* end of it in front of Elizabeth, I suggest you *drop* it and we pay attention to the problem at hand."

"*This* conversation?" Elizabeth's voice was as mild as Ruxandra's was harsh, but it was no less deadly. "Which conversation?"

"Ask Dorotyas." Ruxandra turned back to Kade. "What do we do?"

"Newspapers take time to print," he said. "If we get a list of papers and photographers, we can suppress the photos before they see the light of day."

"I'll go to the task force," Ruxandra said. "It's near the theater. They probably have a list of all the papers."

"Good. We will go to the scene. Elizabeth and Dorotyas can talk to people and gather information about the ghouls. Meet us there. Go!"

Ruxandra went, turning unnoticed before she was at the hotel stairs. She reached the task force's office in two minutes. Only a single detective sat there, listening to the radio and making notes. He spun around at the sound of her footsteps.

"*Get me a list of all the newspapers in the city,*" Ruxandra commanded. "*Now.*"

He opened a desk drawer and pulled out a pair of pages. "Here you go."

Ruxandra took the list from his hands and scanned it. "How do the police get information from the newspapers? Or from reporters?"

"We call them and ask."

"Is there another copy of this list?"

"Yes."

"Good." Then Ruxandra commanded, *"Call all the newspapers and let them know you need to talk to the reporters who took the pictures. Get a list of names, make a copy of it, and deliver it to Ruxandra Black at the Ambassador Hotel. Tell no one. Understood?"*

"Yes. I understand."

"Good."

"Now get on it."

The scene around the Chinese theater was chaos. Police had cordoned off the street. Some people stood around crying and shaking. Others craned their necks and gawked as if they were at a carnival freak show. The wounded had been removed, but blood still spattered the streets. The scent of it filled Ruxandra's nostrils along with the lingering scent of the ghouls. The Beast growled inside her, wanting to find the ghouls and rend them limb from limb.

Not tonight. But I may just turn you loose once I find this stupid vampire.

"Ruxandra!" Kade stood across the street, talking to two police officers. He waved her over and then turned back to the police. *"You need to bring all the officers from this scene together for a debriefing tomorrow night at your station. Understood?"*

"Yes, sir," both men said.

Kade left them alone and went to Ruxandra. "You have it?"

She nodded. "I've got the police detective calling them all to get the names of any reporters with the pictures. They'll deliver the list to me tomorrow."

"Well done." He patted her shoulder, then raised his voice and went to vampire frequencies. "Elizabeth! Dorotyas! Back to the hotel. Quickly!"

He vanished from human notice and ran. Ruxandra followed. It was two minutes to the hotel, then ten more to wait for Elizabeth and Dorotyas. By the time the two women arrived, Ruxandra and Kade had the locations of all the papers pinned to the map.

"I expected you to be here sooner," Kade said when Elizabeth and Dorotyas came in.

Elizabeth smiled. She had blood on her lips. "We cleaned up some witnesses. Two drunks in the alley. Now they're in the sewer."

Ruxandra's mouth dropped open. *Of all the stupid, asinine, careless things . . .* "You have *got* to be kidding."

"How else were we supposed to get rid of them?"

"Command them, you idiot!"

"Command doesn't last. Especially over something traumatic like this."

"It didn't *need* to last forever! Just long enough for us to hide the evidence!"

"Enough!" Kade's voice was loud enough to rattle the windows in their hotel room. "There is no time for squabbling right now. Elizabeth, you take the places downtown, all right?"

"Fine."

"Dorotyas, take the south, Ruxandra the north, and I will go west and visit those papers. Please do them in this order."

He pointed at the pins on the map one at a time. "If you finish yours, go to whichever section is closest, and start helping there. Do you all understand?"

"Yes," Ruxandra said. Dorotyas nodded. Elizabeth just sighed.

"At each paper, speak to the night editor or the editor-in-chief. Command them to freeze the story and to destroy all the pictures they received and newspaper copies they made. Make them introduce you to the reporters who wrote the stories and command them not to talk about what they've seen and to destroy anything they wrote. Then have them give you a list of every photographer who tried to sell them pictures."

"This is a waste of time," Elizabeth declared, handing the list to Dorotyas. "We should just leave the city."

"It worked before, and it will work now." Kade's voice didn't leave room for argument. "The commands should last two days, three at most. But by then there will be no evidence of anything and nothing to write except speculation. Now let us go. And please, no hunting, no stopping. Just run and get it finished before the sun rises, because then everything becomes much more difficult."

Ruxandra's first paper was easy, a small one in a storefront. The place smelled of ink and old paper, and she saw the hand-cranked printing press that they used to print. Ruxandra spoke to the editor and found out no one had offered to sell him photos. She commanded him not to take any and left.

The second one was a proper newspaper in its own building. Ruxandra stepped through the door into a large foyer with an impressive front desk and an even more impressive night secretary who looked more than ready to send Ruxandra on her way.

Ruxandra commanded her way past the woman, consulted the directory, and went upstairs to the editor's office.

The floor was wide open with pillars holding up the ceiling and windows to let in light during the day. There were a dozen desks, most empty this time of night. A few lamps shone where men worked on their stories. At the far side, behind a wall of glass, sat the editor's office.

"Hey!" A reporter stood up. "You can't be in here."

Ruxandra sighed and two commands later stepped into the night editor's office. It was the size of the last newspaper's entire operation. And the man within had no intention of stopping his paper from getting out. He was, in fact, on his way to the printing room and not in the mood to stop and chat.

Ruxandra started with a command. *"You will listen to me."*

"Of course, but you'll need to walk with me." He took her arm and led her out of his office. "We got a big story breaking right now."

"You need to stop printing."

He shook his head. "I'm not the one printing, lady. The presses are printing. I'm just the one who tells them to start. Once they start, they're all on their own down there."

"Make them stop."

"Oh, the printing only stops when the run finishes or something happens that makes it worth crying, 'Stop the presses.' But that never happens."

"It's happening today." Ruxandra ground the words out between clenched teeth. "Take me to the presses. *Now!*"

"Sure thing, little lady." He took her arm and led her down the hall. "But let me tell you, you should feel very privileged because nobody gets to come down to the printing room. It can be dangerous there if you're not careful around the machines. Why, once a young man who worked for us—"

"*Shut up.*"

He fell silent and took Ruxandra down through the type-foundry, where they made the pages, then into the room where enormous machines churned out the papers. They stretched the length of the building. Ruxandra watched in awe as the machines pulled the newsprint off the huge rolls of paper. The machines printed, cut, and smoothed the papers before folding them twice and dumping them in neat piles to be picked up and stacked by a dozen men. The noise was terrifying. The machines clacked and whirled and groaned and clattered as the papers whizzed through. The room smelled of diesel fuel and ink and machine oil. Every now and then, a blast of steam hissed into the air when the boilers got too hot. Ruxandra's eyes almost bulged out of her head at the sight of it all.

Then she took a deep breath and screamed out, "Stop the presses!"

Ten minutes later the night manager announced that their cover story had been a hoax and was not to be printed. The printers started destroying the papers and the editor sent reporters to burn all the photos and negatives.

She had four more newspapers to reach before sunrise.

The next two were small, with only a few people working at each. She commanded them not to print anything about the ghouls or the attacks at the theater. The last one on her list was a larger operation. This time, Ruxandra went straight to the printing press. Her shouted command brought the entire line to a halt and brought everyone over to her to see what was going on. In short order, she told everyone what she needed to tell them and commanded those who needed to forget.

Finished. Time to go east and see what Elizabeth has done. Then we figure out how to stop the ghouls from attacking again. Maybe I can find the vampire and get her to stop being such a . . .

She went unnoticed and ran across the city. The closest newspaper on Elizabeth's list wasn't as large as some but was still respectable. It was a four-story building with two apartment buildings on either side of it and a sign above the door declaring it the *Los Angeles Daily Gleaner.*

It was also on fire.

Ruxandra stopped in the street, staring. Flames belched out of the basement and first floor. On the second and third floors, people stood at the windows trying to breathe in whatever fresh air they could get. Several prepared to jump. More men and women stood below, yelling at them to stay there and wait until help arrived. Sirens rang out in the near distance.

The fire department. Good. Who did this?

She extended her mind and her senses. Elizabeth was a mile away, Dorotyas two. Kade wasn't even in the range. She couldn't sense any other vampire.

A group of men and women huddled together across the street, nursing burns and other injuries. Ruxandra knelt beside a man covered head to foot with soot and cradling his arm. Ruxandra knelt beside him. *"Tell me what happened."*

"I . . . I don't know. I was in the printing room. Everything was fine. We were packing up the papers to get them ready for the morning edition. Then something exploded . . . the boiler or something. I ran in to try and help, but I couldn't see through the smoke. Then something landed on my arm and—"

"*Did you see anyone you didn't know in there?*"

He shook his head. "I was too busy trying to save the papers."

"Save the papers?" Ruxandra felt her stomach sink. "How many?"

"Some. Not enough. I don't know."The man started trembling. *Face pale, shaking, breath short.* "You're going into shock. You need to lie down. You there!"

One of the people tending the other injured turned her way. Ruxandra gestured him over. "This man is going into shock."

"He's not the only one," the man said. "Help me lay him down with the other injured."

Ruxandra helped set the injured man down in the recovery position, his broken arm on top so his weight wouldn't rest on it. Two years on the battlefields of the Great War made her nursing skills near automatic.

When they finished, she asked the man, "Did you used to work in there?"

He nodded.

"Good. *Tell me where the editor's office is and where they load up the newspapers. Now.*"

She went to the loading dock first. The lane for the trucks was half-blocked by debris, enough to keep any vehicles from getting through. Behind the building Ruxandra found a large lot. The trucks had all been pulled as far from the fire as possible, but warehouses surrounded the lot, the spaces between them wide enough for men, but not vehicles. The drivers stood beside their trucks, watching the fire with grim faces. Ruxandra ran straight at them. "Why are you still here?"

"Got to protect the trucks," said one. "That's our jobs in those trucks."

"It's your lives if you stay here," Ruxandra snapped. "Are the trucks loaded with papers?"

"Yes."

Which means the edition still goes out if they manage to put out the fire.

She ran to the back of the truck. The papers blazed with the words:

"Crazed Fiends Stalk Opening Gala! Six Hurt, Three Killed"

A picture of a ghoul filled the rest of the front page.

Shit, shit, shit, shit, shit!

"Lady, you shouldn't be here. It's too dangerous."

"Neither should any of you." Ruxandra raised her voice and commanded, "*Everyone get out of the lot. Now. Get to safety. Fast!*"

They ran.

Ruxandra waited until the last one ran out. Then she grabbed the truck's front bumper and dragged it toward the building. Metal screeched and the newspapers in the back shifted. Ruxandra put her strength into it and pulled it up to the loading dock in seconds. She did the same with the others. Then she steeled herself and stepped inside the building.

The heat slammed into her, turning her flesh red and sending pain like a thousand needles pushing into her skin. Bundles of newspapers still lay piled high on the loading docks, flames licking at their edges. She grabbed stacks already on fire and threw them into the trucks. Then she stuck her head inside the printing room.

Instantly her skin began erupting into blisters from the heat. The smoke stank of chemicals; any human who breathed it would die. Ruxandra retreated across the parking lot. Her skin began healing at once, the burning pain of the blisters subsided into itching in the cool predawn air.

Predawn? Ruxandra glanced up. The eastern sky was growing lighter. *At least there's no way the photographs will survive the fire. I doubt there'll be anything left of the building at this rate.*

"Help! Please, help us!"

Ruxandra looked up. A dozen people on the roof waved and shouted. A woman screamed, "Please! Tell the firemen we're here! Please! We can't get down without them!"

There's no way the fire trucks can get here, either. Poor bastards.

The first newspaper truck exploded. Ruxandra dove for cover as flaming debris and shards of metal flew everywhere. The second one exploded a moment later, its transmission flying through the air and slamming against the newspaper building's wall. Flames reached for the roof.

Ruxandra heard more cries for help, both from inside the building and from the roof above. The woman who had screamed before leaped from the roof, her hair and clothes streaming flames like a meteor as she smashed onto the concrete below. A man, also on fire, followed her. Then Ruxandra heard nothing but the sound of metal tearing and stone crumbling as the roof collapsed. The screaming stopped, replaced by the roaring flames and explosions as the chemicals inside caught fire.

Ruxandra ran back across a lot between two warehouses and out the other side. The buildings blocked the worst of the fire's heat, though the fumes left everyone coughing. Ruxandra leaned against a wall across the street. *What a stupid waste. When I find out which of them did this I am shoving a pike up their ass.*

She extended her senses again. Elizabeth was still two miles away, Dorotyas half a mile, but neither were moving fast. Kade was at the edge of her reach, running. *No doubt to see how his plan got messed up. Can't wait to hear what he says about* . . .

Massive rage, fueled by hatred and pain, and a desperate hunger filled her senses from all directions. Ruxandra pushed off the wall and stood. Her teeth and talons came out. Inside, the Beast howled with fear and anger.

Ghouls swarmed out of the alleys and buildings, howling and charging straight at her.

O H, FUCK!

Ruxandra leaped twenty feet up and jammed her talons into the wall. For a moment she hung there, eyes wide and breath coming in short, snarling pants like a wolf surrounded by hounds. The Beast filled Ruxandra's mind with screams for blood.

Ten ghouls circled and snarled at her from the ground below.

How can anyone make ten of them? Kade had made three and said that the effort of keeping them from attacking him left him exhausted. *It must drive the vampire insane. If she wasn't there already.*

The closest ghoul took a running jump, climbing the wall as if it were flat. Ruxandra kicked it in the head just before it reached her, sending it flying. The Beast howled with glee. Then five more leaped up the wall, clawing at Ruxandra with their ragged nails, snapping with their teeth. She managed to kick two, but two more latched onto her legs. The third dug its claws into her body, trying to crawl up her and sink its teeth into her throat.

Ruxandra pulled her claws free and dropped like a stone. She drove her knees into the ones grabbing her. They hit the ground and her knees slammed through their ribs, smashing bone and making the ghouls scream. The one that tried to bite her fell onto Ruxandra's raised hand. She made her fingers stiff as boards, and the talons went through the ghoul's flesh like steel through paper. It convulsed and screamed like its brethren. Ruxandra tossed it off her arm and jumped to her feet.

Seven ghouls closed in on her. A gust of wind blew through, bringing with it the smell of blood and death and burned meat. The Beast howled, wanting to be free, to fight and slaughter, but Ruxandra held it at bay. *I won't lose control here. I won't.*

Instead, she moved.

The Chinese martial arts focused on fluidity, the ability to flow from one stance to another, from one motion to another with a minimum of wasted movement. In the fifty years she studied in Asia before the Opium Wars, kung fu had been her favorite activity.

And so she flowed.

When the two closest ghouls closed in on her, she slipped through their outstretched arms and attacked the two ghouls behind them. Two slashes of her clawed hands tore off an arm from each, and a kick stove in the rib cage of the one behind them. Two others charged in, and Ruxandra redirected one into the other, adding her strength so they slammed hard together and crashed to the ground.

The other ghouls charged.

This time, Ruxandra moved in a circle, clawed hands tearing and feet smashing into one ghoul after another. None laid a hand on her, but she couldn't get close enough to drive a killing blow into any of them. They leaped in again and again, heedless of the damage she inflicted. The two with the missing arms howled in agony but didn't stop their attack.

The Beast could deal with them all.

The thought slipped in like an intruder, throwing Ruxandra into confusion just long enough for the ghouls to pile onto her. She spun in place, hurling them off. Their claws tore her clothes and the flesh beneath. Silver blood oozed from a dozen scratches as her dress tore apart. The skin healed at once, but it wasn't fast enough to stop the ambrosial smell of her vampire blood from reaching the ghouls' noses.

The ghouls screamed in frenzied ecstasy. They tried to pile on Ruxandra and fought one another to sink their teeth into her flesh and drink her blood. Each time she threw one off, two more tried to jump on her.

I'll die at this rate.

The thought spurred the Beast to try to break free. Ruxandra held onto control and threw the three ghouls off. She leaped straight up fifty feet into the air. Below her, the ghouls howled and jumped and slashed at the air with their claws.

Ruxandra's eyes narrowed. *If I time this right . . .*

She twisted her body in the air, shifting her descent path. Then gravity took her, and she plunged down into the screaming, clawing mass of bodies.

She landed feet first on one ghoul's head, smashing it into the ground. That gave her just enough space to reach out with her talons, catch the next closest ghoul by the throat, and tear its head off. Blood fountained into the air. The other ghouls howled with delight. Ruxandra threw the head at another ghoul's face, the two skulls connecting with a sharp crack. She jumped back, clearing space between her and the other ghouls. Then she ran straight toward the fire.

The ghouls chased after her. Ruxandra put on a burst of speed to take her out the other end of the alley and give her enough room to fight. She spun and met their charge head-on.

Two ghouls launched at her. One lost its head; the other had its guts torn out, a spray of blood and filth and flesh covering her and the walls around them. Three more came. Ruxandra fell back, slashing one hard enough to take off the top of its head, spattering bits of brain and blood over the ghouls behind it. She kicked another in the thigh. The crack of its leg breaking sounded even over the roaring flames, and jagged bone poked through its flesh. It kept coming, hobbling on the broken limb. The one behind them leaped over the others. Ruxandra caught it and threw it into the flaming building.

It burst into flames the moment it hit the loading dock, its flesh lighting like a gasoline-soaked torch, making a blazing, screaming pyre of its flesh.

The ghouls kept coming, trampling the one with its head open and the one with the broken leg in their eagerness to reach Ruxandra. Even the one with its guts spilling out ran at her, loops of intestines dragging behind it. Ruxandra skipped backward until she felt fire's heat burning her skin. The ghouls charged again, fangs bared and claws slashing, trying to rend her flesh and drink her blood.

They didn't stand a chance.

She threw three ghouls into the fire on the first charge. She heard them screaming and their flesh catching fire. On the second charge, she sent one into the flame and took the head of another. For the last two, she picked up the broken axle from an exploded newspaper truck and smashed their skulls as if they were overripe melons, leaving their twitching corpses on the ground.

Thank God they're stupid. She scanned the area, both with her eyes and her senses, but couldn't see another ghoul for miles. *Just like me not to keep my senses open. They almost had me.*

Ruxandra collapsed, her entire body shaking.

I can't let Elizabeth see me like this. She pressed her hands to her head to silence the still-screaming Beast inside. The animal went quiet, but its rage raced through Ruxandra. She wanted to slash out and kill anything that came close.

What the hell is the matter with me? I've been fighting abominations for a week and they almost killed me, that's what.

Ruxandra rose on unsteady feet and began to collect the ghouls' bodies. She grabbed the ones from the streets first, then the ones in the lot.

God, this is like Fleury-devant-Douaumont before the battle of Verdun.

She had hunted that village during the Great War. After the Allied artillery barrage, the Germans piled the villagers' bodies in the street. Now, Los Angeles smelled the same—of fire and burned bodies and oily smoke and death.

One by one she tossed the ghouls' corpses into the blazing building, watching each one burst into a white-hot ball of flame. When the last ghoul disappeared into the fire, Ruxandra turned unnoticed and slipped back out through the laneway.

A dozen fire trucks sat in front of the building, with more pulling up around the perimeter. Men ran into the buildings on either side, bringing out the residents and hustling them away. Ambulance drivers loaded up the injured and took them away. The dead still lay in the street covered with blankets. Ruxandra wondered how many buildings would catch fire before they brought it under control.

Kade tore around the corner, unnoticeable to the humans. He bounced off a wall and came to a skidding stop in front of Ruxandra. When he spoke, he used vampire frequencies. "Are you all right?"

"Barely." Ruxandra leaned against the wall. She made her voice match his. "I got all my newspapers done."

"So did I." Kade's eyes went to the burning building and the scrambling firemen. "Did you . . .?"

"No." Ruxandra managed not to growl the word. "Not my style. At all."

"Too bad," Elizabeth said. She walked toward them, fully visible. "Fire is always an elegant solution to one's problems."

Ruxandra pushed off the wall. "You did this?"

"Of course," Elizabeth said. "There wasn't time to summon everyone involved to stop the presses. This was the simplest solution."

"Modify your voice and vanish from notice, Elizabeth," said Kade, "before someone hears you."

"My apologies." Elizabeth did as he asked. "I just didn't expect to fight over a few humans."

"A few?" Ruxandra pointed at the blazing building. "Look at it! You must have killed fifty people!"

"Fifty, five hundred, five thousand! What do you care? You're a Blood Royal!"

"Enough with the Blood Royal!" Ruxandra screamed the words. "We're vampires! Nothing else!"

"Fine!" Elizabeth's shouted back. "Then we're *vampires.* Humans are *prey;* they are what we *eat.* So don't you act all high and mighty, *princess*, because you chose to be a vampire just like the rest of us!"

"I didn't choose! A fucking *demon* turned me, remember? You three are the ones who had a choice!"

"Then why didn't you kill yourself, if you feel so guilty about it?" Elizabeth sneered.

"I tried. It doesn't work."

"Try harder or grow up and accept who you are, Ruxandra!"

"Grow up?" Ruxandra advanced on Elizabeth. The Beast snarled inside her, and she was getting damn tempted to let it out. "Don't you dare tell me to grow up, you arrogant, outdated bitch. You lit this place on fire because you were too lazy to do the job right. And don't tell me you didn't have the time. *I* had time. *Kade* had time. *Dorotyas* had time. You lit the damn building on fire because you wanted to!"

"Yes." Elizabeth didn't back away. "We wanted to keep our secret. This is the easiest way."

"*This* was unnecessary!"

"What happened, Ruxandra?" Dorotyas appeared at the corner, unnoticeable and speaking in vampire frequencies. She was looking Ruxandra up and down as if she were something to be wiped off a shoe. "You look like you spent the night fucking a troop ship."

Ruxandra looked down. Her dress was shredded, her underpants torn away. Her shirt and bra were torn open, and the nipple of one breast poked through the fabric. "I got into a fight with some ghouls."

"Ghouls?" Dorotyas sneered. "There aren't any ghouls here."

"There were ten."

"Then why didn't I detect them?"

"I assume because you were too busy killing some poor bastard." Ruxandra glared at Elizabeth. "Just like your owner, here."

"Owner?" Dorotyas voice came out in a low, harsh growl. "You fucking dare . . ."

"I fucking dare!" Ruxandra screamed the words. "Ten of them! Ten fucking ghouls attacked me! They almost killed me! You two were close enough to help if you'd bothered to keep your fucking senses open!"

"Ruxandra." Kade laid a hand on her arm.

She knocked it off. Ruxandra glared at Elizabeth. "Why do this?"

"Because I am trying to *save* us all, remember?" Elizabeth stepped closer, her fangs coming out. "I wanted to go to the ranch. I wanted us all out of here, but *Kade* said we needed to clean up the mess. So I cleaned it!"

"You're batty. This isn't cleaning! This is attracting attention!"

"How?" Elizabeth's voice rose in volume. "Who can say that we had anything to do with this? Who can connect us to it? An unfortunate accident is what the papers will say, what the radio will say, and what *everyone* will agree on."

"She is right, Ruxandra," Kade said.

"How?" Ruxandra spat the word into Kade's face. "How is this right? How is this anything except a waste?"

"It did what needed to be done." Kade's tone was quiet and placating and infuriating.

"This did not need to be done," hissed Ruxandra. "This is a fucking *beacon* telling everyone what we're up to. No wonder the vampire sent ten fucking ghouls. She thought she could kill you and solve her problem!"

Dorotyas grabbed her arm and spun her around. "Don't you blame Elizabeth for this!"

Ruxandra broke the grip with a single twist of her arm and sank her talons into Dorotyas's throat. "How about I blame you?"

"Ruxandra!" Elizabeth's voice slashed through the air. "Dorotyas is not the cause of your failures!"

"Failures?" Ruxandra shoved Dorotyas away and rounded on Elizabeth. "I didn't fail at anything! I took care of my newspapers. I burned the papers in the trucks of *your* newspaper that *you* didn't bother destroying. I killed ten ghouls *by myself* because you were too slow to come help."

"You didn't catch the vampire who caused this whole mess, did you? You didn't do the one thing I brought you here for!"

"Because you were too incompetent to do it yourself!" Ruxandra jabbed her finger into Elizabeth's chest. "Why didn't you help me? You were less than a mile away!"

"I didn't feel any ghouls, Ruxandra. I was busy stopping another paper from printing the pictures."

"How? By torturing all the women until the men capitulated?"

"Ruxandra!" Kade stepped between them. "Not now."

"Yes, now! Everything that has gone wrong here is Elizabeth's fault, and I'm the one who's dealing with the mess! I'm the one who's had to fix everything and stop the ghouls while that selfish *thing* and her bitch sit on their asses!"

"I don't think you fought any ghouls," Dorotyas said nastily. "I think you're making it up because you're looking for an excuse to run away."

"*What?*"

"You haven't wanted to be here from the beginning." Dorotyas's voice dripped with acid, and a smile worked its way across her face. "Now, suddenly, ghouls appear that only *you* get to fight. Ten of them, but of course you managed to win."

"You." A terrible thought bloomed inside Ruxandra. The Beast growled, low and deadly, hungering for a fight. "You conniving, self-serving little bitch. You sent them after me."

"Me?" Dorotyas eyes went wide, her voice high and loud with anger. "You miserable—"

"Dorotyas did not create any ghouls," Elizabeth snapped. "She was with *me.*"

"Oh, and I should listen to you?" Ruxandra snarled. "Because you're so respectable?"

"The sun is coming up!" Kade's voice broke through Ruxandra's rage. Dorotyas looked over her shoulder at the far-too-bright sky. Kade raised his voice. "We have minutes before we all burn to death, so I suggest . . ."

Ruxandra didn't wait to hear the rest. She ran back to the Ambassador Hotel, the sun scorching the earth behind her. *I hope Elizabeth and Dorotyas burn up. Maybe then the vampire will stop this stupidity and let me alone. Kade needs to stop with his being Switzerland, routine.*

Ruxandra made it inside with moments to spare. The smell of humans filled her nose. She began drooling, and her fangs started coming out. The Beast licked its lips in anticipation, and Ruxandra felt her tongue come out.

No! She ran from the lobby, up to her room. It had been years since the Beast had taken enough control of her mind to move her body at its will. That it managed to do so this time terrified her. *I won't let it take over. Not now. Not here. I'll hunt tomorrow.*

She slipped into her room and closed the door tightly behind her. The Beast growled in discontent. Ruxandra ignored it, let the remains of her clothes drop to the floor, and turned the shower on. She sat in the tub while the water streamed over her.

Could Dorotyas have done it? To get at Elizabeth, perhaps? Except that Dorotyas wants Elizabeth for herself. She said so. Unless she wants me and Kade gone, so she can take her revenge on Elizabeth for making her a slave. Ruxandra bowed her head and let the shower pound down. The hot water began pushing the blood and brains from her hair, sending a stream of red and gray down the drain. *Is Dorotyas smart enough for that?*

Ruxandra never thought of Dorotyas as her own person, never thought of her as anything other than an attachment of Elizabeth's to be used when needed then ignored. Dorotyas never left Elizabeth's side, never once tried to get away after Elizabeth made her a slave.

As far as I know, Ruxandra corrected. *I haven't been with them for three hundred years. Their relationship might have changed. But then we never really change, any of us.*

She sat up and reached for the soap. She began rubbing it over her now unblemished skin. The cuts and bruises on her flesh had healed, leaving her nothing to show of what she had done that night, or any of the other fights she'd survived over the centuries.

If Dorotyas loves Elizabeth, then maybe Dorotyas didn't start the vampire attacks. Maybe there's another one out there who's responsible, and Dorotyas is taking advantage of it to get rid of me . . . So tired of this whole situation.

Ruxandra turned her back and let the water rinse away the soap. She shampooed her hair, rubbing deep and finding bits and pieces of ghoul flesh and ash and wood and brick from the explosion. All of it hit the tub and washed away down the drain until all evidence of what had happened vanished.

That's the problem. No evidence of anything at all. She stepped out, grabbed a towel, and started rubbing away the water. She wanted to feed, to distract her brain and appease the Beast and slake her thirst. *Too bad there's no way to get anything to eat until tomorrow night.*

Kade knocked on the door. Ruxandra considered not answering, but in the end she wrapped the towel around her body, went to the sitting room, and opened the door. In her most dismissive tone, she said, "You want what, exactly?"

"To come in, for a start."

She shook her head. "I'm not in the mood for company."

"But you need it."

"No, I really don't."

"I felt the ghouls," Kade said. "The ones Dorotyas said you made up."

Ruxandra's eyes narrowed. "You didn't say anything. Why?"

"Because Dorotyas is not stupid." He glanced down the hall. "May I come in, rather than having this discussion here?"

Ruxandra stepped back and gestured him inside. Kade went over to the small couch and sat down. "I sensed some ghouls, but not how many."

"Ten."

"Yes, you said." Kade rubbed at his chin. "Do you think I would let you die rather than help you?"

"I think Dorotyas would let the world die if she thought she could get Elizabeth for her very own." Ruxandra sat in the chair. "I don't know. The Beast was still angry and still wanted to fight when Dorotyas showed up and accused me of making things up . . ."

"So you could be wrong?"

"I could also be right." Ruxandra leaned forward. "The ghouls targeted me from the moment I arrived. Every ghoul attack that happened since I arrived happened while I'm around. That seems like something far more than coincidence, doesn't it?"

"But that doesn't mean Dorotyas did it."

"It means that someone is tracking what I am doing and sending out the ghouls. Right now, there're only three people who know what I'm up to. And since you weren't around for the first week, that leaves two."

"Or the other vampire."

"*If* she exists."

"If," Kade sighed and stood up. "Elizabeth still wants to leave tomorrow."

"Of course." Ruxandra shook her head.

"If Elizabeth is the target, as she says she is, then leaving town might lure the vampire to her." Kade said. "If Dorotyas is involved or behind it all, then we need to keep a close eye on them both."

"Then let's keep a close eye on them *here*." Ruxandra rose and headed for the bedroom. "I need to sleep and feed before. We'll talk about this tomorrow night."

"Elizabeth wants to leave tomorrow night."

"Well, Elizabeth can bloody well wait." Ruxandra stopped in the bedroom door. "I need to go to bed."

"Me too," Kade said. "Do you want company?"

"After you took Elizabeth's side? No."

"I did not take Elizabeth's side." Kade sighed. "If one is short of time, then, yes, fire does the trick. If she did it just to see the place burn, then, no, she shouldn't have. Either way, it is done, and now no one will print the pictures."

"No one in town," Ruxandra corrected. "There are still the out-of-town newspapers."

"Tomorrow, when the police deliver the list, we will collect all the pictures and make sure they are destroyed before the out-of-town papers get them, all right?"

Ruxandra glared. "She had the time."

"Then it was a stupid decision lacking in subtlety!" Kade dropped his voice. "Believe me when I say I am not on Elizabeth's side in this. In any of this. But we need to see it through."

"I believe you." Ruxandra put enough feeling into the words for him to know she meant it. "We will discuss it tomorrow. Good night, Kade."

"Good night, Ruxandra."

She let him go and crawled into bed. The hunger inside her kept growing stronger, brought on by the battle and the constant internal fight against the Beast. She closed her eyes and laid back, sprawled like a starfish. She tried to relax and sleep, but her mind kept spinning. Again and again, she played over the fight in her mind, and Dorotyas's sneering reaction.

She knows something. Maybe about the vampire, maybe about the ghouls. I don't trust her or Elizabeth enough to be out in the country with them. Not unless I absolutely must.

She woke in the early afternoon to someone pounding on the door. Ruxandra blinked awake and slid out of the bed. She reached out with her mind and found two men, both healthy and strong and smelling of cigarettes and bad coffee.

The hunger rose again, and the Beast grumbled inside, reminding her she hadn't eaten. She smelled the blood of both men through their skin. She considered inviting them in and making them both disappear. Instead, she slipped on the kimono, tied it tight and opened the door.

The two men on the other side wore suits with guns tucked under their armpits. Both were built solidly and watched her with intense, glittering eyes.

"Yes, gentlemen?"

"You Ruxandra Black?" asked the taller and slightly older one.

"Yes."

"Los Angeles Police, Miss Black. We'd like you to come with us."

CHAPTER
THIRTEEN

RUXANDRA WAS SURPRISED enough that it took her a moment to gather her wits and say, "I beg your pardon?" "We need you to come with us. Now."

The man's tone held no room for argument. Ruxandra put on the pretty, confused expression she used to lure predators into alleys and kill them. "But why? Why do you need me to come with you?"

The big detective looked unimpressed. "We'll talk about it at the station."

So much for that. The other detective sized Ruxandra up and reached into one of his pockets—*probably for his handcuffs.* The first cop took a step closer, trying to intimidate her with his size. "*Now,* miss."

"*We'll talk about it here,*" Ruxandra commanded. "*Come in and sit on the couch.*"

She stepped back and held the door open. The two detectives filed inside, went to the couch, and sat. Ruxandra took the chair. Inside her, the Beast slavered, doubling her hunger and pushing her to drink both men where they sat. Ruxandra leaned forward, her eyes on the big man's throat. When she realized what she was doing, she sat back abruptly. *They are police. Drinking them is a stupid idea.*

"So, miss," said the big one. "What were you doing at the *Los Angeles Daily Gleaner* last night?"

The words hit her like a slap. Ruxandra kept her face clear of any expression at all. "I'm sorry. Where?"

"Don't fuck with us, lady." The second detective leaned forward, his hands clenching and unclenching as if he'd like nothing better than to beat the answers out of her—if only he could leave the couch. "You wouldn't last two days in prison, so tell us what we want to know."

"*How about you answer all my questions instead?*"

"Fine," the first detective said. "We'll answer your questions."

"Who told you I was staying here?"

"Our captain."

"Why does he care?"

"Because he knows you lit the fire at the *Los Angeles Daily Gleaner.*"

"What?" Shock brought Ruxandra to her feet. "Who told him that?"

"Dunno," the second one said. "We just got our orders to come here, pick you up, and take you in."

"And if I refuse to go?"

"Then the captain will be plenty mad," the first one said. "He said if we come back without you or if we're not back by six, he's sending a squad of uniforms to take you in, dead or alive."

"Was that his idea or someone else's?"

"Lady, he don't tell us where he gets his ideas from."

Dammit, dammit, dammit.

"You got any more questions, or can I ask mine now?"

"Just one." Ruxandra stood up and headed for the bedroom. "How far is it to the station?"

Everyone stared as Ruxandra crossed the hotel lobby in her long coat and dress, with her wide hat and sunglasses and gloves and the escort of two police officers. Heads turned and eyebrows rose, but no one said anything.

The advantage of staying in the better class of hotel.

She sat in the middle of the back seat for the entire drive. It was a bright, clear day, and the sun beat down on the car, heating it like an oven. When they turned corners, the sunlight slipped across the seats as if searching for Ruxandra's flesh. She slid back and forth on the seat, avoiding the light.

When they reached the station, she commanded, "*Through the rear entrance, please, and straight to your captain.*"

The station was gritty with dirt on the floors and dust on the windows. Graffiti covered the walls in the back stairwell. Ruxandra extended her senses. She found desperation, despair, and anger, and, in one room, a man being savagely beaten. There was no sign of a vampire or ghouls.

The detectives led her up three flights to an annoyingly bright office, where the captain sat behind a large, paper-covered desk. He took one look and growled. "Why the hell is she in here?"

"She's Ruxandra Black, Captain," said the first detective. "You wanted her brought in."

"Into an interrogation room, not into my office! Get her out of here!"

"Do the interrogation rooms have windows?" Ruxandra asked.

The captain's eyebrows went down, and his face scrunched up. He looked like a bulldog ready to attack. "Some do, some don't, and you don't get to choose which."

"Take me to one without any windows. Come with us, Captain."

Two minutes later, Ruxandra sat in the darkest interrogation room. The three police officers stood against the wall, staring. She felt their pulses, heard them loud enough to fill her ears in the silent room. *I could drink all three and be miles away before anyone realized they're missing.*

Inside her, the Beast rumbled its agreement.

Stop that. She glared at the policemen. *"Tell me why you think I started the newspaper fire."*

"I got a phone call," said the captain. "A very reliable source described you and put you at the scene. Said he saw you coming out of the building just before the fire."

Ruxandra frowned. "And?"

"He said that since you're the only one who doesn't work there that came out, there's a good chance you're the one who burned the place down."

"I wasn't. Who was the source?"

"It's a source. I protect their names."

"Tell me."

"I don't know the name," the captain said. "But I know it's a good source."

"Of course." Ruxandra bit her lip as she thought about it. "And this source told you my name, my hotel, and what I looked like?"

"That's right."

"And was the source a man or a woman?"

"A man," the captain said. "German accent. Said to arrest you and put you under watch."

Rage, powerful enough that it sent the Beast howling, flared up inside her. "When did he call?"

"Eight this morning."

He's taking Elizabeth's side to get me out of the city. The Beast howled again, but the anger Ruxandra felt wasn't animal rage. It was pure human fury at his betrayal.

"Why did he say so if you didn't?" the captain asked. "Who is he?"

"*Not your business.*" Ruxandra snarled the words between fangs she didn't realize had sprung out. The men stepped back, their eyes going wide. The detectives reached for their guns. "*Everyone stay still and calm down.*"

The men nodded and the fear melted from their faces. Ruxandra picked up the table and hurled it against the wall. It cracked in two. She wanted to pick up the pieces and throw them again and again until the entire thing turned to kindling. She wanted to kill everyone within range; wanted to face down Kade and listen to him scream as she ripped his arms off. *Not that it would kill him, but it would make me feel better.*

She paced back and forth across the room, growling. Her arms swung in helpless circles, the talons slicing the air. She willed the talons to retract, willed her fangs back into her head. She needed to stop being so angry and start thinking.

I need blood, I need to rest, and I need to think. And I can't do it back at my hotel if he's got all the police in Los Angeles looking for me.

She turned back to the detectives. "What's the worst bar in the city?"

They all looked startled and glanced at one another. The first detective said, "The Mitchell Saloon, off Hollywood Boulevard. We don't go there unless there're twenty or thirty of us. Even then, it's a fifty-fifty chance we'll lose the fight."

"Take me there," Ruxandra growled. "*Now.*"

She had the detectives drop her off at the saloon and leave. Inside, the place was dark and almost empty. Three men nursed beers in the corners. Behind the bar a large woman with a scarred face and tattoos on her arms polished glasses. Ruxandra went straight toward her. The scarred woman looked down her nose and sneered. "We don't serve fancy drinks here, girl."

"Whiskey."

The woman leaned in close. "There're some men coming tonight that would just love to take a turn at a pretty thing like you. So unless you want your cunt spread so hard you piss blood for a month—"

Ruxandra grabbed the other woman's collar and pulled her down until their faces were level. "I said whiskey. *Now.*"

She shoved the bartender back. The woman glared at Ruxandra but put a glass in front of her and poured a whiskey. Ruxandra drank down the shot, enjoying the burn, wishing she could get drunk. "Leave the bottle."

The bartender left the bottle. Ruxandra shot back three more in rapid succession. She surveyed the others in the room. Five men sat drinking alone. No one made a move toward her or even looked her way. Ruxandra growled and shot back a fourth. *All I want is someone to eat. This should not be that hard.*

"Hey, Lucy," called one regular. "Turn on the radio. I want to hear what happened with that big fire."

"Learn to say please, why don't you?" the bartender grumped, but she turned on the radio.

"To repeat our top story, following the attacks and fire last night, the mayor of Los Angeles declared a curfew for the next three nights. Anyone on the street after eight p.m. will be arrested and detained for the night, as well as receive a five-dollar fine."

"Well, shit." Lucy said. "There goes business for the next three days."

"Does this mean you'll give it away for free?" asked another regular. The other three men in the room laughed like the question was the height of hilarity.

"Means it costs twice as much." Lucy raised her voice. "In fact, since you're all I'm getting today, I'm closing down until the curfew lifts. Finish your drinks and get out."

The regulars grumbled. Ruxandra didn't move. Lucy tapped her elbow. "Especially you. I don't need your sort of trouble in here anyway."

Ruxandra ignored her and poured another whiskey. *Shit, shit, shit.*

Something hard poked Ruxandra's elbow. She looked up and saw the baseball bat in Lucy's hand. Lucy poked her elbow again. "You hear me?"

"I heard you."

"Then fuck off."

"Don't think so."

Ruxandra threw back her drink. *"I'm staying until the sun sets. And you're staying open until then."*

With luck, someone worth killing will come in. She cast her eyes over the other patrons. *Otherwise, one of them is lunch.*

An hour later, Kade walked in.

He wore a new suit as well as a heavy coat, hat, and sunglasses. He cast his eyes around the room, then onto her. "Hunting?"

Ruxandra put down her glass and stood up. Her voice carried through the bar. "*Everyone. Get out. Now.*"

The men in the bar scrambled to leave. Lucy retreated through a back door. Ruxandra heard the lock click when she closed it. Kade's eyes narrowed as he watched. "What is the reason for this?"

"How did you find me?" Ruxandra's words came out so angry, so filled with violence, that Kade took a half step back.

"I wanted to talk to you and sensed that you weren't in the hotel," he said. "You weren't in range, so I asked at the front desk. They said you left with two policemen. After that, it took a pair of phone calls."

Liar. Ruxandra held her temper in tight check and didn't move.

"The front desk told me the list of photographers arrived." Kade held up a piece of paper. "I thought that we could track them down tonight."

"Before that." Ruxandra's words came out like bursts of flame. "*Why* did you want to talk to me? How come the police knew where to find me, knew my *name*, and knew what I looked like?"

Kade took another step back. He spoke in slow, measured tones. "I wanted to talk to you about the way Dorotyas behaved at the fire. As for the police, I have no idea."

"And I suppose you have no idea how they connected me to the newspaper fire, either?"

"I don't." Kade stopped backing up. "Ruxandra, what's going on?"

"Someone *called* them, Kade. They told me so. The captain called it a reliable source."

Kade frowned. He rubbed his chin. "You think Dorotyas set you up?"

Not Dorotyas. Ruxandra didn't say a word.

"Or Elizabeth?" Kade rubbed his chin some more. "They're trying to drive you out of town."

Them or you? Ruxandra wanted to scream what she'd learned, but Kade looked genuinely confused. *Of course, he's a better liar than I am.*

"I suspect that now you really don't want to leave town." Kade went to the bar and hopped over it. "So if it was one of them, their plan backfired."

"It certainly did."

"I always loved the way bad rum feels going down." He opened a bottle and drank half of it. "I still think you should go to Elizabeth's ranch."

"Of course."

He frowned. "Why of course?"

"How stupid do you think I am?" The words came out in a shout that rattled the glasses along the bar. "Did you think I wouldn't ask who called?"

"Why are you yelling—"

Ruxandra's glass flew at his head. He ducked, and it smashed against the bottle shelf. She picked up the bottle. "A man. With a *German* accent. Know anyone who fits that description, *Kade?*"

Kade's eyes glinted red. "I did not call the police."

The bottle flew. Kade caught it. Ruxandra threw her stool. "Then who the *fuck* did?"

Kade smashed the stool to pieces in the air. "I don't know what you think you're playing at—"

The Beast howled and Ruxandra dropped into a crouch, ready to spring. "Playing at? Why don't you tell me what you and Elizabeth are 'playing at,' since you're so desperate to get me out to her ranch."

"I am not desperate to get you out to her ranch!" Kade's own fangs came out. He jumped the bar and landed across the room from Ruxandra. "I want Elizabeth and Dorotyas out of the city and neither will go without *you!*"

"So you called the *police* on me?"

Kade threw up his hands. "That wasn't me!"

"Bullshit!"

"Dammit, Ruxandra!"

"Fuck you! Fuck you and Elizabeth both! I'm not leaving the city, you hear me?"

"Then what's your plan, Ruxandra?" Kade's words came out loud and hard. "Stay here? Chase ghouls around the city with no hope of finding where they came from? You won't find anything like that, and you know it! If we all leave, the vampire will come after us."

"Assuming Dorotyas isn't the vampire. Or in league with the vampire." Ruxandra looked for something else to throw. "Assuming *you're* not in league with her."

"How could I be in league with her?" Kade demanded. "I just got here, remember?"

"And suddenly the ghouls went public. How convenient!"

"The vampire is desperate!" Kade's fist slammed onto a table, cracking the wood. "And *if* Dorotyas is helping her, then she must be desperate, too! So let's get out of the city and watch her. If she makes a move, we know that she's part of it."

"And if she doesn't? What then?" Ruxandra circled him. "What if more people die?"

"Then they die!" Kade thundered. "But at least we'll know who is or isn't responsible."

"How, if it's ghoul attacks? You said you could control your thralls from half a world away. From how far away can someone control a ghoul?"

"I don't know."

"Then how do we know they can't control the ghouls from the ranch?"

"We watch them."

"You think that will work?"

"I don't know, but it's better than any other idea we've got right now!"

"So good that you used the cops to get me going?"

Kade's hand smashed down on the table, this time hard enough to snap it in two. "That wasn't me!"

"Then who was it?" Ruxandra's voice came out as sharp and deadly as a razor.

"I don't know." Kade spoke in slow, measured tones again, his anger held in tight rein. "Someone who commanded them to say that the informant was a man with a German accent, perhaps."

Ruxandra's eyes narrowed. "You're reaching."

"I have to reach! I can't get you to trust me any other way!"

You're not getting me to trust you this way, either.

He must have seen her distrust in her face. "Fine. Don't trust me. Don't believe me about the police. That doesn't matter. What matters right now is that we stop the reporters from showing their pictures. Then we'll argue about this, all right?"

Ruxandra glared some more. She ached to attack him, to sink her teeth into his throat and tear the flesh from his face. The only thing that stopped her was that he was right. She straightened up and pulled in her fangs and talons. "Yes, we will."

"There are phone numbers on the list," Kade said. "Why don't we bring them all here and deal with them all at once?"

"Tell them we're from the *New York Times*," Ruxandra said. "That we want the prints and the negatives. We'll barely need to command them."

Kade nodded. "Can I go to the phone without getting my face destroyed?"

"For the moment."

Kade nodded again and began making the calls.

It was midnight by the time all the reporters gathered. They all handed over the photos and negatives. Kade commanded them to remember only that they didn't get any decent pictures. And because of the curfew, Ruxandra ordered them all to stay in the bar drinking until morning. Then she and Kade made themselves unnoticed and stepped out into the night.

Halfway to Elizabeth's apartment, Kade asked, "Are you still planning not to come with us?"

"Yes."

"I'll let you explain that to Elizabeth," Kade said. "One fight today is enough."

Ruxandra glared but didn't say anything more. She spread her senses wide, looking for someone breaking the curfew to eat. The streets were empty, even of the usual muggers and prostitutes and thugs that roamed the night. Ruxandra growled in frustration. *At this rate, I'm going to need to break into someone's house.*

On the edge of her senses, she felt Dorotyas in agony.

Ruxandra stretched her mind as far as she could. Dorotyas was in Elizabeth's apartment and Elizabeth was with her. No one else was there. Dorotyas pain was so great that Ruxandra was amazed the woman wasn't screaming.

What the hell did Elizabeth do to her?

They slipped in past the concierge and up the stairs. Kade knocked at the apartment door. The door swung wide and Dorotyas glared at them. "About time."

She turned and walked away. And because Ruxandra was looking for it she could see the pain in Dorotyas's movements. She glanced around the apartment, looking for any sign of spilled silver blood.

"About time," Elizabeth said from the balcony. She stepped in and closed the door behind her. "Sit down, everyone."

Ruxandra watched Dorotyas hide the pain that sitting down cost her. *She should be healed by now unless Elizabeth used fire.*

"Where have you been?" Elizabeth demanded. "We need to go."

"Cleaning up the last of your mess," Ruxandra said before Kade opened his mouth. "We got all the pictures and convinced all the reporters they didn't see anything. What have *you* been doing?"

"Preparing for the journey. Dorotyas cleaned the apartment of any evidence, and we are packed and ready to go. You?"

"Ruxandra doesn't want to go," Kade said. "She thinks she'd be better here."

"Well, she's wrong." Elizabeth glared at Ruxandra. "Too much happened in the city. We need to keep a low profile for a while and distance ourselves from it."

"You couldn't have thought of that *before* you burned the newspaper down?"

"It would not have been necessary to burn it if you found the vampire!"

It took a great deal of restraint for Ruxandra not to jump across the table and rip her throat out. She suspected that Kade and Dorotyas would try to stop her, and she'd need to fight them all. While she had no doubt she could beat Elizabeth or Dorotyas, she wasn't ready to take on all three at once. Instead, she stood up and said, "I need some air."

Elizabeth glared as Ruxandra stepped out on the balcony. The smell of charred meat filled Ruxandra's nose. She slid the door shut behind her. A small charcoal brazier sat on the balcony—the type used for cooking outside. The coals in it still glowed red. And though the fireplace poker beside them wasn't hot anymore, Ruxandra saw the burned flesh that still stuck to it and the blood— once silver, now gray—that covered the eight inches closest to the point. She winced. *Why would Dorotyas let her do that?*

And why does Elizabeth want us out of town? She leaned against the balcony rail and looked out over the city. She could see the lights of Hollywood Boulevard and the dark hills beyond. *She doesn't care about keeping a low profile, and she doesn't care about more people dying. So why does she want us out at the ranch?*

Control.

That piece fit. Ruxandra had stayed away from Elizabeth's control since she arrived. And with Kade there, it was even easier. Going to the ranch would put them in a place where Elizabeth had control. And *Kade will be more than happy to agree, so long as it got him what he wants.*

Dorotyas opened the door behind her. "Elizabeth says that if you're not going to go, at least help carry the bags."

"But you're so good at it," Ruxandra said without turning around. "Carry the bags, dispose of the bodies, clean up her messes."

"Which you've proved totally incapable of doing," Dorotyas replied, her voice honey infused with cyanide. "No wonder she likes Kade better now. At least he has brains."

"At least I tried, instead of sitting around listening to the radio."

The moment the words left her mouth a thought raced through Ruxandra's head, *electrifying her* like lightning. She put on a calm face and turned around. "But since Elizabeth's decided you're too incompetent to even carry the bags after this last fiasco, I'll help, just to stop her whining."

They finally slipped up.

Ruxandra swept past Dorotyas, glancing into the kitchen as she went, and past Elizabeth and Kade still poring over maps in the dining room. She went to the bedroom and grabbed two bags, leaving the larger and more awkward pieces for Dorotyas.

"Finally doing what I ask?" Elizabeth called from the dining room. "How refreshing."

"Ruxandra." Kade stood up and went to her. "I think we should all go. I think it will stop the slaughter in Los Angeles and help answer our questions."

The last words accompanied a barely visible nod toward Dorotyas.

"Yes." Ruxandra kept her voice grudging and angry. "It would."

"So will you?" Kade put his hand on her arm. "Please?"

Ruxandra looked at Elizabeth, whose eyes sparkled with anticipation. "All right, Kade. I'll go. Since *you're* the one asking."

CHAPTER
FOURTEEN

GOD, *I SHOULD have drunk someone first.*

It was a long, slow drive through the country, and Ruxandra grew hungrier with each passing hour. Normally she would have lasted at least one more day without having to slake the thirst, but the last few days were as far from normal as she could get. She was hungry, still angry with Kade, and the Beast still rumbled inside her, trying to break free.

And now I'm on my way to an abattoir. The perfect place to try to contain a blood-crazed animal.

"Here we are," Elizabeth announced as her driver and thrall, Mason, turned the car off the dirt road and drove under a large sign that said "Joyous Waters" in very pretty cursive. "With an hour to spare before dawn, too. Excellent driving, Mason."

"Thank you, ma'am."

"Joyous Waters?" Kade smiled. He was sitting in the middle seat between Elizabeth and Ruxandra, his arms around each one's shoulders to give them all room. "I take it you didn't name it."

Elizabeth chuckled. "The first owners found a spring here. They claimed the land and made it into a ranch. The next ones decided it was better suited to wine. So far the grapes have done remarkably well, haven't they, Dorotyas?"

"Very well, my lady." Dorotyas said from the front seat beside Mason. "Last year's crop commanded high prices at market."

"One hundred acres of grapes," Elizabeth said. "Fifty acres of fruit trees, a hundred of vegetables, and another five hundred for cattle."

"Impressive," Kade said.

Elizabeth patted his thigh. "Land is power. The crops generate money and feed the peasants."

"Peasants?" Kade laughed. "How old-fashioned. Where do you find peasants in America?"

"Mexico, mostly. Though there are some wandering ranch hands looking for work. You won't see most of them, of course. They work during the day and live apart from the house staff. But the ones that tend house are ready to serve at all hours. The ones in the games room, well . . . they're always available. There's the house."

It was huge and white, covering half an acre, though it stood only two stories high. The house was done in the Spanish Colonial style, with balconies and wide windows to let in the breezes. Crushed gravel covered the ground around it for thirty feet in every direction. Mason pulled the car up in front of the ornate doors and honked three times. He opened Elizabeth's door and gave her a hand out, then did the same for Dorotyas, leaving Ruxandra and Kade to climb out on their own.

Ruxandra opened her senses wide. Sixteen humans in the house, ten female, six male, all smelling of fear and blood. A mile away, she sensed the barracks where the farmhands slept, men and women together in each building.

"I don't feel your games room," Kade said. "Where is it?"

"Below ground." Elizabeth smiled. "Rather far below, in fact. The previous owners found natural caverns when they dug their wine cellar. Now, come inside."

The foyer stretched up the full height of the house, with twin stairs leading up to balconies on the floor above. The floor was tile, and the walls painted pristine white.

Six naked men and ten naked women stood in a line by the door. All had been beautiful once. Now, their strong features looked worn down from fear. Bruises and scabbed-over wounds covered their bodies.

"I keep them chained when we're not here," Elizabeth explained. "Save for Barbara."

Barbara, a dark-haired woman with small breasts and deeply sunken eyes, had two scabbed-over punctures in her neck where Elizabeth had made her a thrall. She stepped forward, knelt, and presented Elizabeth with a flail whose lashes glittered with the metal embedded in them. Elizabeth took it and patted the woman's head.

"Now, I know you're both hungry," Elizabeth said. "Which ones would you like?"

Kade walked down the line of humans, examining them all. He stopped in front of a buxom young woman with dark skin and long, flowing black hair. She had more bruises than most, with dark shadows under her eyes and a dead expression on her face. He pulled her out of the line. "This one."

"Excellent choice." Elizabeth turned and gave Ruxandra a smile that could wither flowers. "I suppose you're too good to drink from my slaves?"

"Yes." Ruxandra said, hoping Elizabeth didn't see the fear she hid with the lie. The Beast reveled in the smell of blood and fear that permeated the building. It pushed harder against the walls in Ruxandra's mind. The slightest slip would allow it to break free, and Ruxandra was terrified she wouldn't regain control.

"As you wish." If Elizabeth sensed Ruxandra's feelings, she showed no sign. "I'll show Kade to his room, then. Dorotyas, show Ruxandra to hers."

"Yes, my lady."

Dorotyas led Ruxandra out to the courtyard in the middle of the building. It looked very pleasant at first glance. Large pots filled with blooming desert plants and raised gardens of fragrant flowers stood along the paths that led from each side to the large tiled fountain in the center. The path was swept clean, and the plants were attended to with near-fanatical care. At the end of each path, just before the fountain, stood an execution station.

In front of them sat a cross wrapped in barbed wire. Spikes stained red with blood stuck out from the wood, the last victim's hands and feet still attached. Across the yard stood a ten-foot-high sharpened wooden stake. Circles of nails protruded upward for all but the last foot and a half of the post, to slow and prolong the agony of whomever they impaled on it. On one side sat a wheel on a post with a bloody mallet leaning on it for breaking a man's bones before weaving them through the wheel and leaving him to die. On the other stood a large frame with manacles, each big enough for a man's ankle, hanging down from the top corners, and a bloody two-handed saw beside it.

Leave it to Elizabeth to have sawing as the most merciful way to die in her house.

"We keep these as a reminder to our workers of what happens to those who disobey," Dorotyas said over her shoulder as she led Ruxandra past the cross. "We've been busy, so it's empty. But we try to use it once or twice a week to keep them in line."

"Lovely." Ruxandra kept her emotions out of her voice. "Does Elizabeth make you do all the dirty work, or does she kill the girls herself?"

"We make them execute each other." Dorotyas looked smug and satisfied. She led Ruxandra around the fountain and down the path. "It reminds them why they're here, and their terror is exquisite."

Ruxandra's bedroom faced the courtyard. It had a bed, a chair, and wide windows with thin curtains and an eastern exposure. Dorotyas saw Ruxandra eying them and smiled. "The sun hits the bed every morning. So as far as I'm concerned, you can lie there to your heart's content."

As soon as she left, Ruxandra pulled the bed away from the window to a corner that the sun wouldn't touch. She lay down, trying to calm her mind and the Beast that growled and paced inside it. She felt tired and angry and the hunger gnawed at her insides, all of which gave the Beast strength. She ignored it and cast out her senses again, this time stretching them as far into the earth as she could manage, which wasn't very far at all.

The torture chambers were fifty feet belowground, near the edge of her reach. It held eleven men and forty-five women. All radiated terror and pain, even the ones sleeping. Ruxandra sensed Elizabeth's blazing presence entering the chamber. The fear in the prisoners skyrocketed, and one started screaming loud enough for Ruxandra to hear.

Ruxandra yanked her senses away. She turned her mind outward, away from Elizabeth's games, scanning to the horizon in every direction. Aside from the barracks, she sensed no humans within five miles. No ghouls, either.

But then, there wouldn't be.

Just before dawn, a man began screaming in the courtyard.

HUNGER, HUNGER, KILL, KILL, KILL, the Beast howled back. Ruxandra sat bolt upright in bed and slammed the Beast back into its cage in her mind. The fresh smells of blood and terror filled the air. She extended her senses and found Dorotyas with the household slaves in the courtyard. Ruxandra growled and stomped down the stairs. *There's no way I can sleep through that and she knows it.*

They had impaled one of the men.

He hung in the air, the post buried in his backside. The first circle of nails stopped his descent, holding him in place even as they dug into his flesh. They'd chained his hands behind him and left his legs free. He scrabbled and pushed against the stake, his feet bloody and torn from the nails around the post.

Dorotyas stood in the doorway, naked, surrounded by three naked men. They caressed her flesh as if she were the most desirable of women, even as they shook with fear and despair.

She smiled at Ruxandra. "Given your father's reputation, I thought you'd appreciate this one."

Ruxandra refused to acknowledge the Beast's eager reaction and her own hunger. "What did he do?"

"He didn't fuck me well enough. I don't think he knew how."
Dorotyas caressed the men's faces. "But now they see what happens
if I am not satisfied, so I'm sure they will do a *much* better job."

"I'm amazed you can take anything," Ruxandra ground out,
"given what Elizabeth did to you."

Dorotyas eyes flashed red, even as her face went expression-
less. "Fuck you."

"Not even with Elizabeth's fingers." Ruxandra tilted her head
toward the screaming, impaled man. "Is that why you did this to
him? Because she did that to you?"

"I should kill you!" Dorotyas hissed. Her eyes turned red again,
and her fangs and claws came out. She shoved the men way from
her, sending them sprawling. "I should kill you right here!"

Before the men landed on the ground, Ruxandra stepped in
front of her, her own talons out and her fangs bared and ready.
"You can't and you know it. Elizabeth won't let you. Is that why
you were so pissy when the ghouls failed?"

Dorotyas stiffened. A deep growl resonated in her throat.
Ruxandra waited for her attack, but it never came. Instead, Dorotyas stepped away from her, and her fangs and talons retreated
back into her flesh. Her voice came out low and vicious. "Tell me,
did you come down here because the screams bothered you, or
because you smelled the blood and the Beast won't let you sleep
until you've drunk some?"

It hit close enough that Ruxandra couldn't answer. Dorotyas
bared her teeth in a grin. "I remember when you used to *like* the
screaming. When you used to circle them on your hands and
knees, growling and snarling and sniffing like an animal. Your
mind was like a ghoul's."

"Trust me, it wasn't."

"Oh, of course not." Dorotyas sneered. "*You're* the one who made a ghoul. *You're* the one who figured out everything about being a vampire, and God forbid you share any of it instead of making everyone else figure it all out alone. But no, you *won't*—because under it all you're just the Beast!"

Ruxandra forced herself to be still, to not answer the animal raging inside her. Dorotyas pointed at the man on the stake. "That's why you don't like hearing this. Because it reminds you that you're just another animal."

"I don't like *this* because it's barbaric and stupid."

"Well, here, let me help." Dorotyas strolled over to the man on the stake, grabbed one of his legs and yanked it hard. The nails holding him in place tore through his flesh and went inside. The man screeched at the new terrible pain as pointed steel gouged through his bowels and he dropped the six inches down onto the next set. His legs flailed and his body convulsed. Fresh blood spurted out on the ground beneath him.

"There." Dorotyas sauntered back. "He'll be hoarse in a half hour or so. Then you can sleep. Unless you want to drink him and put him out of his misery."

The worst of it was that Ruxandra *wanted* to drink him. The Beast screamed for it. Her own hunger demanded it. The scent of blood and the sense of his agony washed over her in waves.

I won't feed off a slave. It's stupid and it's wrong. I am better than this.

Even if it's a mercy killing? The thought came unbidden from some dark, hungry recess of her brain that would do anything to justify the blood. *Even if it stops his pain? Even if the blood keeps me from being stupid? Even if—*

Ruxandra dropped to a crouch and dug her talons into the ground. She ripped a rock from the path, spun, and hurled it in one motion. The impaled man's head exploded. Brains and bone and blood went flying, and the rock embedded into the white plaster across the courtyard.

"My, my," Dorotyas said in the sudden silence. "The animal has such a temper."

And because Ruxandra knew Dorotyas wanted her to attack, knew she was trying to make her lose control, she turned and walked away. Dorotyas's laugh followed her up the stairs to her room. Ruxandra slammed the door shut and paced.

I need to talk to Kade. I need to find out if he's on my side in all this, because if he isn't . . . If he isn't, I'm screwed. I can't kill all three at once. I don't think.

She expanded her senses again. Dorotyas had the three men in her room. The other servants were dispersed around the house. Kade wasn't in his room or anywhere aboveground. Ruxandra turned unnoticed and walked through the buildings, staying inside and away from the growing sunlight. She got her first sense of him in the kitchen, though he wasn't there. He was belowground, his bright presence standing next to Elizabeth's. *Dammit, dammit, dammit. What are they talking about?*

The door down to a wine cellar also led down to Elizabeth's "playroom." The problem was that if Ruxandra went close enough to hear them, Elizabeth would know she was there. *And knowing Elizabeth, she's listening for me.*

She walked back down the corridor, her mind open. Soon, her sense of Elizabeth and Kade vanished. *And if I can't sense them, they can't sense me. Fortunately, I don't need to.*

The sun was well up now, but the light hadn't hit the court-yard. Ruxandra slipped outside, ignoring the heat, and picked a spot near the eastern wall. She couldn't sense Kade or Eliza-beth, which was what she wanted. She knelt down in the flow-erbed and put her ear against the ground. Then she closed her eyes and listened.

"That's quite something," Kade said, his voice raised over the sound of a woman crying out in pain.

"Isn't it?" Elizabeth sounded pleased. The woman's cries turned to sobs as Elizabeth removed whatever implement she'd been torturing the woman with. "Heat creates a long-lasting agony."

"Indeed." He fell silent a moment. Then, "Is that why you used it on Dorotyas?"

"You noticed?" Elizabeth sounded impressed. "I thought she concealed it rather well."

"Not as well as all that. Why?"

"She disobeyed me." Elizabeth sounded quite put out. "I told her before there are consequences for that."

"I thought she *couldn't* disobey you."

"Well, not outright. But sometimes she tries to go around my wishes."

"It would be a shame if her actions led to my plans being ruined."

"They won't. Nor will our vampire problem." Elizabeth said. "I don't see how it *could* cause harm to your plans. We're on the other side of the world, after all."

"News travels faster these days. I wasn't planning to move for at least another five years. This . . . makes things difficult."

"Does it, now?" Elizabeth's voice became serious. "I suppose you want it to stop."

"Yes."

"Well, then, you'll just need to convince Ruxandra to search harder, won't you?"

"You know that's not the solution."

"I do." Elizabeth's voice turned sharp. "Just as I know that I would prefer to discuss this matter tomorrow night, after everyone feeds and rests."

"Of course." Kade said. "If you'll excuse me, that woman still awaits me in my room."

"Of course. And if you'll excuse me . . ." The human woman cried in pain again.

Ruxandra rose and went back inside. Her mind was still open, and she could sense Dorotyas and the three men up in her room. On impulse, Ruxandra walked toward them. She heard Dorotyas grunting with pleasure and one of the men trying to scream, though his voice was muffled. She found the room, its door wide open, and looked in.

Dorotyas was riding one of the men. He lay on the edge of the bed, his legs wide to accommodate the second man. That one caressed Dorotyas's breasts from behind. The third man stood above the first, a wad of rags stuffed into his mouth. Dorotyas grabbed his backside with both hands, talons digging in, to pull him close.

Blood overflowed from her mouth, spattering the man's face below her.

Ruxandra shook her head and looked over the room. Dorotyas had no other furniture save a dressing table covered in small, delicate glass bottles.

"What the fuck do you want?" Dorotyas demanded. Blood streamed down her chin. "Can't find a man of your own to ride?"

Ruxandra took a deep breath as if to answer, then turned her back and walked to her room. She lay on the bed, pulling the blanket over her head, and closed her eyes. The Beast inside her screamed and fought, but she clamped down on it hard.

Just a little longer. Then we feed. I promise.

As soon as the sun disappeared behind the horizon, Ruxandra stepped outside. A breeze blowing from the Pacific carried cool, clean air with it. Ruxandra circled the house, listening to the night animals' cries as they hunted or fled their hunters. In the garage behind the building, she heard Mason polishing the car and whistling. Ruxandra followed the sound and found the man running a cloth over the shining hood of the Stutz.

"Good evening, Mason."

The man turned. "Good evening, Miss Ruxandra."

She walked forward, keeping her hands behind her back, to admire the gleaming chrome and painted steel. "It is a beauty, isn't it? Stutz limousine."

Mason's eyebrows went up. "You know cars, miss?"

"I do." Ruxandra flashed him a smile. "Guess what kind."

"Ooh. A lady like you? Let me think." Mason pursed his lips and looked her up and down. "A Packard. Maybe a Chrysler. Definitely a two-seater."

Ruxandra grinned. "A Bugatti."

"A Bugatti?" Mason's mouth fell open, and he laughed. "How did you get your hands on a Bugatti?"

"Man in New York brought it over," Ruxandra said. "His wife didn't like it, and he had to sell. I snapped it up, and for a pretty penny, too."

Mason looked at her slyly. "Does it really go as fast as all that?"

"Ninety miles an hour," Ruxandra said. "Seventy for cruising if you want to go a long way."

"That is magnificent!" Mason smiled widely. "Bet you painted it red."

"That's a bet you win." Ruxandra looked at the Stutz. "This must go pretty fast, too. Do you get to take it out much?"

"Oh, lots," said Mason. "The lady visits Los Angeles three times a week, except when she went out of town to fetch you."

"I didn't think there was that much to see in Los Angeles. Does she have a favorite spot?"

"Griffith Park. She loves to go there and walk among the trees."

"Well, I can't blame her. It's beautiful." Ruxandra walked around the car, pretending to admire the polish on it. "Does she go alone? Or bring friends?"

"Always with friends, miss. Usually folks from the ranch."

"Good to hear." Ruxandra smiled. "I should go back in. Thanks for letting me look."

"Anytime, miss. Anytime."

"Ruxandra!" Dorotyas pounced on her the moment she walked in the door. "Where have you been?"

"Breathing clean air," Ruxandra said. "Where are Kade and Elizabeth?"

"In the dining room, waiting for *you.*"

"Well, we'd hate to keep them waiting, wouldn't we?" She let Dorotyas lead her into the dining room. Kade and Elizabeth sat on either side of a long dark-mahogany table. A pair of women, naked and bearing the marks of a fresh beating, stood beside Elizabeth. Ruxandra stood as far from them as possible. "I don't suppose there's any coffee?"

Elizabeth put on a small, patient smile as if she were talking to a two-year-old. "No, Ruxandra, we don't have coffee."

"But there is an excellent selection of red wine," Kade said, holding up his glass. "Leftovers from the previous owner. Shall I pour you one?"

"No, thanks."

"All of us together," Elizabeth said. "When was the last time this happened?"

"Castle Csejte," Ruxandra said. "Just before King Rudolph broke through the gates."

"Back when you tried to kill us all," Dorotyas said.

"Pity I failed."

"Ruxandra." Kade's voice held a warning. "That was more than three hundred years ago."

"Things are different now," Elizabeth said.

"How?" Ruxandra demanded. "You're an insane, bloodthirsty maniac, Dorotyas is still your lickspittle, and Kade still keeps secrets from everybody. Nothing's changed at all."

"One thing has," Kade said. "I no longer suspect Dorotyas."

"I know." Ruxandra said. "I'm going back to Los Angeles."

"*What?*" Elizabeth's surprise propelled her to her feet. "What do you mean you're going back?"

"I mean that I am hungry, I am tired, and I am in no mood to be lied to or bossed around, so I am going back to Los Angeles. Now."

Elizabeth and Dorotyas just stared in shock. Ruxandra reached the door before Kade caught up to her.

"I thought you *wanted* to be here," he hissed.

"No," Ruxandra said. "*You* wanted to be here. *I* wanted to find the vampire who's sending ghouls into Los Angeles."

"I thought that's why we came here."

Ruxandra took his hand. "Did you know that sound travels faster through earth than through air? Especially if you put your ear to the ground?"

"What?"

She raised his hand to her lip and kissed it, then pushed back the sleeve of his shirt. "Places to go and things to do."

Kade shook his head. "I don't understand."

"I know." Ruxandra dropped his hand and ran off. She looked over her shoulder once and saw him staring at his arm, where she'd scratched: *No radio.*

CHAPTER

FIFTEEN

ALFWAY BACK TO Los Angeles, Ruxandra caught the
scent of men. They stank of unwashed bodies, cheap
whiskey, and harsh tobacco. She tracked the smells to a
hobo camp in a shallow depression near the railway tracks. Seven
men: six drunk and asleep, the seventh awake and alone, radiating pain and anger.

He was older than the others. He had blood on his unshaven
face and fresh bruises. He was in the bushes near the camp mum-
bling and whetting a rusty knife against a grindstone.

"Assholes," he muttered. "Assholes, assholes, assholes. Bastards. Take my booze. Cunts. Cunts, cunts, cunts. I'll show them.
I'll show them all. I'll gut them and cut them and make them
bleed. I'll—"

Ruxandra stepped out of the shadows. "Make who bleed?"

He jumped and swore and turned around. Then he saw her,
and his lips pulled back in a smile showing yellow rotted teeth.
He began fumbling with the front of his pants. "Lady. Gotta love

the ladies. Gotta love them all the time. Come here, lady. Come give me a rub 'n' tug."

Her fangs and talons came out, and his eyes went wide. Then her teeth sunk deep into his throat, his blood gushing into her mouth as he gasped with pain and pleasure. He died with his hand still in his pants.

Ruxandra dropped him and wiped her face. The man had been foul to touch and foul to taste, but he served the purpose. She took his knife, slit his throat and put the blade in his hand. Then she slipped through the hobo camp, stealing the bottle of rotgut out of one sleeping man's arms as she went. She wiped off the bottle and took a long swig, swishing the burning whiskey around to take the foul taste of the man's skin off her lips and tongue before she spat it out.

For the first time in days, her head felt clear.

I wonder if Kade figured it out yet. He was smart and the pieces were there to be put together if he wanted. The problem was that if he was on Elizabeth's side, he might ignore what she had shown him. *Or worse, come after me with them.*

She broke into a run again, eating up the miles between her and Los Angeles.

She reached the city after midnight. The streets were deserted, the only movement from police cars patrolling in pairs, with four officers in each. She sensed anger and fear from each man in the cars. She turned unnoticed and walked through the streets. Men in military uniforms with rifles and machine guns stood at every intersection.

Martial law? What the hell happened last night?

She spotted an officer and slipped up behind him. Two whispered commands got him alone with her. One quick conversation later, she sent him back to his men and headed for the Ambassador Hotel, fury bubbling up inside her.

That stupid, arrogant, self-serving, miserable . . .

Five people had died, all torn apart. Two died in front of police officers, who managed to bring down one attacker by blowing its head off with a shotgun. The opinion going around was that the Mexican underclass had attempted a revolution, and a new drug on the streets was turning them into insanely strong psychopathic killing machines. The mayor asked the governor for National Guard units to help. They had taken the headless body to the morgue to examine it.

If one person in charge believes what they find, everything will be even worse than we had thought.

Housekeeping had made the bed and changed the towels and even folded the clothes she'd left on the floor. She spent a half hour under the shower, rinsing away the dust and dirt and the stink of the hobo and the perfume of terror and death that lingered from Elizabeth's ranch. The last was only a memory, rather than a true scent, but it, too, faded away as the hot water pounded down on her.

She put the plug in the tub and soaked in the bath for an hour. She let her mind relax the way she had learned in Japan, let go of one thought after another until her mind floated, detached from hope and worry, immersed in the unbound experience of consciousness.

As the water turned cold she came back to earth, wrapped a kimono around her body, put her hair in a towel, and sat in the chair in her sitting room. She looked at the map. Griffith Park was surrounded by houses on three sides, plus the river on the west and hills to the north.

The whole park is groomed. There's no easy place to hide anyone. The airfield? Someone would hear the noise inside a hangar. No, it must be underground somewhere. Which means the hills or the river. Tomorrow night, I'll find out which.

The next evening, dressed in her blacks and unnoticed by any human, Ruxandra slipped out and ran to Griffith Park. She opened her senses wide, reaching down as well as around, searching for something—anything—that might lead her to the ghouls. She jogged through the park, sweeping the length and breadth of it five times. The golf course was pristine and well maintained, the airfield quiet and all the hangars closed. No one was in the park, and there was neither sight nor scent of any ghouls.

Of course.

It was one in the morning when she climbed to the top of Mount Hollywood. The moonlight glinted off the river and cast a silver glow over the trees and plants below. She closed her eyes and paid attention with her other senses. Night animals ran through the grasses. The leaves stirred as the wind blew through them. Outside the park, she heard the humans in the nearby houses, talking, making love, or snoring.

She opened her eyes and watched the way the moonlight sparkled against the shallow river. *Every ghoul I've fought used the river one way or another. Last night five ghouls were out and attacking people. In those numbers, they must have left some sign . . .*

An hour later, she found it.

The cave entrance stood two feet high and four wide, hidden by trees and right at the waterline. The ground around it was marshy and beginning to wash away. The cave looked ready to collapse in the next flood. From the outside, it looked hardly big enough to hold a single ghoul, let alone five or ten. But air from deep in the earth had its own scent—of rock and earth and stale stillness. Ruxandra smelled it in the air coming from inside.

A shiver ran down her back, anticipation and dread making her skin tingle and the hair on the back of her neck stand up. She crouched down and slipped inside, staying low to avoid hitting the cave ceiling. The cave sloped down, and the ceiling grew higher the farther she went. She smelled dirty human flesh and rot. Footprints on the ground led out, but none came in. She followed them back to the end of the cave. There, boulders lay piled on top of one another.

"They're stacked."

Ruxandra yelped, jumped, hit her head on the cave ceiling, and spun all in the same moment. Kade walked forward and frowned at her. "We're deeper than I thought if you couldn't hear me coming."

"You think?" Ruxandra rubbed her head. "Why are you here?"

"Looking for you." Kade had to bend farther than Ruxandra and crouched down when he reached the end. "Rocks don't fall like that. Someone stacked those the way farmers stack rocks when they clear a field."

Ruxandra backed away from him. "Why are you here?"

Kade's eyebrows came down and his eyes narrowed. "Why do you think?"

"Not good enough," Ruxandra growled. "Nowhere near good enough. Not after dragging me to Elizabeth's place so she could unleash her monsters on Los Angeles. *Why* are you here?"

Kade sighed. "I got your message."

"It took you a whole day to figure it out?"

"No, it took a whole day to convince Elizabeth to let me come alone to talk to you. She made Mason drive me."

Ruxandra's hackles stood on end again. Anger and panic flared up together in her stomach. "Did you lead him here?"

"He's at the Ambassador. I sensed you in the park just before you went in. How did *you* figure it out?"

"Elizabeth said they heard about the ghouls on the radio. They don't *have* a radio at the apartment. Then Dorotyas made snarky remarks about my being the only one who'd figured out ghouls. That meant she'd figured them out, which meant Elizabeth figured them out, too. Also, one of Dorotyas's perfumes matched the smell on a ghoul. Why should these ghouls destroy your plans?"

Kade's eyes went wide. "That's what you meant about sound carrying through the ground. You heard us talking."

Ruxandra waited.

Kade shrugged. "Dorotyas hates you. She wanted you dead and that seemed a perfect time to try it. And as near as I can tell, Dorotyas's 'love' for Elizabeth is rooted in being a slave vampire. She's jealous and hateful to anyone else getting close."

"Which is why she tried to kill me." Ruxandra sat on the ground, cupping her chin in her hands. "That's why the ghouls kept trying to lead me into the desert and why the ten ghouls attacked me. When Elizabeth figured it out, she fucked Dorotyas front and back with a hot fireplace poker."

"Yes." Kade looked around the small, dark cave. "Now, would you tell me why we're here?"

"Because Mason told me Elizabeth likes to visit the park. With friends."

Kade nodded. "Elizabeth doesn't have friends."

"So chances are this is where she makes her ghouls."

"And behind there?" Kade pointed at the rock pile.

"Is most likely where she keeps them." Ruxandra picked the top rock off the pile and tossed it aside. "Remember you said you needed to feed to keep control of your thralls? How much more did you need to feed to keep control of those ghouls you made in Ireland?"

"Every second day, without fail." Kade stepped beside her and started removing rocks. "It exhausted me. I constantly felt their anger and their hunger. Most of the time I just left them alone."

"Elizabeth feeds at least twice a day, every day."

Realization and a faint horror dawned in Kade's eye. "How many does she have?"

"I don't know." Ruxandra tossed another rock aside. "But if it's as many as I think, it makes sense to put them someplace where she doesn't need to control them when she's not using them."

They cleared the last rocks away, revealing a long, narrow chimney of stone that sank deep into the earth. Ruxandra looked down. "There are handholds."

Kade tried to peer past her. "If you say so."

"Try them yourself." Ruxandra found the first holds on the wall and began descending. "You are coming, aren't you?"

"Oh yes." Kade's voice was grim. "I want to see just how much trouble we're in."

The rock was slippery with moisture, and the handholds were less than an inch deep. If it weren't for vampire strength to grip the rocks, Ruxandra suspected she'd have gone down much faster and probably not in one piece. The darkness grew deeper as they went down. Ruxandra's eyes adjusted, seeing the energy and heat that radiated from inside things rather than visible light. Kade, above her, shone brightest of all, but even the rocks glowed with their own slow, stagnant energy.

They went down well over a hundred feet before the shaft flattened into a low, narrow tunnel. Ruxandra stooped to walk through it. Kade was almost doubled over. He grunted as he grazed his head on the ceiling. "Any chance this is getting wider? Or higher?"

"No. But it branches into two tunnels. Stay together?"

"Yes." They walked on. "I can't sense anything yet."

"There's so much stone around us, I doubt I could sense even Elizabeth before I was on top of her." Ruxandra stood before the left tunnel and sniffed. "I think . . . I'm sure. There's something down this one."

"Something?" asked Kade, coming close behind her. "Or someone?"

"Both, I think," Ruxandra said. "This way."

She sped up, moving unerringly through the tunnel, following the scent of blood and unwashed flesh. Deeper and deeper they went, sometimes crouching, sometimes moving on all fours like animals stalking prey. The tunnel ceiling never rose high enough to allow her to stand upright.

"There're more than one," Kade said. "Lots more."

"I know." Ruxandra heard snarls and hisses somewhere up ahead. The smell of many unwashed bodies and blood and rotting flesh filled her nose. A moment later, she sensed emotions as well: anger and hunger greater than any she had felt before. "How many . . .?"

The tunnel opened up into a huge cavern that rose high above their heads. Its smooth walls spoke of the water that once carved out the stone. Ruxandra stepped out into it and the hisses and growls turned into howls and snarls. She heard scrabbling and the sounds of fingernails tearing as they scraped hard against rock.

A huge pit lay in the cavern ahead of them.

The Beast, still and quiet inside her since she had fed, began to growl in alarm. Ruxandra's talons and fangs came out. Her body tensed, ready to spring at any moment. Behind her, Kade growled in anticipation.

They crept forward. A ledge, only wide enough for one person at a time, circled the pit. The noises from below grew to deafening. Together they reached the edge of it and looked over.

"My God," Kade whispered.

The pit was filled with ghouls.

The walls of the pit went down forty feet, its sides smooth and straight. At the bottom, ghouls clawed and fought with one another to get at them. The ghouls were strong, but not strong enough to dig into the solid rock to pull themselves up. And if any ghoul tried to climb up on the shoulders of the others, the rest pulled it back down.

"How many?" Ruxandra breathed. "I see . . . two hundred . . . something?"

"At least." Disgust laced Kade's words.

"This is insane, Kade." The horror of what she saw made Ruxandra's voice shake. "No wonder Elizabeth and Dorotyas need to feed all the time. No wonder she acted so recklessly. This . . . this is madness. Even for her."

Kade nodded. He looked down at the mass of writhing, fighting bodies. "What's that on the ground?"

Ruxandra walked around the pit, one hand on the wall as she stared down. The ghouls followed her, racing back and forth between her and Kade, desperate to kill them both, unable to reach either. Bones and the dismembered remains of bodies littered the pit floor. The ghouls trampled them as they raced back and forth, unable to decide which vampire they wanted to rip apart more.

"They're all Mexican," Kade said. "Just like the ones on Elizabeth's farm."

"Peasants, Elizabeth called them." Ruxandra's stomach turned at the sheer amount of waste the bodies below represented. "Elizabeth always thought of her peasants as cattle she could slaughter at her whim."

They reached the far side, where another tunnel led off into the darkness. Looking back, Ruxandra saw two tunnels in the direction they had come. "I wonder where that one leads?"

"Nowhere, I think," Kade said. "There's no air movement from it."

"Or from the one behind us." Ruxandra examined the pit walls. "There's no way they can climb out, is there?"

"I don't think so."

"So someone had to come in and let them out."

"Unless they controlled them to make one climb out over the others?" Kade shook his head. "But I don't think anyone could control that many. So how do they get them out?"

"Ladder," Dorotyas said from the other side of the cavern. "You're wrong about the other tunnel. It's where we keep the food supplies . . ." Four Mexican men stumbled out from the other tunnel, their hands against the walls to feel their way forward in the pitch-black cave. All had holes in their necks. "Like them? They're mine. All the men are, except Mason. He's Elizabeth's. She always likes the personal servants to be hers, just to keep them from running away." The Mexican men began walking around toward the edge of the pit, smiles on their faces. "Thralls are so fun, aren't they? These ones think they're living to please me."

"How did you get down here?" Ruxandra demanded.

"Idiot." Dorotyas caressed one man's faces as he went by. "We followed Kade. When he came here, we came here."

Ruxandra's eyes went to Kade, her lips curling back over her fangs.

"I didn't know," Kade said. "I swear."

"Of course *he* didn't know," Dorotyas sneered. "He thinks he's so smart, thinks he knows all of Elizabeth's ideas, thinks he knows everything with his grand plans. Well, Elizabeth has plans, too, and she's smarter than him. Smarter than *either* of you!"

"What are Elizabeth's plans?" Ruxandra asked.

"I'm not stupid!" Dorotyas shouted. "Everyone thinks I'm stupid, but I'm not. I'm not telling you anything!"

"Then why are you here?" Kade asked. "Where's Elizabeth?"

"I'm here because it's feeding time." The four Mexican men reached the edge and stopped. "After all, we can't let our army starve."

"Dorotyas," Ruxandra spoke slowly, as if to an uncomprehending child, "this needs to stop."

"Oh, you'd like that, wouldn't you?" Dorotyas backed away from the pit. "We've got fifty more people in the other cave tied to the walls, eating cold porridge. You going to let them go?"

"How the hell did you get fifty people in here?" Ruxandra demanded. "How did you get this many ghouls in here?"

"Wouldn't you like to know?"

"We would," Kade said. "So tell us."

"Go fuck yourself." The Mexicans stopped moving. The ghouls below ran frantically, bouncing off the pit walls.

"Why do this?" Ruxandra asked. "You can't control all these ghouls. Why make them?"

"Tsk, tsk, tsk." Dorotyas shook her head. Sarcasm oozed from her voice. "You never listen, Ruxandra. Elizabeth told you her plans."

"Things were better before," Elizabeth had said, *"and I think we should make them better again."*

Oh God. Ruxandra looked down at the fighting, slavering ghouls. *She's making an army to terrify the humans and make them kowtow to her wishes.*

"Real fear comes from not knowing," Dorotyas said, triumph in her voice. "Remember? The humans will never figure out how to stop us. All they can do is bow to our wishes and hope we let them survive!"

"No." Ruxandra could imagine the slaughter that would take place. The idea made her sick in a way she hadn't felt since the battlefields of the Great War. "We can't take over the human world. We don't *need* to. We already have everything we need—wealth, abundant prey, and so many luxuries and pleasures that never existed before. The humans made all this. But even if there was a reason to rule them—we can't. There're too many. It won't work!"

"You have no faith in her!" Dorotyas spat the words. "You never have! Well, I believe in her!"

"Dorotyas." Kade's said gently. "Elizabeth can't win. Not like this."

"Shut up." Dorotyas snapped out the words. "She knew you would side with Ruxandra! You always side with Ruxandra!"

"That's not true."

"*Shut up!*" She jabbed a finger toward Ruxandra. "How can you side with that bitch? She's the reason we lost the castle! She's the reason we were forced from our home, and she's the reason Elizabeth did this! She thought she still needed you! Both of you! Well, she doesn't! She doesn't need anyone but me! *Jump!*"

On her command, the four men all jumped forward and into the pits. For a split second, they hung in the air, they flailed in the darkness, terror on their faces. Then the ghouls leaped up, catching them before they hit the ground below. Fangs and claws flashed. The men's screams echoed over the ghoul's howling. The ghouls climbed over one another to reach them, fighting and biting and scratching. Blood sprayed in all directions over the mass of flailing, fighting bodies.

In the split second Ruxandra and Kade were distracted, Dorotyas slid a long ladder from the second tunnel and shoved it over the edge.

"Die here, both of you!" Dorotyas screamed as she ran away. The ladder clattered and slid and wedged against the side of the pit some ten feet below the ledge. The ghouls howled with glee and fury and swarmed up the ladder,

"Run!" Ruxandra raced across the cavern even as the words left her mouth. Kade reached the tunnel before her, his longer legs making up for her head start.

They raced through the tunnels. Kade tried to stay upright, but the low tunnels forced him into a crouching, unnatural run. Ruxandra gave up running like a human and dropped to all fours, bounding with a motion she'd learned in the woods four hundred years before. It wasn't natural, but a hundred years as the Beast made it faster than trying to run upright in the tunnels. They heard Dorotyas racing ahead, but the tunnel's twists and turns kept her out of sight.

Behind them, they heard screams and snarls and scrabbling claws as the ghouls jumped up from the ladder and escaped the pit.

The screech of talon digging into rock replaced the sound of Dorotyas's footsteps as she went up the rock chimney. Kade put on a burst of speed and reached the bottom.

"I wouldn't try it," Elizabeth said from above.

Kade froze. "Elizabeth! What are you doing?"

"Following my plan, of course," she said. "A little earlier than I wanted, but still, *my* plan. Not yours, and certainly not Ruxandra's."

The ghoul's snarls grew louder, and Ruxandra heard the scraping of claws against the tunnel wall and floor.

"You didn't say anything about killing us," shouted Kade.

"Well, Ruxandra didn't say anything about learning my little secret. So I guess we're even."

"Elizabeth, we talked about—"

"You wouldn't stay with me!" Elizabeth screamed. "You didn't trust me, and you wouldn't listen to me, either of you!"

Ruxandra grabbed Kade and hauled him back. Something bounced its way down the rock chimney, its fuse hissing. Then the dynamite went off, the explosion ripped through the tunnels, deafening them both and sending rock and dust flying.

CHAPTER
SIXTEEN

*O*H GOD, *I'm alive.*

Every inch of her body hurt. She felt like a gigantic iron fist had punched a brick wall with her in the middle. She couldn't see at all, and her ears rang loud enough to block out any other sound. The ghouls could be on top of them, and she wouldn't know it. She groped her hands over her body. Dozens of cuts and major bruising covered her, but she wasn't buried under rock. *Which is something close to a miracle.*

The sharp pain in her eyes faded when her sight returned. She blinked, and the stone that had blinded her fell to the ground. Around her, dust whirled and danced in the low, narrow tunnel. The way to the ghoul's pit was still open. *Of course.*

She looked the other way. Kade was bleeding, his chest caved in and one of his arms bent at the wrong angle. His silver blood glowed bright on the dark cave floor.

Beyond him, hundreds of tons of rock blocked their way out. *Shit.*

The ringing in her ears faded. She heard distant howls and screams of pain and terror. Her stomach tightened and her shoulders tensed as she realized what it meant. *The ghouls found the food supplies. Wonder how much time that buys us?*

Ruxandra crawled over to Kade. She shoved him, but he didn't move. She growled under her breath and punched him hard. He grunted. She hit him again. "Get up. Come on. Get up. Now."

He groaned and pushed against the cavern floor with his good arm until he sat up. "*Gott*, that took me back to the war."

Ruxandra shook her head, wincing as the movement sent pain through her skull. "At least in the war, the explosion had someplace to go."

"You weren't there when they mined the German trenches." Kade stretched up, stifling a curse as his ribs crunched back into place. He looked at the rock pile. "Trapped?"

"There were other tunnels," Ruxandra said. "I'm hoping one leads out."

"Trapped, then. Ow." His arm straightened, the bones clacking back together.

"I'd rather not say that until we've tried to get out."

"You think we can?"

"Unless you want to give up and get eaten by ghouls."

"True." He rose to a crouch. "After you."

Ruxandra stayed on all fours. In the low tunnel, it was easier to run like an animal than crouch like a human. Every movement hurt, but became less painful with every second. She would heal soon, and so would Kade.

Which is good, because if we can't get out of here . . .

The screaming grew fainter, the howls and snarls louder as the ghouls fought over the humans.

"They're eating?" Kade asked.

"Yes."

"Good. My hearing is back, and I'm not imagining things. How much longer do you think?"

"Not long enough," Ruxandra said grimly. "So let's find another way out before they swarm us and get a taste of our blood. If that happens, we are in very deep trouble."

She started moving at a loping run. The screams grew louder as she reached the first branch in the tunnels. She took the one that led away from the ghouls. It dead-ended after thirty feet. "Fuck."

"Dead end?"

Ruxandra pushed Kade in the other direction. "Get a wiggle on. We'll try the next one."

The next one turned a corner and stopped ten feet later. Ruxandra punched the stone. "*Cacat cu ochi!* Back!"

Kade backed out. "There's no way out."

"There's that tunnel on the other side of the ghoul pit. It has to go somewhere."

Kade shook his head. "These didn't."

"Well, this one better, because I don't feel like fighting two hundred ghouls today."

The screams stopped. The snarls and howls grew louder and more frantic as the ghouls fought over the bodies. *They're going to come after us sooner rather than later.*

She ran faster, bouncing off the rock walls and feeling the stone abrade her flesh as she charged down the low, narrow tunnel. Kade grunted in pain as he hit the same obstacles. Then the tunnel opened out into the cavern, and the smells of blood and death hit Ruxandra's nose. The howls and snarls of the ghouls fighting were now interspersed with the sounds of bodies hitting walls and teeth tearing flesh as they fought one another.

"Faster!" She pitched her voice for vampire ears. She had no idea if ghouls heard the same way as vampires, but she would try anything to keep them unnoticed for a little longer. She jumped to her feet and raced around the pit. The tunnel on the other side was high enough to run through, and Ruxandra bolted down it.

"There's no air flow," Kade said from behind her.

Ruxandra sniffed the air as she ran. "Shit."

"We should make a stand here."

"Too tall, too wide, too many. Maybe there're more caverns beyond. Maybe we can lose them."

"Unlikely."

The Beast inside her howled, wanting to turn and fight. She clamped down on it. "We're not fighting them here."

She dashed through the tunnel, dropping to all fours where it got low, sprinting when it grew tall enough and squeezing through narrow spots. In one place she used her talons, jammed into the stone, to crawl across the wall when the cavern floor dropped away into a deep pit. She looked down into it as she went, hoping for a way out. A crack ran down one side of it, but stones blocked it up. Ruxandra snarled in fury and kept going. Behind her, she heard Kade pause, then jump and scrabble along the wall with his talons to catch up.

Ten yards farther along, the tunnel stopped dead.

Ruxandra's fist slammed against the wall. "*Phai shaa za mkban!*"

"What language is that?" Kade asked.

"Tibetan." Ruxandra hit the wall again. From far behind them, she heard the scrape of claws across stone and the hissing of ghouls on the move. "*Fuck!*"

"That one I recognized."

Ruxandra jabbed two fingers in the air in a rude gesture older than both of them. "The pit had a crack blocked with rocks. Maybe we can dig our way out there."

"And if not?"

"Then we die here!" Ruxandra snapped. "I'll hold them off, you go look. If there's no way out, we fall back to this side pit and make our stand. If worse comes to worst, we bring the ceiling down on ourselves."

"So they won't get our blood?" Kade frowned. "How bad is it, exactly, when that happens?"

"Imagine one of us," Ruxandra said. "Insane, without thought, without remorse, without anything in its head but to kill and drink."

"Worse than Elizabeth, then?"

Ruxandra couldn't manage a smile at his attempt at humor. She remembered the boy she had turned into a ghoul. Dozens had died while they battled through a village. "Much worse."

Kade turned around and headed back. "Then let's hope that there's an exit to the tunnels down there, because I have no desire to spend eternity buried under a pile of rocks."

They reached the pit, and Kade went down. Ruxandra went over it and forward until she reached a bend in the tunnel. The hissing snarls grew louder with each passing second. She let her fangs and talons come out and felt the Beast inside her, raging for a fight. *Not yet. Not unless there's no choice.*

The snarls turned to howls. The ghouls had their scent.

KILL! The Beast howled inside her head.

Oh, don't worry. We'll definitely do that.

The first ghoul turned the corner.

Ruxandra punched it in the face hard enough to cave in its skull. The creature stumbled back and the others that followed dragged it under. She punched and kicked and clawed as they came around the corner, sending them reeling back or smashing them to the ground. But for every ghoul she stopped, three more pushed forward to get to her, forcing her back inch by inch.

KILL! KILL!

I'm trying! Now shut up!

"I feel air!" Kade shouted. "There's a way through here. I just need to clear it!"

Ruxandra broke a ghoul's leg with a kick, then grabbed its hair and slammed its face onto the tunnel floor. "Well, hurry up!"

The noise of rocks smashing against the wall below filled the tunnel, giving a staccato, arrhythmic backbeat to the snarls and hisses and screams of pain. The ghouls kept pushing, driving her inch by inch back from the bend in the tunnel. They rounded the corner, arms and claws slashing as they tried to reach her. Teeth snapped in the air or gouged into other ghouls' flesh as they fought to get in front. Ruxandra lashed out with fists and talons and stomping boots, trying to slow them down.

KILL, KILL, KILL!

Too many. There're too many. They're going to overwhelm me!

KILL!

She crushed another ghoul's head into mush beneath her boots and dodged back from the snapping teeth of the next one. She shoved two fingers into its eyes and pulled down, ripping the front of its skull off. It fell, and two more squirmed forward to take its place. "Hurry!"

"Just about . . ." There came the sound of rocks and gravel falling. "*Fotze! Deine oma masturbiert im stehen!*"

More rocks flew, and gravel and sand rattled against the walls of the pit. Ruxandra kicked a ghoul in the ribs, crushing its chest. She used her claws to tear open the neck of another one that tried to bite her leg. It cost her another step backward, though. "Fucking hurry!"

"*Ich eile!*"

"*Schneller!*"

Stones rumbled and crashed down. "Got it!"

Two ghouls squirmed forward together, one crawling over the other's back. The one above slashed out with claws, the one below with teeth. Ruxandra grabbed the top one and smashed its head against the head of the one below. "Can we get out?"

"Just a moment!"

She booted the one below, sending it back to be swallowed up by the writhing mass of ghouls behind it. "*Kade!*"

"Twenty-foot drop! Big cavern! Tunnels!"

"*Go!*"

Kade went, his talons screeching against the rock as he pushed through. Ruxandra threw a kick that spattered the closest ghoul's brains over the ones behind it and jumped for the pit. The Beast roared, wanting to fight. Ruxandra heard Kade land far below, barely audible over the frustrated howls above. Ruxandra hit the bottom of the pit and dove through the opening. She bounced off an outcropping of rock and fell, landing on all fours and spitting like an angry cat. Above, the ghouls began fighting for space to get through.

"This way!" Kade ran across the cavern and through a tunnel. "Fresh air!"

The first ghoul hit the ground behind them. Ruxandra gritted her teeth and sprinted after Kade, leaving the creature behind.

The tunnel went on and on through the darkness, sloping down and up, twisting back and forward and never quite straightening out or giving them a chance to move at full speed. Half a dozen tunnels sloped off it, but Kade ignored them, charging straight ahead. Ruxandra dogged his heels, keeping her ears wide open but not looking back. The ghouls fell behind, but they still came on, howling as they gave chase.

"There!" Kade shouted.

Ruxandra looked past him. The tunnel widened and the top rose high enough for them to stand upright. At the far end of it, almost completely blocked by a wall of vegetation, Ruxandra saw the cold light of the night sky.

They sprinted across the cavern, ripped through the foliage, and stepped out into a low gully.

And into a hail of gunfire.

A dozen rounds smashed into them. Silver blood spurted and flew as the bullets ripped flesh and cracked bone. Both yelped in pain and dove to get away, scrabbling for cover where there wasn't any. Any plant life taller than the dry, scrubby grasses had been ripped out long before, leaving scars in the earth. Ruxandra changed direction, preparing to charge the gunman.

"You stay there a moment," Mason said. "We need to talk."

He stood twenty yards away at the top of the gully, holding a Thompson submachine gun. Beyond him were more hills and scrub-covered ground. A quick glance behind showed the same. Ruxandra's eyes went to the gun. She'd seen Thompsons in the trenches at the end of the war—the ammunition drum held a hundred rounds. The bullets wouldn't kill her, but they would hurt like hell and slow her down. And given what was behind them, she had no desire to be slowed down.

Kade rose to his feet, growling, "You need to die."

Mason pointed the submachine gun at him. "Elizabeth has messages for you two. Said I should tell you before you do anything else. Gave me this to make sure you would listen. Are you listening?"

"Mason." Ruxandra tried to keep her voice steady. "There are ghouls after us. Lots and lots of ghouls. We need to block off the cave and get out of here."

"But you can't, dear." Mason's voice changed timbre and cadence, his posture shifting, becoming more languid. "I made sure of that when we dug it out."

Ruxandra frowned. "Elizabeth?"

"Speaking through my thrall. Neat trick, isn't it?"

"Elizabeth, what the *fuck*—"

"Shut up, Ruxandra!" Mason screamed. "Just shut up! You *betrayed* me! You left me! You always leave me, and you always ruin everything when you go! So you just shut up!"

"Elizabeth, stop!" Kade started up the hill, stopping a moment later when Mason raised the Thompson. "Do you know what's going to happen when the ghouls get loose?"

"Oh, I know," Mason said in Elizabeth's tones. "I planned it. I wanted a hundred more, but I realized I could barely keep sane holding on to this many. Dorotyas and I feed twice a day, just to keep them quiet in our heads, and when we want to control some, well, that requires a bit more feeding. Fortunately, no one misses the ones we take."

"You need to stop them, Elizabeth."

"There're too many. That's the point. All I can do is guide them, let them know where to find you two. Or where the best prey is." Mason shook his head, the movement a near-perfect imitation of Elizabeth. "No, I'm afraid events are now in motion, and there's nothing you can do to stop them."

Kade began swearing in low, guttural German.

"Tut-tut, Kade." Mason shook a finger. "You had your chance to join us, and you didn't take it. Now you must deal with the consequences."

"If I get the machine gun from him," Kade said, "I can kill twenty or thirty."

"You won't, dear," Mason said. "Besides, you and Ruxandra have a much larger problem."

"What is that?" Ruxandra asked.

"That isn't the only exit."

Ruxandra's stomach dropped. She realized the growling wasn't just from the cave but from woods all around them. *Oh, crap.*

"I'm going to go. You can eat Mason, if you need a snack. I'm done with him and don't want to feel what happens to him when the ghouls get him." He smiled. "But first . . ."

Mason pointed the Thompson at Kade and let it rip. Kade dodged and zigzagged, but bullets still managed to pierce his flesh, their force sending him sprawling. Ruxandra ran up the hill, grabbing for the weapon. Mason turned it on her and four rounds slammed through her belly and out her back before the magazine went dry with a loud click. Ruxandra shoved Mason, sending him sprawling. Her stomach burned red. The Beast screamed for his blood. It would have killed Mason on the spot save that Ruxandra pushed him out of reach. She fell to her knees, groaning as her flesh healed.

The growling turned into howls as the ghouls caught the scent of their blood.

Ruxandra stood up, ignoring the burning in her stomach. "Kade?"

"I'm fine! I just need a second."

"Well, that's all you've got, so hurry up."

"Oh God." Ruxandra turned back. Mason fell to his hands and knees, his eyes wide and staring. He scrambled backward. "What did she make me do?"

"Nothing!" Ruxandra snarled. "Get a hold of yourself."

"Those girls . . . all those girls." Mason buried his face in the dirt and started pounding at his own skull with his fists.

"Shit." Ruxandra closed the distance between them in seconds. She grabbed him by the scruff of the neck and pulled him up. "You need to get out of here, all right? You need to warn people."

Mason shook his head. "That woman! She made me do things for her. She made me . . ." Tears filled his eyes. He threw his head back and howled in despair and grief.

And then the ghouls came.

They charged from all directions, rolling over the hills in waves of death. They moved at a stumbling animal run. Their red eyes shone with hatred and hunger. Blood stained their jagged fangs and long nails, and spatters of it covered their clothes. The males wore the white pants and shirts of Mexican peasants or the coveralls of working men. The women wore long dresses and once-colorful blouses. Their hair had once been hung in long, silky streamers, hairpins still tangled in their tresses. All their clothes were filthy and ragged. The ghouls looked emaciated, as if they had gone far too long without feeding. She felt the rage consuming them, and their hunger, greater than even their anger.

Then they charged. Mason disappeared beneath the wall of flesh. Ruxandra barely heard his screams before the ghouls surrounded them and the Beast howled and her world became a whirling mess of slashing claws and snapping teeth. Kade jumped away out of sight.

KILL!

Ruxandra spun, whirling like the kung fu master she'd met in Xaimen, her talons moving like his swords. Blood and flesh tore away from the ghouls' bodies as they screamed in agony. Other ghouls shoved past them, their own claws out and tearing. One laid a hand on her, tried to drag her forward to its mouth to sink teeth into her flesh. She tore her arm from his grip and leaped. Ghouls grabbed at her legs and gouged her flesh as she flew.

In the split second she flew through the air, she saw Kade standing on the top of a hill, fifty ghouls around him. His jacket and shirt were already rent open. He fought with cold efficiency, not a single wasted motion as he forced them back, only to have more charge in each time.

DIE?

A fear that wasn't hers rose inside Ruxandra. Terror filled the Beast, doubling its fury. Ruxandra felt it struggling for control of her limbs, trying to take over and destroy all the threats that surrounded her. She fought it back even as she landed feet first on the head of one of the ghouls. One jumped at her face, spit flying from its mouth as it howled and tried to dig its claws into her head. Another dove for her legs, hands grasping and teeth snapping. She dodged them both and managed to spin away from a third trying to grab at her arms.

STOP, STOP, STOP! KILL!

Each time she tried for a finishing blow, to get close enough to tear off a head or smash open a skull, three other ghouls would attack, driving her back. Again and again, she tried it, and each time another ghoul got in the way. In desperation, she jumped again, aiming for Kade. The ghouls bounded after. She landed on another one, smashing it to the ground with a crunch of bones. She speared one ghoul in the throat, trying to take its head off. It stumbled back and two more drove in.

"This won't work," Kade shouted as he threw a ghoul fifty feet and broke the leg of another one with a hard kick. "There're too many!"

NO DIE, NO DIE, NO DIE!

Shut up! She ripped the throat out of one ghoul, stove in the chest of another, and cracked open the skull of a third. A set of teeth just missed her fingers, and claws raked open her arms as she attacked.

NO DIE!

"We need to get out of here!" Kade shouted.

"We can't!" Ruxandra caught a reaching ghoul's arm, slashed out with her talons, and pulled. The ghoul's arm tore apart at the elbow. The creature screamed and swung its other hand. She blocked and booted it backward. "If we leave, the ghouls go into Los Angeles!"

"If we don't, they'll kill us!"

NO DIE!

Fuck off!

The distraction was enough to let a ghoul get through her guard and slash open her face. The claws scored deep. Silver blood spattered over the closest ghouls. All the others caught the scent and went into a frenzy.

NO DIE, NO DIE, NO DIE, KILL, KILL, KILL!

"Ruxandra, stay with it!" Kade screamed. He smashed the face of a ghoul charging her and kicked away another. "That hill to the east! Jump!"

They jumped, sailing over the crowd around them and landing on top of another hill. Both their clothes were in tatters now, and Ruxandra's face burned where the ghoul's claws had dug in. A hundred ghouls swarmed up the hill after them.

A hundred? Where are . . .

She saw them. A swarming pack of howling death running over the hills west toward the city lights of Los Angeles only a few miles away.

"Oh, fuck." The words came out as a whisper. "Kade, they're heading for the city. We have to stop them"

"How?" Kade demanded. "We can't get away long enough to do anything."

Ruxandra looked at the swarm of ghouls charging up the hill "We can if you go."

"What?"

"You go. I stay." She ran forward and kicked the first ghoul to crest the hill hard enough to send it flying. "Get to the city. Warn them."

"You'll die."

NO DIE! NO DIE, NO DIE, NO DIE!

Ruxandra sent another ghoul tumbling down the hill with a boot to the chest. "I won't."

Kade caught another ghoul and tore its head off. The thing collapsed to the ground, dead. "You can't fight them all!"

"*I* won't be fighting," Ruxandra snarled. "Go warn the humans!"

"But—"

"Go!"

Kade glared but jumped away. Ruxandra slashed open her own arm with her talons, sending out a fresh spray of silver blood, dragging the ghouls' attention away from Kade and back to her.

NO DIE!

No dying. Please, no dying. Fear, stronger than any she'd felt in years rose inside her. Her stomach clenched and her hands shook even as they smashed into the nearest ghoul's face.

NO DIE, NO DIE, NO DIE! The Beast screamed in a pathetic, continuous chant. The Beast fought harder and harder to escape the cage of her will. The ghouls crested the hill on all sides now. They charged forward, claws slashing and teeth bared, ready to sink into her flesh.

Please let me come back from this.

Then Ruxandra wasn't there anymore. In her place, wearing her skin and baring her fangs, was the Beast.

KILL.

CHAPTER

SEVENTEEN

T HE BEAST HIT the ground, its body changing shape as
it took control. Its arms grew longer, its legs shortened,
its neck shifted, and it became an animal once more.
The Things closed in.

BAD! WRONG!

The Beast roared. The things didn't shy away. They didn't run.
They didn't smell like fear. They smelled like blood and rotten
meat, like prey that lay still on the forest floor, insects crawling
out of it.

DEAD.

A shiver ran through the Beast. It knew these things. It had
faced them a hundred years ago. They had attacked the Woman
who kept the Beast imprisoned, and had frightened her enough
that the Beast got free. The Beast grinned even as it snarled.
The last time, the Beast ran free for days before the Woman got
control again.

The Beast bared its fangs and leaped on the closest Thing,
sinking its teeth into its throat. The flesh tore away from the

Thing's throat in a spray of blood. It spat the mouthful at the next one. The second Thing didn't blink, didn't flinch as blood and rotting flesh splashed it. The first Thing still tried to grab the Beast, tried to slash it with its claws.

WRONG! BAD!

The Beast jumped off the Thing, hit the ground and leaped away. It landed on the slope behind another Thing and pounced. The Beast's claws ripped out the Thing's hamstrings. Its teeth sank into the Thing's neck. Bones crunched in its mouth. The Beast sank claws into either side of the Thing's head and pulled as it twisted the spine out with its teeth. The head ripped off.

The Thing collapsed.

THING, DIE!

The Things on the hill ran up behind the Beast. It leaped again trying to put distance between them. The Things chased after it, howling and snarling. The Beast didn't snarl back. Snarls were warning. Snarls said stay back. The Things didn't listen.

THINGS STUPID. THINGS SLOW.

THINGS DIE.

ALL THINGS DIE.

KILL ALL.

KILL!

The Beast laughed and jumped away from the Things.

JUMPING WRONG.

FEET WRONG.

Thick dead skins wrapped the Beast's feet. It leaped high in the air and hacked the skins off with its claws. They fell away. Talons came out of its toes and dug into the earth when it landed. The Beast howled victory. It jumped onto a Thing, back claws ripping open the middle of it, sticking into its pelvis. Front claws stabbed through its throat. It pushed off the ghoul's body and pulled at the same time. The Thing's head ripped off with a wet tearing and a spout of black-red blood. The Beast tossed it away, spun, and landed on another Thing's shoulders. Back claws into shoulders. Front claws into neck. Jump. Rip.

DIE!

The Beast landed. A Thing jumped on it, claws cutting into its skin. The Beast rolled and spun in the dirt, tearing the Thing off. Two more came. It batted them out of the air, claws ripping out one's eyes, tearing off another's jaw. The Things screamed in pain.

TOO MANY, TOO MANY, MUST KILL.

Leap again. Land again. Kill again. Leap again.

RUN, CIRCLE, RUN.

The Beast took off. The Things roared and charged. The Beast dodged and darted between them. Its teeth sank into ankles and hamstrings. Its claws ripped through legs. Things tried to grab, tried to hold. Claws ripped into its flesh, and pain flared along its back. The Beast snarled and kept moving, up to the top of a hill and down the other side.

It ran around the hill, behind the crowd of Things running for the top. It caught one at the back, tore its head off. The Beast used its falling body as a springboard to grab the next. The Things chased, howling and screaming. The Beast howled back and dove into another ravine.

The sun was coming.

SUN BAD.

The Beast smelled the heat touching the land. It could see the first lights in the sky. The Things saw it, too. They began to scatter, running away from the Beast. It followed, snapping at their heels. The Beast caught the slow ones, crippling them with teeth and claws and tearing off their heads.

The Things ran into the gully, fought to get into the caves. The Beast attacked from behind, killing more and more. Each time it got one, they all turned to fight. It would jump away, and they'd run back to the cave. More and more bodies piled up outside until the sun broke the edge of the horizon.

SUNLIGHT BAD. LIGHT HURT. HIDE.

The Beast ran away from the Things, away from the sun. It found a gully and dug a cave in the dirt of one side. It made a long curved tunnel so no light could come in, digging deep into the hill to a place where the sun's heat wouldn't touch. It hollowed out a space for its body, shoving the dirt back along the tunnel, blocking up the entrance so no Things could follow. Then the Beast curled up in a ball and closed its eyes.

Somewhere deep inside the Beast, the Woman called to it, telling it to listen, to let go and relax. The Beast snarled at the voice.

WON'T. WON'T GO. WON'T SLEEP. STAY.
STAY!

Night.

The Beast had not slept at all. Every time it wanted to relax, to close its eyes, it heard the Woman's voice calling it to give up and go back to its cage. The Beast snarled and clawed at the dirt, refusing to sleep, refusing to let go.

When it felt the sun sink below the horizon, the Beast dug out from its cave, sniffing the air and listening, but it sensed no threats nearby. It slid, stretched, and shook off the dirt. It still had the cloth on that the Woman had worn. With a hiss, it ripped at the fabric until the cloth shredded away and it felt the warm evening breeze over its skin. The Beast shook again and stretched and howled its presence, daring anything to challenge it.

HUNGRY.

HUNT.

The Beast breathed deeply, smelling small animals nearby emerging from their day burrows to seek seeds and grasses. It sniffed again and smelled the Things.

THINGS BAD.

THINGS DIE.

KILL THINGS.

HUNT.

The Beast went to the Things' cave and found footprints and scent, fresh but not new. It followed them over the hills, across the dry ground. The Beast didn't like the hills here; too few trees, too little cover. Not enough food for an easy kill and a quick meal. No other predators to fight.

WANT FOREST.

KILL THINGS.

FIND FOREST.

The Beast ran, hands and feet hitting the ground in long bounding strides that covered ground faster than anything on two legs. The Things' stench covered the ground. Their footprints crushed the bushes and left trails through the dirt. The Beast couldn't smell them on the air yet, but it knew it would soon.

Instead, it smelled humans. Many humans. It smelled wood and foul burning smells, sharp and tangy and harsh. The Beast went over a hill and screeched to a stop. The sky was bright with the lights of the city. In places the Beast saw flashes, and in the distance it heard popping sounds. It ran closer and heard humans screaming and Things snarling and growling.

The Beast howled out a challenge, its voice echoing for miles. The Things didn't howl back. It kept running, heading toward the loudest screams. The popping noises grew louder. Something even noisier sounded a rapid bang-bang-bang-bang-bang-bang-bang. The scent, sharp and acrid, burned the Beast's nostrils.

GUNS.

The Beast knew guns. Knew guns hurt. Knew it should stay away. But the Things were killing its prey. The Things were not allowed to kill the Beast's prey.

KILL ALL THINGS.

The Beast left behind the dirt of the hills, running on the foul-smelling solid stuff, like rock but wrong, which covered the streets where the humans lived. No humans were in the streets. No Things were in sight, but it smelled them. The Things were in the bright places, where humans put their lights to hide from the night. The Beast ran faster.

"Ruxandra!"

The Beast spun. The Man stood there. The one the Woman fucked. He smelled of Things and blood and death. The Beast crouched low and snarled.

"Ruxandra?" The Man sounded less certain. "Are you in there?"

The Beast had a long memory. It remembered the hundred years it ran in the forest, remembered every time it broke free, and remembered the time when it had killed three Things in the woods.

Those Things smelled like the Man.

Now this Man smelled of the Things.

DIE!

The Beast roared and charged.

"*Scheisse!*" The Man moved as fast as the Beast, caught it and spun, sending it flying. The Beast landed on all fours and sprang again.

"Ruxandra, stop!" The Man dropped into a crouch. Teeth and talons came out. The Beast roared out its challenge and charged once more. The Man tried to attack, but the Beast clawed and slashed with front legs and back and sank teeth into his arm. The Man bellowed and twisted and smashed the Beast into the ground. It let go, leaped again, and scored more slashes into his flesh.

"Ruxandra! Listen!"

Please, listen, came the Woman's voice from inside the Beast's head. The Beast ignored her. The Woman wanted to imprison the Beast again.

"The ghouls!" the Man shouted. "You need to hunt the ghouls!"

The Beast's back claws ripped open his belly. Its front claws tore open his arms. It climbed him, mouth wide to sink teeth into his face.

The Man hit it harder than any Thing, harder than the bear it once fought. His fist smashed against the Beast's face, blinding one eye. It landed in a heap, screaming in pain.

KILL, KILL, KILL!

But the Man ran fast away. The Beast followed, the pain of its healing face making it yelp with each jolt even as it added to its fury. The Beast ran faster and almost caught him. He kept changing directions, kept dodging between the humans' tall houses and the metal squares sitting in the long, hard path. The Man ran toward the guns. The Beast heard the Things roar and howl and snarl and humans screaming in pain as they fought. The Man sprinted around the corner, and the Beast put on another burst of speed, trying to catch him.

It ran around the corner and straight into a pack of the Things.

The Man jumped away, springing high up to the roof of the nearest building and disappearing from sight. The Things descended on the Beast, snarling and snapping. The Beast howled and leaped at the nearest one.

KILL MAN LATER.

KILL THINGS.

KILL ALL THINGS.

Half the Things attacked the Beast. The others fought the humans and their guns. Many humans in brown cloth fired at the Things. Some Things fell, but most howled and kept going, tearing into the humans and drinking them. On a big metal box, two humans used the noisy gun.

Bang-bang-bang-bang-bang-bang-bang-bang-bang-bang-bang-bang-bang-bang-bang-bang-bang-bang.

Everywhere the noisy gun hit, the Things screamed. The noisy gun shot through their bodies and broke their legs, making them easy prey. The Beast danced through the pack. It tore the heads off the wounded, dodged the ones trying to fight, and ran circles around them all. It bounced off the big houses on either side, using the walls to spring it again and again into the pack of Things.

A bullet tore and burned through the Beast's shoulder. It screamed and tumbled to the ground. The Things piled on, biting and clawing. The Beast screamed louder and thrashed in panic. Its claws moved faster than any Thing could manage, tearing out guts and ripping off arms and faces until it scrambled to its feet. It scuttled out of the pile, leaped on one of the smaller boxes of steel, and dove at the human who shot it. He raised his weapon again, but the Beast leaped before he used it. The first swipe of its claws took off one of his hands; the next ripped open his face. It grabbed his head, sank its teeth into his neck.

Bang-bang-bang-bang-bang-bang-bang-bang-bang-bang-bang-bang.

HURT!

The Beast screamed again and jumped away from the dying human. The big gun hurt was much worse than the small guns. This gun blew holes into the Beast's body and broke two ribs. The six with the smaller guns fired too, the smaller bullets tracing lines of fire on the Beast's arms and legs. One bullet smashed into its face, tearing open its cheek and smashing two teeth. The Beast screeched and leaped back, ready to attack again.

The Things got there first.

The man on the big gun died screaming as three Things swarmed over him, teeth sinking into his throat. The other humans shot their guns and stabbed with knives but the Things kept coming. Blood spattered everywhere, and humans screamed and died.

RUN! HIDE!

The Beast jumped onto a wall, claws digging into the joints between the small rocks as it scaled the building. It cowered on the rooftop behind a tall, warm stack of rocks. The Beast writhed on the ground, crying as its body pushed out the bullets and healed its wounds. It howled in agony as the teeth grew back and shoved through its gums.

When the pain ended, the Beast gasped in relief. It rose on its haunches and growled, low and long.

KILL.

PAIN!

Something hard and sharp hit the back of its head. The Beast spun around just in time to see the Man that smelled of Things throw a second rock from the next roof. The Beast charged and leaped. The Man jumped to the next roof over. The Beast followed, roof after roof, until the Man jumped down to the streets.

The Beast leaped after him straight into a pack of the Things.

The Man landed on one, smashing its bones and flattening it, then jumped away. All the Things attacked the Beast. It roared and fought, dodging them, jumping from one to the next, tearing off heads whenever it had a moment long enough. The Things died one by one, and the Beast howled with delight.

Then the Things all ran.

They took different directions, spreading out and vanishing among the buildings. The Beast chased down the closest one, cut out its hamstrings and ripped off its head. The next one turned to fight, and the Beast chewed through its neck until the head popped off.

Bang-bang-bang-bang-bang-bang-bang-bang-bang.

The Beast spun, ducked, and dove across the street as another big gun opened fire. Bullets ripped into the ground and the buildings, but none touched it. It leaped up to the nearest roof, then across the others toward the noise. It found a dozen men around a truck with the big gun mounted on the back.

Don't, the Woman begged from inside the Beast's head. *Don't kill them. Kill the ghouls. Don't touch the humans.*

QUIET!

The Beast dropped on the men like an angry god of death. Blood covered the streets as it tore off limbs and ripped through intestines, killing one after the other before they could turn around. The Woman screamed at it to stop. The Beast ignored her, reveling in the humans' screams and the scent of their blood. It sank its teeth into the last man's throat, draining half his blood in less than five heartbeats.

Then another pack of Things came around the corner and the fight began all over again.

The Beast hunted up and down streets and across the rooftops, killing Thing and human alike. Every time it stopped, the Man would appear, throwing stones and leading it to more Things. Each time the Beast drove through them like a starving wolf through a pen of rabbits, slaughtering as many as possible before the men turned their guns on it. Then once more, the Beast went after the men.

Halfway through the night, the fires started.

The Beast was stalking a pack through the street, slashing at legs and taking heads, when the Things shifted their direction, jumping and smashing through the windows of a building. The Beast followed, slashing the ones caught, chasing the others through doors and upstairs, slaughtering them one after the other, leaving the building dripping with the blood of Things and humans.

It reached the fourth floor when it smelled the smoke.

FIRE!

The Beast ran back down. Humans crowded the stairs, struggling to flee the Things. The Beast bowled them over; ignoring the screams of pain and cracks of bones as some tumbled down the steps. Flames rose from below. It turned and ran back, bouncing off walls, scaling the outside of the banisters and once shoving off a human's head. The human hit the wall with a crunch, and fell to the ground. The Beast reached the top floor and found an open door and a woman screaming as a Thing tore out the throat of a little boy in front of her. The Beast bounded around them all and raced for the window. It hurled its body through the glass, knowing it would hurt and knowing it had no choice.

The Beast plummeted down into a waiting mass of Things below.

They attacked the moment the Beast hit the ground. Two dove at it legs, claws and fangs snapping. Two more went for its body. The Beast jumped above the first two, slashed at the second pair. Blood spattered, and the Things screamed, and another one hit the Beast from behind, knocking it out of the air. The Beast howled and spun, taking off the Thing's face as it fell, rolled, and jumped up on its feet again. Three more Things charged from the front, one from each side and two from behind. The others faded back, forming a ring to keep it from escaping.

NOT THINGS!

They smelled like Things. They moved like Things. But the Things did not fight like that.

The Beast jumped high. From the building across the street, another Thing dropped, matching its jump and smashing into it in midair. It plummeted down, spinning as it did, so the Thing hit the ground first. The Beast bolted, heading for what looked like a gap in the circle.

A barrel filled with burning wood smashed down in front of the Beast, making it jump sideways into three waiting Things. They fell on the Beast, and for the first time, teeth dug into its flesh. The Beast grabbed a Thing's neck and spun its head backward. The neck snapped with a noise like twigs wrapped in moss, and the Thing collapsed in a heap on the ground. The other Things tried to bite, too, but it ripped off both their jaws and ran again.

THINGS FIGHT WRONG.

It's Dorotyas and Elizabeth, the Woman said. *They're controlling the ghouls.*

PACK LEADER?

NOT THINGS.

WOLVES.

The Beast knew about wolves. It fought them a dozen times in the woods. They operated as a single creature, working together to force their prey down. They had patterns and plans and made events happen as they wanted. These Things were acting like wolves. Even if they still looked like Things.

KILL THING-WOLVES.

The Beast turned back, leaped over the burning barrel, and ran straight through the Thing-Wolves. They attacked from four sides. The Beast changed directions, jumping and spinning and grabbing the head of one behind. It ripped the Thing's head from its shoulders with a spray of blood and a howl of delight. The Beast landed, jumped again, and attacked another. Every time they pushed it in a direction, the Beast went the other way. Every time the Things left an opening, it attacked the thickest crowd instead.

By the time the Things broke and ran, their dead covered the street.

The Beast howled and chased. Three more times they tried ambushes, but now the Beast knew what to expect. It ran into the traps, howling with glee as it slaughtered.

The fourth time, the Things led it to the big human guns.

Bang-bang-bang-bang-bang-bang-bang-bang-bang.

Bang-bang-bang-bang-bang-bang-bang-bang-bang.

Bang-bang-bang-bang-bang-bang-bang-bang-bang.

Bang-bang-bang-bang-bang-bang-bang-bang-bang.

Bang-bang-bang-bang-bang-bang-bang-bang-bang.

The Things fell to the ground, writhing as big bullets from the five loud guns smashed into them. The Beast dashed away, zigzagging and ducking as the bullets stitched holes into the walls and ground. It ducked away from the men, away from the noise, and right into another pack of Things.

KILL, KILL, KILL!

These were not Wolf-Things. They used no plans or tactics, only fury and brute force. The Things and the Beast fought with the pure animal hatred of a pack of hyenas facing a lion. Teeth flashed and snapped, claws ripped and tore. Blood and intestines spilled out and limbs flew off screaming Things as the Beast tore into them. One by one, it ripped and clawed and chewed their heads from their bodies.

SUN!

The Beast sensed it coming, smelled it coming. It saw the light in the sky and knew it had to get away. It needed to find shelter and food and a place where humans wouldn't look for it.

Go to the docks, whispered the Woman. *Find a warehouse. Hide until morning.*

HUNGRY!

The Beast felt the need gnawing at its insides. It wanted blood and it wanted it *now*. The Beast ran hard, heading away from the smaller, squalid dwellings to the larger houses on the hill.

No! Stay away! Stay away from people!

The Beast grinned. It knew how to hunt humans, though it rarely had the chance. It also knew that the more isolated the house, the easier to find prey.

Stay away!

It found a house standing alone inside a large fence. The Beast jumped it with little effort, killed the two barking dogs in less than a second, and charged. It smashed through a window on the main floor, ignoring the glass slashing open its skin. Above, the Beast heard panicked voices and shouts. It raced up the stairs, down the soft hallway. A door opened, and a man stepped out, a small gun in his hand. The Beast slashed open his arm and leaped on him, burying its teeth in his throat. Behind him, a woman screamed. The Beast ignored her and drank until the man's blood went dry.

Enough! The Woman inside screamed. *Stop it! Don't kill anyone else.*

The Beast dropped the body and crossed the room in an eye blink, burying its teeth deep in the woman's throat.

Stop it! Stop it! You don't need that much!

"Mommy? *Mommy!*" Small footsteps dashed across the room, small hands grabbed it, trying to pull it away.

Enough. Please, enough.

The Beast drank the woman's blood. Then it grabbed the small one and dragged it close.

STOP IT! The Woman's screams reverberated through the Beast's skull. *YOU HAVE TO STOP IT! STOP IT!*

The Beast howled and sank its teeth into the small one's neck, drinking until there was nothing left.

It stumbled down into a dark room, deeper underground than any other in the house, with large racks of bottles lining the walls.

KILLED.

HUNTED.

GOOD.

ALL GOOD.

TOMORROW.

MORE.

The Beast stretched, yawned, and closed its eyes. It curled into a ball, hands on forearms, comfortable in the cool darkness.

TOMORROW HUNT.

TOMORROW KILL MAN.

KILL MORE THINGS.

TOMORROW.

The Beast laid its head down and closed its eyes. Sleep stole slowly over it, like a warm blanket, and it let consciousness slip away.

"Got you, bitch," Ruxandra said.

CHAPTER
EIGHTEEN

THE TWO OF THEM fought for control in her head when Ruxandra woke up.

The Beast never went away quietly. Every time it ran free, it took days before it went silent again. And right now, the Beast was furious. It wanted out. It roared and howled and snarled so much that Ruxandra couldn't hear her own thoughts. The Beast still wanted to fight and kill and hunt down everything that moved.

Ruxandra pressed her hands hard against her head, trying to shut out the noise.

KILL!

Shut up. Ruxandra curled tight into a ball against the wine cellar wall. *Just shut up and go away.*

Ruxandra remembered everything the Beast had done in the last two days. She always remembered what the Beast did. It made some days far, far worse than others.

Blood and offal covered Ruxandra from head to foot. The smell of it made her feel ill. She'd killed twenty-seven soldiers in the street battles—young men, all of them. None had seen the Great War or a battlefield or fired a shot in anger. Instead, they died fighting monsters.

She could smell smoke still on her as well.

In the burning building, she'd crushed an old man's skull against the wall, his brains spattering out as she used him as a springboard. She'd sent three old women tumbling headfirst down the stairs. She had heard the crunch of broken vertebrae, the sharp snap of an arm and a leg breaking, and the hollow crack of a fractured pelvis. The sound echoed in her head, along with the screams of the ones the ghouls had slaughtered.

How many died in that fire?

The Beast had run right past the woman and the child in the apartment, leaving them to the ghouls. Ruxandra hadn't even controlled the Beast enough to make it kill the ghoul before it jumped out the window. She'd heard what happened, though; heard the child's flesh ripping as she'd jumped, heard the mother's desperate, horrified screams as the ghoul tore her child in two before her.

Ruxandra's eyes filled with tears. Her body shook with sobs.

I shouldn't be like this. None of us should be like this. None of us should kill the innocent. None of us should kill children. Oh God. The child.

She ground her face against the floor, trying to escape the sights and screams that filled her mind. She had killed innocents before throughout the centuries but never children. She'd made the rule centuries ago, when she first regained her mind.

I should have made the Beast stop.

Ruxandra curled up tighter. She just wanted to sit in the dark and not move for a very, very long time. But ghouls still ran through the streets killing and causing chaos.

The Beast howled for blood and death.

Shut up. Fuck off. Die.

She extended her mind outward and found no one else alive in the house. It gave Ruxandra a moment of relief. She had no idea what she'd do if she found another child in the home. She rose unsteadily on her bare feet, upright for the first time in three days. She walked up the stairs clinging to the banister as her body reshaped to move like a human instead of an animal.

The clean, tidy kitchen had striped dishcloths hanging to dry on a wooden rack and a bowl of oranges on the counter. The sitting room looked neat and well appointed, made cozy by scatter rugs on the polished wood floor, with an overstuffed floral-patterned couch and armchairs. A child's drawing of ships on the ocean hung framed on the wall. The banisters and steps up were immaculate. The upstairs hallway was dusted and swept and tidy. The furnishings, draperies, and decorative objects throughout the house spoke of care and attention to detail and a great love for their home.

I wonder if she had a maid. God, I hope there isn't a maid. I hope it's her day off.

The bedroom on the top floor had surprisingly little mess in it.

The largest pool of blood had spurted from the man's arm after the Beast—*after I*—slashed him open. He lay on the floor beside it, arms and legs akimbo, empty eyes staring into the sky, face still contorted with fear. His wife lay on the bed, the same look of terror on her face. And the small one . . .

The child, Ruxandra corrected. *Their son. I murdered him.*

She found him in the corner below a dent in the wall where she'd thrown him. He looked asleep save for the angle of his neck and the wide-open eyes in the small, angry, terrified face.

Ruxandra wept again and kept weeping the entire time it took to straighten up the room. She put the parents in the bed first, side by side. She picked up the boy and laid him between them as if he had crawled in to sleep there. She pulled up the white sheets over them, covered them all with a thin, silk-edged yellow blanket, and wiped her face. Then she searched the room, finding matches and cigarettes and a bronze ashtray. She dropped the ashtray on the floor beside the curtains. She lit a cigarette and smoked half of it. Then she put the remaining half, still glowing, in between the father's fingers.

Then she picked up the matches and, one thing at a time, lit the room on fire.

The cotton curtains went first, the bedside rug next, then the bedclothes. Then she stood in the doorway and watched as the flames spread up and out.

FIRE! FIRE, FIRE, FIRE!

The Beast's panic rose with the flames. Ruxandra's legs quivered with the desperate urge to run. She refused to give in to it, refused to turn away. She stood and watched as the smoke and flames filled the room and began licking the ceiling. Enveloped in flames, the bed looked like a funeral barge ready to take its passengers in a blaze of light to the underworld. Only when the heat grew so great that her skin blistered did she turn away and leave the house.

She turned unnoticed and walked across the city. The Beast wasn't howling anymore. It still rumbled and growled and demanded release but more like a petulant cat denied a snack than a terrible monster.

Ruxandra needed to clean up. She stank of death and rot and despair. Anyone who saw her would take her for one of the ghouls.

I killed eighty-three ghouls last night. The soldiers killed some, too. Now I need to find the rest of them.

The Ambassador Hotel was as busy as an ant colony. Soldiers marched in and out of the lobby, weapons on their shoulders and grim, tired looks on their faces. She smelled the fear on them, and when she extended her senses, she felt their determination and anger. She heard men talking about lost friends. Heard others swear they would kill anyone who came at them. Officers filled the small hotel bar—kept for those who thought the Cocoanut Grove too loud and too crowded—and were leaning over a large map. In the middle of them, wearing a clean gray suit, stood Kade.

He pointed at the map, saying, "anyplace where someone could hide during the day. That's where they will come from . . ."

Ruxandra walked past without stopping. She wasn't ready to talk to him.

Up the stairs to her room she went to scrub and soak away the dirt and grime and blood and death. She sat in the shower for a long time, letting the water pound down on her, staring at the red and brown streams of filth that sloughed from her body and went down the drain. It took her half an hour before she could pick up the soap and facecloth, and a half hour after that before she stopped scrubbing her skin raw to get the last of the blood off.

But the water won't wash the memories away, will it?

When the filth was gone, she scrubbed out the tub, filled it with water, and lay in it until it became tepid. She dried off and put on her kimono and sank down on her bed. *Now what?*

Kade tapped on her door. "Ruxandra?"

MAN SMELLS LIKE THINGS! KILL! DESTROY!

Ruxandra slumped on the bed. She didn't want to deal with him. Didn't want to deal with anyone.

"Ruxandra, I know you're there . . . are you . . . you?" Kade's voice sounded tentative, nervous. She imagined just how he looked, tensed and ready to spring if the Beast was what was waiting for him.

KILL!

Fuck off.

I need to put an end to this. She pulled the robe tight, went through the sitting room, and swung the door open. "The Beast doesn't like hotels."

She turned away and sunk into the chair, pulling her legs in close and wrapping the kimono around them.

Kade took a spot on the small couch. "Are you all right?"

"Of course not."

"You killed a great number of ghouls."

"Eighty-three." Ruxandra's voice came out flat. "Twenty-seven soldiers, five civilians by my own hands during the fight, dozens more civilians because the Beast didn't stop to help, and after . . ."

Kade waited for her to finish. When she didn't, he shrugged. "Casualties of war."

"Bullshit."

"Casualties of war," Kade repeated, his voice firm. "Civilians die wherever there are battles in the streets. You know that."

"I *know*"—Ruxandra spat the word out like poison—" that *I'm* not supposed to be the one killing them."

"We all kill." Kade's tone didn't change. "Whether one in a night or a hundred in a night doesn't matter."

"It matters to me!" The words tore out of her, raw and loud and shaking the room. She pulled her voice in, switched to vampire frequencies so no one else could hear. "I killed a *child*, Kade."

"Children die."

"This one didn't die. I murdered him. I killed his parents, drained them both, and then drained him." Saying the words out loud made her want to vomit, to shove two fingers down her throat and try to expel the child's blood from her body. It wouldn't work, she knew. The blood had already absorbed into her, become a part of her that she couldn't expel or even cut out.

Kade shrugged—an elegant, unconcerned gesture. "You were hungry."

"I was the *Beast*," Ruxandra snapped. "The Beast wanted a drink, so it did what the Beast does. I found an isolated house, and I killed everyone in it so I could have a safe place to sleep. And the whole time I watched myself and screamed no and tried to make it stop."

"Ruxandra—"

"I don't kill children!" The words ripped out of her. "I don't kill the helpless or the weak because that's what animals do, and I spent too long as an animal already!"

"Get ahold of yourself." Kade's voice went cold. "You are a vampire. You drink blood. You were hungry, and you ate."

"I shouldn't have."

"Are you going to indulge in guilt now, Ruxandra? You who killed thousands over the centuries are going to weep for a single child?" Anger and contempt vied for a place in his voice. "Think about this, then. Your actions last night saved hundreds of lives. Maybe thousands. Yes, the Beast killed humans, but that is what we do, so have done with it."

Ruxandra glared. Self-hatred still filled her, making her want to lash out. "You led me to them."

Kade ignored the accusation in her voice. "Once I saw how the Beast fought, I knew it was the best chance to destroy as many ghouls as possible."

But you didn't fight them yourself, did you? She looked away toward the wall and the map and the bed and anything but Kade's superior, condescending face. She wished she had run as soon as Elizabeth had appeared in New York.

"The Beast is amazing," Kade said, his voice filled with excitement. "I've never seen it in action. Not even after it killed those ghouls I had made in Tuscany. The way it moves, the way it fights. If you could control it—"

"I can't."

"But if—"

"No."

Kade shut his mouth, pressing his lips together so hard they turned white. Ruxandra just stared. At last, Kade shrugged again.

Ruxandra dropped the kimono and rooted through the drawer for clean underwear. "Who do the soldiers think you are?"

"A liaison with the FBI, here to help coordinate against the Mexican insurgency."

"Is that what you told them?"

"It's what they believe. I just agreed."

Ruxandra pulled on a bra and panties. "Do they know to shoot the ghouls in the head?"

"They do now."

"Good." She found a pair of brown britches and a white shirt. "How many did they kill last night?"

"Fifty or more."

"So just over a hundred left."

"Yes."

"Do you have a plan at all?"

"The ghouls come out, and we destroy them."

"That's not a plan."

"No," Kade agreed. "It's reactive. But it is night now, and there is nothing else we can do. The ghouls have already struck in a half dozen neighborhoods. They lit fires, which means either Elizabeth or Dorotyas is controlling them. They're also using the rooftops to cross the city to avoid the patrols. Fortunately, Los Angeles is spaced out enough that it isn't the best method of travel."

"That's something." Ruxandra buttoned up the trousers, then the shirt. "Do I look respectable?"

"Fairly."

"Good." She found her travel shoes. "I'll need some new boots. And a gun."

"A gun?"

"I'm with you, and the FBI does not kill its enemies with their teeth."

"A woman?" The major frowned. "Not sure what use a woman will be here."

"I'll pretend I didn't hear that," Ruxandra said. "*Just listen to us, and have someone get me an M1911 with a holster, ten full magazines, and a hundred rounds extra ammunition, all hollow point. And a machete. Now.*"

The major gave the order. Ruxandra looked at the large map on the table. "How are you dividing your men?"

"Same as last night," the major said. "We have more troops, so we're going to have men at each major intersection with companies in radio contact. When there's an outbreak, we'll close in on the enemy and destroy them."

"Good work," said Kade. "My associate and I will coordinate between groups and—"

"Assign me a squad," Ruxandra said. "Preferably in something fast and mobile. They should have Thompsons and machetes."

"A squad?" The major shook his head. "Miss, I don't know what you're thinking, but—"

"Assign me a squad," Ruxandra commanded. *"With a car. We'll go searching for the enemy and drive them toward the main force. It's a good idea."*

"Good idea," the major agreed. "I'll see it done."

Ruxandra and Kade stood outside the Ambassador waiting for her car. She popped the magazine out of the heavy pistol in her hand, checked the action, and reloaded. She'd carried a Webley revolver in the war, but M1911 had just as much stopping power and one more bullet—two if you started with one in the chamber. It also reloaded a great deal quicker.

Kade frowned as he watched her and kept frowning after she holstered the pistol. He waited until there was no one in earshot and then said, "This is not what I had in mind."

"What *did* you have in mind?" Ruxandra asked. "Sending me into the streets to be bait again?"

"It worked."

Ruxandra glared as the Beast inside her growled its agreement. "No."

"Why not? You were able to come back the last—"

"I said *no.*" Ruxandra put all her hatred for the Beast into the words. "I'm not doing that again, Kade, not unless I am absolutely desperate."

"You'd move faster on your own. You're a better killer with your talons and teeth."

"I need some distance tonight." She tapped her hand against the pistol, secure in the holster at her waist. "That's why I have *this*."

An engine roared and a large, open-topped car with four soldiers inside pulled up to the Ambassador. They got out and one man with sergeant stripes on his arm stepped forward, a swagger in his stride. He had a big jaw, sun-roughened skin, and cold blue eyes. "Are you the chicky we're supposed to escort, then?"

Ruxandra smiled at the disdain in his voice. "*Attention!*"

By midnight, Ruxandra stood in the back of the car as it drove through Los Angeles, a soldier holding onto each leg. She opened her senses wide as they crisscrossed the city using the big boulevards. Each man carried a Thompson. *Now, if I were Elizabeth, what would I be—*

There. "South to the railway station."

The driver looked unsure. "Railway station is guarded, miss."

"*Now.*"

He drove.

A block from the railway station, Ruxandra called out a halt. She stepped out and pointed at a warehouse. "In there."

"With respect, miss," began the sergeant, before seven ghouls leaped off the building and charged.

"Shoot them in the head!" Ruxandra yelled, bringing up her pistol. The Thompsons chattered around her, bullets spewing out and smashing into the ghouls. Ruxandra emptied her magazine, reloaded, and shouted, "Cease fire!"

The soldiers stared with wide eyes at the ghouls. Each one had a hole in between the eyes and the back of its skull blown out. Ruxandra pulled out her machete and advanced. "Sergeant, help me take the heads. The rest, keep an eye out."

The sergeant swallowed hard and nodded. "Yes, ma'am."

They racked up twenty-two more kills that night. Ruxandra felt a grim, hard satisfaction from it. She'd learned to use pistols in the Great War, had fired more than once in self-defense, though not to kill. This night, though, the pistol was more than just defending her body. It was a line in the sand, a civilized form of murder, distant and precise, that took away the hot-blooded, desperate fight for the kill that the Beast relished.

They drove back to the Ambassador as dawn came. The soldiers—who had killed eight ghouls themselves—felt quite happy and even saluted her. The sergeant had lost his swagger and looked like a tired boy. She thanked them and went inside, where Kade and the major waited.

Ruxandra nodded at them. "How did it go?"

"Badly." The major sounded grim and tired. "We've had a dozen fires set, and by the time we reached them, the insurgents vanished. We've found corpses in the street, and no sign of who killed them. We have fought a losing battle all night, and the best we can say is that fewer people died tonight than last night."

"How many?" Kade asked Ruxandra.

"Twenty-nine," Ruxandra said. "We have the heads in the trunk as proof. They're a good squad. What's the plan now?"

"Sweep the city during the day," said the major. "Find their hiding places, and root them all out. God help us."

"They'll be underground."

"I know." The major inclined his head toward Kade. "Your partner here said as much. We'll search every basement, coal cellar, root cellar, and gin mill in the city. We'll find them."

"Then I'll go with them," Ruxandra said. "I'll need a different car. One with a roof and curtains. And a fresh squad of men."

The major's eyebrows went up. "Think you'll have the same results?"

"I think I'll do better than all of yours," Ruxandra said. "Care to wager?"

"Two dollars."

"Done. I'll get changed."

She headed for the elevator with Kade looking very unhappy beside her. "You shouldn't hunt them in daylight. Let the humans do it."

"How many will they flush out, Kade?" She shook her head. "The humans don't know where to look. We do. We can scour the city."

"In daylight?" Kade asked. "With the California sun shining on us? How much do you think the humans will trust us if they see us burn as soon as the sun touches our skin?"

"I'm going to sit in a car, in the shade, and only get out when I need to. It will be fine."

"Still . . ."

"Still," Ruxandra echoed, "we need to stop the ghouls, and someone needs to collect heads and keep the soldiers under control when the bodies burst into flame in the sunlight. Have you figured out how we're going to explain that yet?"

"What do you think I was doing while you played soldier?" Kade still sounded quite disapproving of Ruxandra's actions. "The major is ordering all soldiers to behead the 'insurgents' and leave them where they lie for later pickup. He'll send out retrieval teams tonight to take all the bodies that survive the sunlight out to the desert for burning."

"Makes sense," Ruxandra said. The elevator stopped and opened. "You go keep the major company. I'll be back early afternoon to sleep and get cleaned up. With luck, we'll get the rest tonight."

Ruxandra spent the next six hours overheated, miserable, and moderately successful. Most of the ghouls went too deep for her to detect as they slept. Even so, she found several nests in abandoned warehouses and several more in homes where the ghouls had slaughtered everything before hiding in the basements. Ruxandra's squad beheaded the bodies and left them there, making notes of addresses for the pickup teams.

They'd found fifteen more ghouls in total.

At three, Ruxandra went back to the Ambassador. She collected on her bet, grabbed a quick shower, and slept until nightfall. She felt better than she had in days. Maybe with their strategy and coordination, the entire mess would be finished tonight, and she could get back to her life in New York. *Right after I deal with Elizabeth.*

Deal how?

The Beast would have killed the woman without thought, but Ruxandra . . .

I've known her for so long. There're so few of us. She still tried to kill me and turn me into a monster for her own benefit. And as much as I loved her once, I hate her more.

She woke to Kade knocking at her door. She reached out with her mind, found the hallway empty except for him. She opened the door without bothering to get dressed.

"I see you're feeling better." Kade smiled and stepped inside.

"Somewhat." Ruxandra closed the door behind him. "I'll be ready to go in a few minutes."

"We need to talk first."

Ruxandra headed for her room. "About?"

"Getting Elizabeth out of the country. She can't stay in America. Not after this."

Ruxandra's mouth fell open. Her eyes went wide and her stomach roiled. "America? She can't stay *alive* after this."

"We can't kill her."

Ruxandra, who'd doubted her own ability to kill the woman the night before, felt her anger rising. "Why not?"

"Because she's one of us." Kade sat down on the couch, his elbows on his knees. "For the danger she's put us all in, she should definitely be punished."

"Punished? She and Dorotyas are trying to kill me. And you. And everyone else, for that matter."

"I can't kill her." Kade enunciated every word.

"Look around!" Ruxandra shouted. "Look how many people are dead! She dumped a load of shit all over the city, and we're the ones who have to clean it up."

"Her blood made me a vampire," Kade said. "She's been my friend—our friend—for more than three hundred years. I can't just—"

"I can." Ruxandra realized she was certain of it. "I *will* kill her. And Dorotyas."

"Dorotyas is a slave."

"Dorotyas tried to murder me a half dozen times."

"She's paid for it. Or did you forget what Elizabeth did to her?"

"I'll still kill her."

"Elizabeth is the reason you're alive."

Elizabeth is the reason the Beast hunts the earth. Ruxandra felt her hands clenching. *Elizabeth tortured and murdered thousands of young girls. She's killed more humans than influenza. She deserves—*

"Elizabeth is one of us," Kade said. "She's Blood Royal."

"Blood Royal." Ruxandra scoffed. "That's Elizabeth's term, not mine, not yours. We're just vampires, Kade."

"Ruxandra . . ."

Someone knocked, surprising them both. Ruxandra picked up the pistol and extended her senses. "Two girls."

Kade listened a moment, then opened the door.

Two little girls, one blonde, the other brunette, stood in the doorway. Each looked twelve or thirteen; both wore filthy nightdresses. They stank of unwashed bodies and fear and urine. A yellow stain ran down the front of the brunette's nightdress. They clung to each other's hands. Both looked terrified. Each girl had an ugly red pair of holes in her neck.

The blonde girl smiled and in Elizabeth's tones said, "Well, haven't you two caused me trouble?"

CHAPTER
NINETEEN

RUXANDRA'S HAIR stood on end. She stared at the two children, horror catching in her throat. She had to swallow twice before she said, "When did you do this?"

"Just before we left for the ranch," Elizabeth said through the pretty blonde child. "I thought I might need to talk to you. Terribly difficult to arrange though, wasn't it, Dorotyas?"

"Very," said the little brunette girl. "We hid them in a storage room. Fortunately, they found a toilet in the basement or they would have had nothing to drink. Isn't that right?"

"It is," agreed the blonde. "Now be a dear and let us in."

Ruxandra stepped back and watched as the two filthy children walked across the room and sat on the couch. Both were shaking, their eyes wide.

"I told them what you would to do with them," Elizabeth said. "It was most amusing. This one wet herself like a little baby."

Tears pooled in the little blonde girl's eyes and began dripping down her face. She didn't move, otherwise. Rage, strong and bright enough that even the Beast quailed before it, burned in Ruxandra. "Let them go."

"Oh, I don't think so," Elizabeth said. "After all the trouble we took getting them here?"

"What do you want, Elizabeth?" Kade asked.

"Me? I want us all together again. I want us to share you." The girl's hands ran up her body in a terrible caricature of an adult's gesture. The movement pulled the dress up over her legs, revealing bite marks on both thighs. She saw Ruxandra looking. "The poor dears got bored, so I had them play some games. Delightful, isn't it? Just like in Castle Csejte. You both remember that, don't you?"

"I remember being an animal." Ruxandra's voice came out sharp and clipped. She wanted to tear Elizabeth's head off and throw her out in the sunlight. "I remember being stuck inside the castle for months because you didn't want me to go anywhere. I remember having to listen to you torturing—"

"Oh, you weren't stuck." The little blonde girl tilted her head and blinked coquettishly, though fear filled her face, and her eyes still ran with tears. "You were bound. Wasn't she, Kade?"

"I know." Ruxandra ground the word out between her teeth. "I remember."

"A tragic failure in the end, of course." Elizabeth leaned the little girl's elbows on her knees and put her chin on top. "I mean, who knew that vampires couldn't use human magic? As soon as he drank my blood, the curse broke, and you left. Good thing Kade stayed around for a while to fill me up."

"They were so loud." The little brunette rolled her eyes and looked at Ruxandra. "Those two fucked like wildcats. Moaning and yelling. You'd have thought his cock was magic the way she carried on."

"Stop it." Ruxandra's words came out in a harsh whisper.

"Well, not magic," the blonde said, "but large. And he really knew—"

"Stop it."

"And there's this thing where I'd lay on my stomach and he'd put his fingers—"

"*Stop it!*" Ruxandra's hands clenched tight into fists. "These are children, for God's sake. Stop it."

The little blonde girl smiled at Ruxandra, her eyes cold and calculating and far, far older than they should be. "Make me."

Ruxandra stood there, shaking. The little blonde girl leaned back on the couch, her legs spread wide. She ran her hands up the inside of her thighs. "You don't hurt children, remember? So you need to sit here and listen."

"I hurt children." Kade stepped in front of the couch. "I have no problem dispatching these two if necessary."

Ruxandra opened her mouth to tell him no when the sharp smell of urine filled the room. Wetness spread over the blonde girl's nightdress. She looked down, and Elizabeth said, "Now see what you've done. You know the hotel charges extra to clean that."

"What do you want, Elizabeth?" Kade's voice was cold as ice. "Tell me, right here and now. And tell me why you sent these thralls in here instead of coming yourself."

"Well, I couldn't, could I?" Elizabeth said. "Ruxandra's going to kill me."

"Ruxandra will not kill you."

Yes, I will. Ruxandra held her tongue. *Especially for this.*

"Oh, please." The little girl pointed at her. "Look at that face. She's more than ready to commit murder. What's it going to be Ruxandra, fire? Or staking me out in the sun?"

"Neither," Kade said. "I promised you I would keep you safe."

"Your promises are worth nothing." The little girl's voice was sharp. "You promised to stay by me in Castle Csejte. You promised to protect me in South America. You promised to help me win Ruxandra back to my side, and you did *nothing*!"

Ruxandra's talons started extending, digging into the palms of her hands as her fists stayed clenched. "When did you promise that, Kade?"

"Tell her, Kade," the little girl said. "Tell her all about how you said we could all be together again."

Kade didn't. "Come with us, Elizabeth. Away from America. Come to Germany."

"I don't want her with us." Ruxandra hissed the words. "I want her dead."

"See?" Elizabeth said. "She wants me dead. No doubt she wants poor Dorotyas dead, too. She'll want you dead, too, Kade, soon enough."

"I have done nothing to her," Kade said. "Unlike you. Why are you here?"

"To play games? To have fun?" The little girl shrugged. "To have one last attempt at reconciliation?"

"To waste our time?" The moment the words left Ruxandra's mouth, she realized that's exactly what she's doing.

She spread her mind and sensed. Elizabeth and Dorotyas less than five miles away, moving at high speed. And worse . . . "The ghouls! They're on their way here!"

"Oh, that's the least of your problems," Elizabeth said. "Just wait until they arrive. But while you're waiting, Dorotyas?"

The brunette girl raised her head and turned to the little blonde girl. Then she screamed—a wordless, gurgling screech.

Blood sprayed out of her wide-open mouth and all over the blonde girl. A small piece of red flesh fell onto the brunette's lap.

"God!" Kade leaped forward, clamping a hand over her mouth. "She's bitten out her tongue!"

The little blonde jumped off the couch. "Now if you'll excuse me, I'm going down to the lobby. They'll love my tale of what you've done to me. Especially when I describe Kade's—"

"Ruxandra, stop the ghouls!" Kade grabbed the little blonde's arm. The brunette started to run. Kade caught her collar. "I'll take care of these!"

"But—"

"Go!"

The little brunette started to scream again. Kade pulled her close and put his mouth over hers, catching the blood and silencing her in a hideous parody of a kiss. He dragged them toward the bathroom, pulling them like a pair of dolls.

"There's a lovely party at Pickfair tonight!" the little blonde shouted just before Kade threw her inside the bathroom.

"Don't hurt them!" Ruxandra dressed in five seconds flat and sprinted down the stairs, pistol and machete in her hands, ammunition bandolier over her shoulder. She hit the main floor and threw open the door calling, "Major!"

She almost ran into him coming out of the bar.

"What's going on?" he demanded.

"Ghouls. Coming here. Fast."

"What?" the major frowned. "How do you—"

"*Get your troops outside! Now!*"

Someone screamed, and the ghouls came pouring inside. Ruxandra drew her pistol and fired two shots, hitting the first ghoul twice in the head and blowing out the back of its skull. Three others dashed off to the sides, one leaping for the front desk, the other two charging the guests sitting in the lobby. Ruxandra took out the first one with a single round. The major fumbled for his own weapon as the other two ghouls jumped on an elderly couple and started feasting. Ruxandra charged.

"Fire! Fire!"

Shit. Ruxandra stabbed her fingers into the first ghoul's eyes and ripped it off its victim. The second ghoul tried to jump on her back, but she had the pistol ready and put three rounds into its mouth. She threw the other ghoul across the room and fired the last round. It collapsed.

"Holy hell, that's good shooting," the major said. "Where are they coming from?"

Ruxandra ran out the door, reloading as she went. Flames leaped up from the door of the Cocoanut Grove, and more from the side of the hotel. Gunfire echoed all around the building as the major's troops fired into a charging pack of ghouls.

"*Shoot the heads!*" Ruxandra commanded. "*Shoot the heads and then cut them off!*"

Then she vanished from notice and ran.

It's fifteen miles to Pickfair. Ten minutes at best.

The streets of Los Angeles were still empty, which made it much easier. She dashed past the checkpoints and the darkened buildings, through the city streets and the hills beyond. She cast her mind wide and spotted Pickfair. It was full of people—fifty or sixty at least. Beyond it, in the hills and drawing closer, came twenty ghouls.

Three miles away. Shit, shit, shit.

KILL, screamed the Beast. *KILL, KILL, KILL.*

Shut up! Ruxandra blocked it out and ran faster. She reached Pickfair first and turned visible as she ran up the driveway.

"Ruxandra?" Joseph's incredulous voice rose above the hubbub. "What are you doing here?"

"*Everyone inside!*" Ruxandra commanded, her voice echoing through the house. "*Quickly. And lock the doors!*"

Joseph and the others sprinted inside. Ruxandra jumped, landing on the roof. Guests scrambled out of the pool and the ones on the patio ran inside as the ghouls came over the hills. *Good.*

It wasn't a fight this time, or even a challenge. It was slaughter, pure and simple. The ghouls charged straight over the hills and straight into Ruxandra's sights. Six of them fell in the first minute, three more in the minute after that. The rest crossed the distance and vanished from sight beneath the eaves. Ruxandra jumped down. For the next two minutes, everything was blood and flashing steel.

Then it ended and Ruxandra stood in the middle of a pile of headless corpses.

Joseph stared out the window at her, his eyes wide. She walked forward and he opened it. "Ruxandra?"

"Yes."

"You . . ." He looked at the pile of corpses. "What . . . what are you?"

"Call the Ambassador Hotel. Ask for the major who is running the operation. Someone will come by soon to pick up the corpses." She leaned in and kissed him on his lips. He didn't kiss her back. "I've got to go now."

"But . . . You were on the roof. How did . . . ?"

Ruxandra smiled and patted his cheek. "Good-bye, Joseph."

Three miles from the Ambassador she sensed Elizabeth and Dorotyas heading in the other direction.

What the fuck?

Her run became a sprint, and she covered the last two miles in less than a minute. Soldiers surrounded the building, rifles ready. A dozen stretchers lay on the ground, the blankets drawn up over the occupants' faces. Two fire trucks sat at the back of the building, lights flashing. The firemen were standing around now, talking and looking relaxed. Kade stood in front of the hotel.

Ruxandra skidded to a stop in front of him. "Where is she?"

Kade frowned. "Who?"

"Elizabeth! She was here!"

Kade shook his head. "She never came near the hotel."

"I sensed her, a mile away. She was here!"

"No." Kade's voice was firm.

"You mean you didn't notice her," Ruxandra snapped.

Kade pointed to the hotel. "We've been fighting fire and ghouls for the last hour. There was no sign of Elizabeth."

A car with four soldiers pulled up. The sergeant she'd worked with the night before leaped out. "Hey, Miss Crackshot! The major inside?"

"He is," said Kade. "What's going on?"

"One of our stations got hit. Everyone killed, and they made off with a carload of weapons." The sergeant ran inside.

Ruxandra's jaw set into a hard line. "Now we know why she came into the city."

"We do indeed," Kade said. "Which way was she heading?"

"Toward the ranch."

Kade frowned. "It'll be dawn before we get there."

"Not if we run."

"You've already been running," he said. "At top speed. How much more before you need to eat?"

Ruxandra sighed, frustration rising up inside. *He's right, dammit.* "I'm already hungry."

Kade pointed at a truck nearby. "There're three soldiers in there getting ready for transport. Two are hurt. One's dying. I suggest you get a drink."

"I'm killing her," Ruxandra warned him. "When we get there, I'm taking her head and putting it in the fire she keeps in her torture chamber."

"No. You won't."

Ruxandra managed not to punch him. Inside of her, the Beast snarled its agreement. "Why the *hell* not? After all this?"

"Because I promised her that I wouldn't." Kade's voice brooked no argument. "I'll find out what weapons they took. You feed yourself. Then we'll go."

Ruxandra headed for the truck, her jaw set in a hard line. *We'll see about that.*

◆ ◆ ◆ ◆

They reached the ranch an hour before dawn. Ruxandra kept her senses wide open from the moment they started running. Five miles out from the ranch, she felt Elizabeth and Dorotyas's presence. The barracks sat empty, and Ruxandra sensed no one else inside the house. She told Kade as much.

"Think they've killed them all?"

"Possibly." Kade looked through the darkness to the house. "They know we're coming."

"Of course."

"They stole a machine gun."

"Lovely." Ruxandra took the pistol out of her holster, checked the action, cocked it, and put it back. "How do we get close?"

"In the war, we'd blast them down with artillery while our troops advanced."

"Well, that's out."

"Then I suggest we run. Zigzag pattern, keep changing direction and hope for the best."

"I hate this plan," muttered Ruxandra. *But not as much as letting her go.* "Ready?"

Kade nodded. "Walk until you hear the first shot."

They walked, straight up the driveway, one on either side, eyes on the house. Ruxandra's nerves were on edge. Inside her the Beast snarled, half in fear, half in anticipation.

The machine gun opened up on them two hundred yards from the house.

"Fuck!" Ruxandra's training from the war came back in a flash. She dove for the ditch as a dozen .303 rounds slammed into the dirt. Two connected, smashing through the bone in her thigh. Through the machine-gun fire, she heard Kade running, then shouting in pain and falling. She crawled along the bottom of the ditch, hoping the earth would shielded her. Her leg burned with agony as the bone knitted back together. She peeked up above the road. "Kade! Can you hear me?"

"Yes." Kade called from a hundred yards away, his voice straining with agony. "I got a few rounds in the ribs."

"Can you move?"

"Yes."

A small black object flew through the sky. Ruxandra's eyes went wide. "Grenade!"

She jumped, using all the force of her good leg to drive her across the road and into the ditch on the other side. She hit hard and the bad leg flared in pain. The grenade exploded in the air, spraying her with hot, fragmented steel. She screamed as the shrapnel tore open her flesh.

"Are you all right?" Kade yelled.

"Of course not!" She started crawling forward as her body began spitting out hunks of hot metal. "It fucking hurts!"

Another hail of bullets rained down upon Kade's position. Red tracers lit the night as the bullets sent clouds of dirt and dust into the air. Then the machine gun swung back toward her, the tracers arcing across the field. She pressed flat to the ground, and the rounds went over her head. Above the noise, she heard Kade shout, "It's Dorotyas on the machine gun! She's in the top window!"

"We both go at once!" Ruxandra yelled back. "Are you ready?"

"I'm ready . . . . Go!"

Kade leaped. Dorotyas opened fire and tracer bullets arced up after him. Ruxandra sprinted straight for the house as the bullets slammed into Kade, sending him tumbling out of the sky. Dorotyas pulled the machine gun down, but she wasn't fast enough. Ruxandra was already beneath her window, out of the line of fire.

Dorotyas stuck her head over the edge and opened up with a Thompson. Ruxandra dove away, zigzagging and rolling to avoid the bullets. Several hit, the pain driving into her like spikes as the bullets tore into her flesh and fractured ribs. She drew her pistol as she rolled, sending all seven rounds straight at Dorotyas's face. The woman's eyes exploded like tomatoes and she fell back screaming. Ruxandra popped out the magazine and put in a new one. She extended her senses, looking for Elizabeth.

Oh, fuck, fuck, fuck, fuck, FUCK! "Kade! Get up! Ghouls!"

They poured from the basement in a wave of malevolence and hunger. The Beast snarled and pushed forward in her mind, trying to take control. Ruxandra shoved it back, ignoring the howls of frustration.

Not this time, animal. Ruxandra kicked in the door and leaped back, giving room for the ghouls to come out. She pulled the machete from its scabbard. It wasn't quite the same weight and size as a Chinese broadsword, but it was close enough. The Chinese broadsword was a cutting weapon, and the machete, designed to hack through trees, was more than suitable to the style.

Before the Opium Wars, a woman named Mai Chu helped Ruxandra become intimately familiar with the Chinese broadsword. Mai Chu had been a dancer as well as a kung fu fighter. She'd shown Ruxandra the balletic nature of the Chinese broadsword.

The ghouls howled and charged through the wide double doors. Ruxandra raised the blade and shouted the famous battle cry of Yuan Chonghuan, just like her teacher had taught her: "*Diào n⊠ mā ding yìng shàng!*"

Then she began dancing and blood sprayed over the clean white gravel surrounding the house.

Ruxandra took five heads in the first second and eight more in the next. More ghouls poured through the door, running straight at her. She spun and whirled, her body bending and dodging as her blade hacked off arms and took heads. Sixteen more ghouls died in the next five seconds.

"Get against the wall!"

Kade's shout broke through Ruxandra's battle trance just as Dorotyas opened up with the machine gun again. Bullets ripped through the ghouls around her. She dove for the house, and a line of bullets stitched down her spine, paralyzing her. She landed in a heap, and the ghouls closed in.

Then Kade grabbed the machete from her hand and stood above her. He hacked at the ghouls, taking heads with brutal efficiency, sending blood spraying everywhere. Ruxandra watched him as her spine pulled back into place, the bullets popping out. She climbed to her feet, staying behind Kade as he cut and slashed through the ghouls.

German saber, she thought, apropos of nothing.

Another grenade dropped down on them. Without thinking, Ruxandra caught it and threw it into the crowd of ghouls. It exploded, shredding bodies and sending them spinning to the ground. Ruxandra jumped high, pulling her pistol. Dorotyas leaped out of the window and right at Ruxandra, attacking with talons and fangs and a meat cleaver all at once. Ruxandra dodged the bite and the talons, but her other arm wasn't working right. The cleaver sunk into her shoulder, catching on the bone and sticking. The two fell hard.

"Die, you fucking whore!" screamed Dorotyas, and she ripped the cleaver out and hacked at Ruxandra. "Die for betraying us! Die for hating her! Die! Die! Die!"

Ruxandra used her good arm on the last "die." She caught Dorotyas's hand and twisted. For a moment, Dorotyas gritted her teeth, frozen in pain. Then Ruxandra pivoted and threw the woman thirty yards away into a cluster of ghouls. Dorotyas hit the ground hard, then screamed as the ghouls descended on her. The cleaver flashed back and forth, hacking at legs and bodies.

Ruxandra didn't stay to watch. She jumped up into the window. The machine gun had a half-full box of ammunition, and three grenades sat beside it. Ruxandra grabbed the machine gun and opened up. Body parts flew as the ghouls disintegrated under the withering fire. Dorotyas's body bucked and twisted as the rounds broke bone and tore open flesh, spattering silver blood across the landscape. Ruxandra kept firing until the belt ran out then grabbed a grenade and leaped down, drawing her pistol as she went. She cleared seven ghouls with seven shots. Then she jumped and landed with both heels driving into Dorotyas's sternum. She heard it crack as she hit.

She dropped to her knees and grabbed Dorotyas's hair. She shoved the grenade hard into Dorotyas's wide-open screaming mouth, breaking her teeth. Then she pulled the pin.

Dorotyas thrashed claws, slashing at Ruxandra, desperately working her jaws to spit the grenade out. Ruxandra grabbed her mouth, held it closed and counted the seconds.

One. Two. Three . . .

At four she leaped off Dorotyas's body.

At four and a half, the grenade exploded, blowing Dorotyas's skull and brains all over the gravel along with the few ghouls left fighting on it. Ruxandra reloaded the pistol, firing again and again. Kade, surrounded by headless corpses, kept cutting until the last ghoul fell.

They stood in the silence, staring at one another. Then Ruxandra turned back to Dorotyas.

"*Mein Gott,*" Kade whispered.

The grenade had done more than blow Dorotyas's skull open. Her head had vaporized, leaving no part of it attached to the body. That, apparently, was too much.

Dorotyas's body did not heal. Her wounds did not seal, and her head did not grow back. Instead, her skin turned gray. The fingers grew wrinkled, and the muscles on the arms atrophied. The skin sagged and grew loose and then fell off the bones.

Ruxandra and Kade watched as Dorotyas's flesh dried out and turned to dust. The muscles beneath dissolved next, then the organs, until only a clean, white skeleton lay on the ground. Then it, too, dissolved.

For a brief moment, Ruxandra felt terrible. To end a human life was one thing, but to end a life three hundred years long . . .

She deserved it. She and Elizabeth both.

Ruxandra turned away and walked toward the house. Kade grabbed her arm. "Where are you going?"

Ruxandra pulled her arm free. She put another magazine into the pistol. *Two magazines left.* "Where do you think?"

It's time to end this.

CHAPTER
TWENTY

S HE STALKED THROUGH the house, Kade on her heels. She sensed Elizabeth upstairs. The woman was in her bedroom, making no attempt to get away. *Good. It'll make it easier to pull her head off her shoulders and stake her out in the dirt for the sun.*

"Ruxandra, please," Kade said. "I made a promise to her. I promised her I wouldn't kill her, no matter what."

"How can you say that?" Ruxandra spun on her heel and ended up nose to nose with him. "Did you see how many people she killed?"

"We *all* kill people," Kade said. "It's how we survive, remember?"

"This isn't about survival!" Ruxandra's temper flared high. All the vitriol she wanted to spit at Elizabeth came pouring out of her. "She tortures for *fun*, Kade! She took two little girls and made them thralls just so she could delay us. She's killed hundreds of people this week, and she's exposed all of us! I am ending her. Now."

Ruxandra stomped away up the stairs. Kade followed on her heels. "Please, Ruxandra, I—"

The machete stopped an inch away from his nose. "One more word, and I'll cut your head in half."

"Oh, dear." Elizabeth leaned out of a doorway ahead, her mouth forming a perfect little moue. "Are the lovers having a quarrel?"

She ducked back in just before Ruxandra fired. Three rounds slammed into the doorframe, blowing holes in wood and plaster.

"Now, Ruxandra, that's enough of that," Elizabeth called from inside the room. "You're not going to kill me, and we all know it."

"I killed Dorotyas!" Ruxandra ran forward. "I'll kill you, too."

She bounced off the doorframe, the .45 in front of her. Half-packed trunks and cases cluttered the room. From one, jewelry spilled onto the floor. A pair of whip handles and manacles dangled from another. Elizabeth sat on the bed, leaning back on her hands. She wore a nightgown, open to show her legs and most of her breasts. "Tried to kill Doro—"

The bullet smashed into Elizabeth's teeth and out the other side of her head. She tumbled over backward with a screech of pain. Ruxandra advanced on her. Elizabeth scrabbled back across the bed and rolled off the other side. She rose to her feet. "For God's sake, Ruxandra!"

Ruxandra's next shot exploded Elizabeth's kneecap. She screamed and fell sideways on the ground, clutching at her leg. Ruxandra walked around the bed. Elizabeth tried to crawl away. Tears ran from her eyes. "Ruxandra, stop it! Please!"

Ruxandra fired again, taking out Elizabeth's other kneecap. Elizabeth wailed and grabbed at it. Ruxandra kicked her in the head, the force of it enough to slam it back against the floor.

Ruxandra straddled her. She dropped the machete and grabbed Elizabeth's hair, hauling her head back up. She pushed the barrel of the pistol into Elizabeth's eye, feeling the soft flesh squish beneath it. Clear fluid dribbled down Elizabeth's cheek.

Ruxandra leaned close to her ear. "Dorotyas is dead. I watched her body turn to dust. And now, I am going to kill you."

Shock filled Elizabeth's face. "You can't have killed—"

Ruxandra pulled the trigger, and bits of Elizabeth's brains and skull spattered onto the wall behind her. Elizabeth convulsed and went limp. Ruxandra dropped her and stood up. She raised her boot and stomped hard on Elizabeth's head, hearing her jaw crack and feeling her skull give. *I'm not letting her wake up until I'm damn well ready for it.*

She raised her boot to stomp again, and Kade grabbed her from behind. He pulled her away and threw her across the room. She hit the wall hard, cracking the plaster. Kade stepped forward, putting his body between Ruxandra and Elizabeth's prone, bleeding form. He raised the machete. "Stop."

"Fuck that!" Ruxandra pushed off the wall. "Get out of the way!"

"No."

"Don't you betray me, Kade!"

"I'm not betraying you."

"Then move!"

"I can't."

"Bullshit!" She started toward him. The machete came up; pointed at her face. "Goddamn it, Kade!"

"I need her, Ruxandra."

"Need her?" Ruxandra batted the machete to the side, stepped in to shove him. He caught her arm, twisted it, and shoved her in the other direction. Ruxandra hit the wall again and bounced off. Her talons came out. "How in hell can you need *her*?"

"If she dies, I die!"

Ruxandra stared, trying to understand. At last she managed, "What?"

Kade sighed and let the machete fall to his side. "There's a bloodline, Ruxandra. When the older vampire dies, the younger one loses its immortality."

"What?"

Ruxandra froze, trying to process what he'd said. "That . . . that doesn't make—"

"I've seen it." Kade said, his voice low and urgent. "Fifty years ago. One of the ones I made turned his lover. Forty years later, they tried to kill me. We fought, I pushed the older one into a blast furnace and . . ."

He stopped and a shudder ran through him. "I watched his lover turn from a beautiful woman into a crone in seconds. She collapsed and died right in front of me."

"But . . ." Ruxandra felt like her head was filling up with cobwebs, trapping her reason in a sticky gray mess. "Why in hell did you never tell me this?"

"I'm so sorry," Kade said.

"Sorry? How the fuck does *sorry* help?"

"When could I tell you?" Kade spread his hands wide. "When could I say, 'Oh, by the way, if Elizabeth dies, I die too' without her hearing it? Can you imagine what she would do to me with that knowledge?"

"*Fuck* you, Kade." Ruxandra turned away, staring out the window just so she wouldn't see his face. The sky outside was dark blue and growing lighter. Ruxandra wrapped her arms around her body, squeezing to keep from exploding with emotions. "Fuck you."

"After everything Elizabeth's done, I want to see her burn, too," Kade said. "I want her to be ash, but . . ."

Ruxandra looked down at Elizabeth's broken body. Her knees and skull were almost healed, and she'd wake up soon. The rage that burned inside Ruxandra flared high as she stared, knowing there was nothing she could do without killing Kade.

God fucking damn you to hell for all eternity, you stupid, arrogant, miserable, torturing bitch. Ruxandra snarled in impotent rage and kicked the bed hard enough to crack the frame. "So now what? Put her at the bottom of a mine shaft and seal her in?"

Kade tossed the machete aside and sat on the mattress. "Magic. I'll make her sleep."

"For how long?"

"As long as you want. A decade, a century, two centuries. I promise to keep her that way until you want to let her wake up." Kade reached for her. "I'm sorry."

Ruxandra stepped away. The bright, burning rage she felt for Elizabeth turned to hot coals deep in her stomach that she could not extinguish. "Me too."

Faster than Kade could react, she jumped forward and slammed both her boots down on Elizabeth's head, squashing her skull. Kade leaped to his feet, but Ruxandra stepped away. "I didn't want her to wake up before you finished."

"Fair."

"How long to cast the spell?"

"Fifteen minutes at most. And the first words render her immobile."

"Do it." Ruxandra headed for the door. "I'll get the Stutz. We'll wait until sunset, light this place on fire, and get the hell out of here."

"Sounds good." Kade reached down and picked Elizabeth up. He set her down on the bed, her silver blood staining the sheets. "Thank you, Ruxandra."

"Don't," Ruxandra warned. "Just get her asleep. Because if she wakes up—"

"She won't." Kade set Elizabeth on the bed and straightened her robe. "I promise."

Ruxandra watched as he crossed Elizabeth's arms in front of her. "I'm going with you."

Kade looked up in surprise. "What?"

"Wherever you're taking her, I want to see it."

"I told you . . ."

"You keep secrets, Kade." Ruxandra's eyes locked onto his. "Too many secrets. You only tell them when you get caught. So I'm going with you, and I'm going to make damn sure you put Elizabeth away somewhere where she can't hurt anyone."

Kade nodded. "Of course."

Ruxandra walked out of the bedroom and out of the house. Bodies lay in piles around the entrance, and blood covered the white gravel. Beyond, the sky was lightening, sunlight hitting the tops of the trees in the orchard. She looked at the pistol in her hand, the end of it still stained silver with Elizabeth's blood. She tossed it away and went to get the car.

How stupid this all was.

Two weeks later, Ruxandra stepped through the ship's doors and out onto the deck. The English Channel roiled beneath the ship's hull, making the big liner sway. The strong, cold wind carried with it not just the smell of the ocean but also the faint scent of farmland and human factories. She leaned against the rail. In the distance, she saw twinkling yellow lights sliding past and fading into darkness. She stood watching for a long time before she heard Kade coming up behind her.

"I smelled the land," Ruxandra said. I wanted to see. There's Calais, I think."

"Yes." Kade leaned on the rail. "How are you?"

"*Very* hungry."

"Ship travel is the worst." Kade rested a hand on her shoulder. "Four days without feeding. Tomorrow night we'll arrive, and then we can eat without attracting attention."

"Good." They stood in silence for a time. "How is Elizabeth?"

"Still sleeping," Kade said. "Still down in the cargo hold and still not conscious."

Ruxandra nodded. "And once we're there?"

"There're rooms in my mansion designed for these situations."

Why, I wonder. Ruxandra watched the shoreline passing by. "I haven't seen Europe since the war."

"It's changed, but not as much as they think."

"Is there jazz?"

"Of course." Kade put his arm around Ruxandra's shoulder and pulled her close. She sighed and leaned against him. "And alcohol isn't illegal, and there's so much more culture than in America." He kissed her on the forehead. "Don't worry. You'll love Germany."

Thank you for reading Beast of Dracula!

Dear Reader,

I hope you enjoyed Beast of Dracula. It was my honor and pleasure to write for you. Of course I was only relaying the information that my Ruxandra was providing, but I hope I did so with clarity and wonder. Thanks for joining me on this fun and wild ride!

Get ready for many more adventures.

Also, if you're so inclined, I'd love a review of Beast of Dracula. Without your support, and feedback my books would be lost under an avalanche of other books. While appreciated, there's only so much praise one can take seriously from family and friends. If you have the time, please visit my author page on both Amazon.com and goodreads.com.

twitter.com/JohnPatKennedy
www.facebook.com/AuthorJohnPatrickKennedy/
johnpatrickkennedy.net

Made in the USA
Las Vegas, NV
08 October 2023

78809527R00192